# Wise Guys Confidential

# A Mafia Story of Industrial Espionage

## John Wooten

*Edited by Rosa Sophia*

Wise Guys Confidential: A Mafia Story of Industrial Espionage

by John Wooten

Edited by Rosa Sophia

Copyright 2016 by John A. Wooten

All rights reserved.

Registered with The Writers Guild of America, West, Inc.

Certificate # 1825370 issued to John A. Wooten for *Wise Guys Confidential: A Mafia Story of Industrial Espionage*

ISBN: 10: 0692583661

ISBN: 13: 978-0692583661

Library of Congress Control Number: 2015921104

John A. Wooten, Riviera Beach, FL

*For my sweetheart, Nancy—the love of my life—for her inspiration.*

*And for my wonderful family, children, and grandchildren for their encouragement.*

# Acknowledgments

With great appreciation to Nancy, my research coordinator, who also spent hours working on my novel typing and completing the first edit.

Many thanks to my wonderful family, children, and grandchildren who provide me with love and support.

Thanks to my friend Lori Oliveira, who went that extra step to help get this project underway.

Thanks to my good friend Grandmaster Kenneth Miarecki, as I remember all the great times we shared together teaching and running seminars all over the country.

A special thank you to our marketing and design team behind the scenes, Heavy Graphics Marketing, Mr. Marketing Tricks, Celebrity Designer Gia and Super Steve, #TEAMHEAVY, for my awesome Wise Guys Confidential book cover and book trailer.

A huge thank you to my editor, Rosa Sophia. You are the best!

A special recognition to a wonderful friend Joe Sorota, who made this endeavor possible.

# Contents

# My Everlasting Love

By John Wooten

They say you can see one hundred miles.

For one hundred miles you can see.

For I can see not one mile, for I am blind you see.

I've wanted to see for oh so long, so long I've wanted to see.

But, now I have seen the hatred of hell, no longer do I wish to see.

I saw my love fall apart at sea, at sea my love fell apart.

Now she has seen the hatred of hell, no longer do we wish to see.

# Chapter 1: Undercover

Johnny Macchia couldn't feel the heat of the summer from where he sat in his air-conditioned SUV, jerking the steering wheel to make a tight left turn before the traffic light turned red. He swerved around a rusted Ford, cutting them off, and the driver slammed on the horn. It was times like this he wished he was driving his Corvette, the car used in his *other* line of business.

"Fuck," he muttered, tightening his large hands around the steering wheel of the beast of a vehicle. He couldn't be late for this meeting, but the digital display on the dash told him he was already late. As if he could afford to make a bad impression.

Despite having gone to school for criminology at MIT, and graduating at the top of his class before joining the Marines, he'd never followed a totally law-abiding path. He'd grown up around older kids like Sonny DeSantis, who went on to become big names in the Mafia, and now he was being pressed to work with the FBI to pin Sonny for something—anything. They just wanted him behind bars, however they could get him. Johnny hated the fact that they wanted him to draw in his old friend.

Even now, in his early fifties, after everything he'd seen in the military, Johnny still felt like that kid who'd admired Sonny DeSantis for his ambition and motivation. But he hadn't kept in touch with him, and because of that, he and Sonny had a falling out. Once, he'd tried to explain to Sonny that it was because he'd been sent to Iraq, he was busy, but Sonny felt *family* should always stay in touch—no matter what.

Now, hesitantly, Johnny played both sides, and couldn't help but fall easily into the role of the wiseguy. Like his friends, they all came from the same place. The same background. This FBI thing—it wasn't Johnny's true nature. But he was undercover, and he was one of the best they had.

He'd just left the martial arts studio he owned in downtown Boston. After ending a class, he'd locked up the building and rushed outside, realizing his watch was five minutes behind. The dark blue button-up shirt he wore presented him as a clean-cut businessman, but the glint in his eye probably told a different story. His past wasn't something he discussed, and his position as an undercover agent for the FBI had been well-concealed by the many students who came in and out of his *dojo* for classes and private instruction. Not even the clients who came to him in his basement office, knowing he was one of the best private investigators in the area, were aware of his dealings with the FBI. Having different aliases, and two vehicles he could switch when needed, helped cover his tracks.

He pulled into the parking lot, hit the brakes, and jumped out of the SUV to hurry into the building. After being ushered toward a door marked Evaluation and Analysis inside a brightly lit hallway, Johnny stepped inside and was met by the stern expressions of four well-dressed agents—along with Richard Brenner, the chief of the FBI's organized crime task force. Richard was in his mid-fifties, but didn't look much older than forty. He pinned Johnny with his intense stare, his face expressionless, his dark hair perfectly combed.

"Mr. Macchia, you are late," he said.

The barren conference room seemed to swallow his voice, and the daylight failed to penetrate the heavy blinds over the far window.

"Traffic's a bitch this mornin'," Johnny quipped, hoping his boss would drop it.

"I was beginning to wonder if you'd make it," Richard said. "Join me at the end of the table, Johnny."

He stood by Richard opposite the projection screen, and the lights were dimmed after a projector was set up using a laptop. An image was displayed on the large screen at the front of the room, and Johnny immediately recognized the Mafia family tree.

Richard began briefing the agents on the situation as he leaned against a podium. First, he gestured to Johnny, who clasped his hands and listened. "For those of you who don't know him, the man to my right is Johnny Macchia," Richard said. "Johnny is a long time member of this task force, working primarily undercover on various mob related assignments around the country. For nearly a year, he's been developing his cover as a part-time private investigator, part-time martial arts instructor with a dojo here in Boston. If you open the folders in front of you, you'll meet the DeSantis family, or at least the key members."

There was a rustling sound as the agents opened their folders, and Johnny glanced at the screen, which showed carefully marked labels of the family tree: boss, underboss, consigliere, and capos. Five capos were listed, along with the boss, underboss, and consigliere.

Richard continued reviewing the material. "Connected to what was once the five families, DeSantis is not as powerful as the old Dons. But he's just as ruthless." He exchanged a glance with Johnny, who kept his expression impassive. "Johnny knew DeSantis growing up, and has been renewing that old acquaintance since coming back to town. Johnny, why don't you take it from here?"

Johnny nodded, stepping up to the podium while Richard took a seat at the table with the agents. Despite being late for the meeting, he never had difficulty switching gears in order to alter his focus on the task at hand. "Gentleman," Johnny began, "Sonny DeSantis knew how to run a gang as a teen back in the neighborhood. I remember it very well. The older he got, the better he was. We know he has revenue from prostitution, loan sharking, gambling, and every other illegal money making activity you can think of. Sonny was always an enterprising fellow, but he has help, too. Let's meet them."

He tapped a key on the laptop computer, and a picture appeared on the Mafia chart already projected on the screen. "This is Alfonzo 'Sonny' DeSantis. He's the boss. He rose through the ranks the old fashioned way, which means he followed orders and killed the competition to get to where he is today." Tapping a key again, another picture appeared beneath the label *underboss*. "Sonny's underboss is Frankie Novello, second in command. When Sonny wants something done, Frankie sees to it. He's been with Sonny since the beginning."

Johnny straightened beside the podium, thinking back. In his youth, he never would've expected he'd be standing here, making a case against his childhood friend. Sonny had been like a big brother to him, and lately it seemed like the lines between good and bad were blurring. That wasn't a good sign; he had to stay on task and get the job done, regardless of his history with Sonny. He tapped a key again and a photo of the consigliere appeared beside its accompanying label, displayed between the photos of Sonny and Frankie. "This is Paul Barone, Sonny's consigliere, or advisor. He reports directly to Sonny," Johnny explained. "Paul is a graduate of an Ivy League law school, courtesy of Sonny. He's smart and cunning, and a big part of the reason Sonny isn't doing life in a federal pen."

One of the agents, a woman with neatly styled brown hair and dark eyes, fixed Johnny with a disbelieving stare. He'd seen her around, but he didn't know her very well. "Is this for real or are these characters from a movie?" she wondered, as if talking to herself.

Johnny smirked. "Oh, it's very real, Agent—"

"Debra. Debra Stewart."

"Well, Agent Stewart, not only is it real, but it's very deadly if you're not careful," he warned. He tapped another key, bringing up yet another photo. "Now we'll take a look at the capos, or captains. There are four of them, and each are responsible for a segment of Sonny's business operations. This man is Peter Bianchi, and he handles loan sharking and shakedowns." It was clear from Peter's steely gaze, sharp eyes, and clean no-nonsense appearance that few would go against his demands unless they had a death wish. "Who's got him?" Johnny asked, surveying the agents in the room.

Larry, one of the younger agents, raised his hand, and Johnny nodded to acknowledge him. "This guy's a mean son of a bitch, and he likes to inflict pain. Word is, he seeks clients he knows can't pay just to have the fun of hammering the crap out of 'em. Good luck, Larry." He exchanged a glance with the agent, who raised an eyebrow in quiet acceptance of his job—hunting down Bianchi himself.

Johnny went on to the next photograph. "This is Cesare Mesopolitti," he said, indicating the heavier, olive-skinned man on the screen. "He runs prostitution, and he's got a weakness for women. He likes to sample the wares before turning them out onto the street. The best way to get close to Cesare is through his broads."

Having caught a murderous glare from Debra, Johnny coughed and hurriedly corrected himself. "Uh, I mean, women. My apologies, Agent Stewart."

Sheila, the only other female agent present, scrunched up her nose and frowned, tucking a strand of dirty blonde hair behind her ear. "*I'm* the one who's got this man's file, Mr. Macchia," she announced. "You're not suggesting I turn tricks to nail this guy, are you?"

"How you do your job is up to you," Johnny said, steeling himself against the expression of disdain on her face. "I'm just telling you how he operates."

Eager to move on, he tapped a key and indicated the next photograph. "This is Maurice 'Mousey' Devito. Gambling is his game. If it moves, he'll take a bet on it." After covering Devito, he moved on to the next picture. "And finally, we have Slavic Androposky. He's relatively new, a Russian import. He specializes in protection and security for the businesses Sonny owns."

Richard rose from his seat, and one of the agents raised a hand. "Yes, Ted?" Richard asked.

"Isn't there a place for him with his own kind?" he inquired, and Johnny scoffed at the tasteless joke.

Richard, however, nodded thoughtfully. "Good question. It's one I want you to be able to answer, so take that seriously."

"Yes, sir."

"Each capo oversees a crew of four to five lieutenants, who oversee lower level soldiers. Right now, they're not on our agenda. Any questions?"

"Now that the introductions are over, what's the game plan?" Debra asked.

Richard joined Johnny at the podium. "DeSantis has been on the taskforce shit list for a long time now," he began, his tone tinged with annoyance. "We've had some luck putting a dent in parts of his organization and reducing his cash flow. He's feeling the pinch and, we believe, branching out in non-traditional ways. Johnny, why don't you tell us a little bit about what you've been doing."

Johnny nodded. "I'm working hard getting back into Sonny's good graces, but he's no fool. He's not gonna trust me simply because we have history." He felt it was important to state that. He was doing his best, but they couldn't rely on false expectations. "That being said, while I work my way into his confidence, each of you will be responsible for keeping tabs on the man in your folder."

Richard placed his hand on the podium, and shut off the laptop. The lights in the room brightened, and the agents blinked, adjusting their vision to the brightness. "Everyone, check in with me daily," he said. "We'll meet back here in two weeks to review our progress." Before anyone could move, Richard raised a hand, adding, "Under no circumstances is anyone to contact Johnny."

"Why not?" Debra asked, her interest piqued.

"We have two priorities." Richard exchanged a glance with Johnny, who had already begun to move toward the door. "Putting Sonny away and keeping Johnny alive."

With that, Johnny left, covering his eyes with dark sunglasses as he walked out into the summer heat. He had a date to keep.

\* \* \*

Every week, he met Melissa Saunders at the same bar downtown for lunch. Together, they would enjoy a meal, catch up on old times, and share news about their lives and families. There was a time, back when they'd been going to MIT together, that Johnny almost imagined marrying Mel. But then again, he wasn't the marrying type—and neither was she. Today, she was clad in business attire, silver hoops hanging from her ears. Her blonde highlighted hair hung around her shoulders, and she sat down at their usual table and smiled warmly at Johnny. He couldn't help but feel protective of her, considering their past. Once, their relationship had been filled with passion. Now, they were close friends with a weekly get-together. Mel played the field just like Johnny did, dating casually, but he couldn't help but scrutinize every man she went out with.

"How was your week?" he asked. "Any hot dates?"

Her perfectly angled eyebrow quirked upward. In the bright light near the window, he could just about see the silver-gray color beginning to show in her hair. Johnny's hair was tinged by a bit of gray on the temples, yet women still commented about his blue eyes and the handsome laugh lines that crinkled when he smiled. They were both older now, both different people. Still, she captivated him. "You just want to know so you can keep an eye on me, Johnny. I know you." She smirked, and when the waiter arrived, she said, "The usual, please."

"Right." The waiter, a young college-aged man, turned to Johnny and said, "Same for you, Mr. Macchia?"

"Yep." The rest of his life was unpredictable, but Johnny loved that this time—this weekly lunch date—was always the same. Just him and Mel sharing stories and catching up.

"How's work?" Mel asked, as she sipped from a glass of water.

"Dojo is good," Johnny said, leaving everything else out. His mind was quickly putting together everything he'd have to do in the coming days, regarding his undercover assignment. He couldn't say a word to his old friend Mel; she didn't know about his position with the FBI.

His kids had guessed, once, that he was an undercover agent. It was hard to hide from his two nosy boys, Mikey and J. J., but they didn't know the details and he'd keep it that way. His secretive nature resulted in few friends—Mel being number one among them—and if it weren't for Kate, his deceased wife's sister, he didn't know what he would do. When it came to his work, he could always count on Kate to not ask questions, and to look after his kids when he had to go out of town. Sometimes, his heart ached thinking of his boys. And his late wife Kimberly. He missed her.

"Boy, you are miles away today," Mel commented. "Wanna talk about it?"

"Nah. How are things with you? Distract me from my thoughts," he added, smiling.

"Oh, the usual." She shrugged. "Work is good."

"Everything at Genzer Labs running smoothly?"

"Yep. No complaints."

There was something about the way she said it that made him wonder if that was true, but he didn't say anything. Were things really going as smoothly as she claimed? He couldn't be sure. However, he didn't want to pry or upset her; they'd been friends long enough that he knew it wasn't wise to press the issue.

As they chatted, Johnny relaxed, and the waiter brought their lunch. The soup and salad increased his appetite, and the roast beef sandwich was delicious. They both ordered coffee, and chatted for some time. Then, Johnny glanced at his watch and announced he had to leave.

"Gotta get back to the office."

Mel pouted, jokingly. "Okay. Same time next week, Johnny?"

"Sure, babe," he said, calling her by one of the many pet names he used in her presence. They hugged and parted ways outside the restaurant.

It was people like Mel who kept him sane. He was glad to have a good friend like her.

# Chapter 2: The First Attack

The following day, Johnny took note of how summer seemed hotter here, in town, where the dojo stood on a busy street across from shops and restaurants. He always parked his Corvette in the lot behind the building, next to the SUV he used when he wasn't out meeting Sonny or Frankie, or doing odd jobs with some exceptions based on the job at hand. Both vehicles remained out of sight.

Besides the fact that the building was spacious, large enough to house the dojo, a martial arts supply store, and the office where he conducted his private investigative business in the basement, the location couldn't have been better. His students often hung out at the eatery across the street, and the local shop owners were accustomed to seeing Johnny. As far as everyone was concerned, he was a martial arts teacher. Others knew about his side business as a private investigator.

But nobody knew he'd been leading a secret double life as an undercover FBI agent.

When he taught his classes, he kept up the façade, and he was a natural at it because teaching was so important to him. Passing on his knowledge of the martial arts was a passion he held close to his heart.

He glanced up at the wall clock. "Okay, everyone, we've only got a few minutes left for today," he announced, facing a room of tired-looking, expectant students. "Let's go through one last thing."

He showed them an additional Judo throw, *O Soto Makikomi*, and corrected a few students on their form and technique. When the class ended, and everyone bowed and left to get changed and collect their things, Johnny wiped the back of his neck with a hand towel and ran his hand through his dark, brown hair. He could do with a shower, but first he had to finish some paperwork.

Taking the steps two at a time, he headed down into the fully refurbished basement and stepped into his office. The open windows above him, which let in daylight from the street, brought him the sounds of his laughing and chattering students as they left the building. Despite the fact that his dojo was part of his cover, he still had students he had to worry about, and that always involved paperwork.

Time passed quickly as he finished things up.

Then, he was startled by the sound of screeching tires in the parking lot. In the past, he'd had students messing around back there, so it was the first thought in his mind as he jumped to his feet and rushed out the back of the building, still clad in his *gi*.

As he stepped outside and rushed up the steps that led into the parking lot, Johnny cast a furtive gaze across the small lot and toward the alley that ran behind the building. The parking lot was empty except for Johnny's car, but in the alley he spotted the source of the commotion. *A crash?*

A limo sat at an angle on the nearby embankment, close to a set of dumpsters. The limo's positioning made it appear as if the driver had been trying to leave, yet a Mack truck in the middle of deliveries had blocked its exit.

At first, Johnny thought it was just an accident, and he could see the driver of the limo was slumped against the steering wheel, apparently unconscious and bleeding. What could have happened to cause this? He hurried toward the car, but there was yet another screech of tires as a third vehicle barreled down the alley, increasing in speed. The driver slammed on the brakes so hard the car jolted forward, and before the vehicle even came to a complete stop, two Asian men shot out of either side and rushed toward the limo, pulling open the passenger side doors.

Johnny was aghast. At first, no one seemed to notice his presence, and he wasn't entirely certain what was unfolding before him. He did the only thing he could think of: he tried to get their attention.

"Hey!" he shouted. "What the hell you think you're doin'?"

The two men, both dressed in dark clothing, snapped their attention to Johnny. Though they seemed surprised at first, they immediately sprung into action and lunged for him. Johnny, well practiced in the art of self-defense, quickly disabled both men. He attacked the first assailant by using an Axe Kick, knocking the man to the ground and throwing the second assailant with an *Ippon seoinage*, the Judo one-arm shoulder throw, then quickly putting him into an Arm Bar, snapping the bone. Though they tried to get the best of him, he emerged victorious, and by the time the fight was over they were running back to their car and speeding away.

Johnny was breathing heavily. *Good thing I didn't bother to shower yet.*

He rushed toward the limo and opened the driver's side door. After quickly surveying the situation, Johnny saw the wound on the man's shoulder, and checked for a pulse, pressing his fingers to the man's clammy neck. While leaning forward, Johnny noticed a figure in the backseat. He hadn't noticed him right away because he was huddled against the door, trembling, glancing wildly out the windows as if expecting the men to return.

"Hey, buddy. You okay?" Johnny asked.

The man in the backseat startled. "Don't hurt me!" he shrieked. "Please, God, don't hurt me, please!" He blubbered, his fists against his mouth, a sheen of sweat spreading across his face.

"Relax," Johnny said, keeping his tone gentle. "I'm not gonna hurt ya. But I can't say the same about the guys who just sped away." Johnny moved slowly to the back of the car and opened the passenger door. "What's your name?" he asked.

The man hesitated as if trying to decide if he could trust him. "It's Joseph," he said, stammering. "Joseph Holmes, the third."

Johnny stepped aside. "Well, Joseph, you wanna come on outta there? Those guys are gone for now."

"How'd you do that...beat them like that?" He looked at Johnny's *gi*, then glanced around as if unsure where he was.

Johnny forced a chuckle. "I don't dress like this every day." He nodded toward the building. "That's my martial arts school. I teach here, and I just finished a class."

"Jesus. How lucky am I? I could have ended up anywhere else."

Johnny acknowledged the truth in that. He was lucky, for sure. Before he could say anything, Joseph hurried to the front of the car and said, "Is he alive?"

Johnny surveyed the driver, who was still unconscious. "Yeah, but he's hurt pretty bad." He crossed his arms over his massive chest. "Now, do you want to fill me in on what I just got myself involved in?"

Sirens wailed in the distance. The law was on its way. Johnny wanted some answers before they arrived, but he wasn't sure he'd get them. The befuddled man before him drew in a few ragged breaths and leaned against the car.

"They came out of nowhere," Joseph gasped, as if on the verge of a panic attack. "We were chased off the highway. They were shooting at us! Who would want me dead?"

Johnny couldn't answer that question, either. He led the man into the building, where he urged him into a chair and brought him a bottle of water. They'd find out soon enough what was going on.

\* \* \*

The day dragged on, and Johnny still hadn't changed out of his *gi*. There hadn't been enough time before the officers arrived on the scene. He kept his arms crossed, fully aware of the distinct odor of sweat that poured off him. He sidled discretely away from Joseph, who had stopped trembling, but now clutched the water Johnny had given him as if his life depended on it.

They watched as the ambulance took the limo driver away, and the tow truck then dragged the car off. After photographing the scene and cleaning up, a number of officers departed, and a plainclothes detective approached. He handed Joseph a business card.

"Hello, gentleman. My name is Detective Casey. I apologize for not introducing myself sooner."

"That's…that's okay," Joseph said, still stammering.

"It's been a long day," Johnny commented.

"Well, we're just about done here." Casey shook Joseph's hand warmly. "If you can think of anything else, Mr. Holmes, just give me a call."

When the detective left, and the alley had been cleared up, the two men were left alone. Johnny rubbed the back of his neck and sighed heavily. "Okay, they're gone now." He knew he couldn't take that shower just yet. He needed to know what was going on. "Spill it," he said.

Joseph's mouth gaped for a moment. "But I…I don't know any more than what I told that detective."

"So, there I was in my office, doing my paperwork after class," Johnny reflected, realizing several hours had passed. "When all of a sudden *this* happens right outside my own damn building. And you expect me to believe that you were run off the highway by someone shooting at you, but you don't know what it's all about?"

Joseph's gaze darted around the alley before he took a long gulp from his water bottle. Annoyed, Johnny huffed and turned to head back to the building. All he could do was hope that none of this came back to bite him in the ass. Before he could get very far, he heard Joseph's resigned sigh. "Okay, okay…look. If you want to help, you can give me the number of a good private investigator. Because I could really use one."

Johnny smirked, turning on his heel. "The universe works in mysterious ways," he said, taking the man's hand and shaking it firmly. "You're looking at one. Johnny Macchia's the name."

"Then, are you interested in getting involved, Mr. Macchia?" Joseph had calmed considerably. Maybe the bottle of water had helped.

"I think I'm already involved," Johnny said, thinking back to the beating he'd given those two men. "Why don't we go inside, and you can fill me in? We'll take it from there." He ushered his newest client toward the back of the dojo. "Come on into my office and make yourself comfortable." Once again, Johnny got a whiff of his own *gi* and grimaced. "Mind if I take a quick shower and change while you wait?"

* * *

In a highly secret location in the city, secluded in a corporate building that no one would have suspected, Kazumi Tabata entered the large office suite on the top floor and sat down behind his desk, adjusting his suit jacket as he did so. Despite his salt and pepper hair, weathered appearance, and small stature, he was a man to be reckoned with. No one dared defy him, and if they did, it was a certain death sentence. The Japanese warlord didn't take kindly to disobedience. The three men standing before him bowed with deep respect.

He cleared his throat. It pleased him that these men trembled before him, and one of them seemed frightened enough that he might've pissed his pants. Kazumi smirked, then wiped any hint of amusement from his features. "I am disappointed, gentlemen. Talk."

Kenzi, the most formidable of the men, his dark hair slicked back and his hands clasped before him, raised his chin high. "We hit the driver and cornered the target in an alley, Tabata-sama…"

"Good. And?"

Beads of sweat appeared on the man's brow. "Someone was there who interrupted our mission," he finished.

"And this intruder is lying in the alley as we speak?" Kazumi doubted this, but it would've been the ideal. He waited to discover the truth of the matter.

The three men exchanged glances as if trying to decide who would explain the truth, and the silence only disappointed Kazumi further. It could only mean one thing: that this mysterious intruder had somehow compromised the mission. Kazumi rose to his feet and moved slowly, like a panther preparing to pounce. He stood before Kenzi, who locked eyes with him briefly before lowering his head.

Kazumi straightened his tie, frowning. "I see. This is very displeasing." Once again, he turned slowly and stepped behind his desk, lowering himself into his leather office chair. He clasped his hands over the ink blotter on the surface of his immaculate desk. "Now, find out who this intruder is," he said, his voice firm and edged with menace. "I would like to know who was able to *interrupt* three of my best men with such success."

Each man uttered an affirmative response in Japanese, then turned to leave the office. They halted for a brief moment when they heard the last thing Kazumi said, which was most certainly a promise:

"Do not dishonor me again. To do so would be fatal."

# Chapter 3: Fishing For Information

The office was a comfortable place to conduct business, and Johnny knew the atmosphere made clients feel at ease. Many of the people who came to him had so many of their own problems that he wanted to make sure they felt comfortable enough to talk to him in his office. The easier it was for them to discuss their situations, the simpler it made the process.

After taking a five-minute shower and hurriedly changing into street clothes, Johnny felt a lot better—and he figured he smelled better, too. He leaned back in his office chair and watched Joseph fumble with his hands in the seat across from him.

"Tell me a bit about yourself, Joseph," he prompted. He had a notepad in case he had to write anything down, but Johnny's memory was such that he almost always *remembered* everything, even the things he'd sooner forget. It was likely that anything Joseph told him would be filed away in his mind for retrieval later on.

"Well," Joseph began, "I work in computer security. In fact, I just left a client. That's why I'm so baffled about this whole incident. I'm worried about my limo driver, he's a good friend of mine. I hope he'll be all right. I just don't understand why anyone would want to hurt me."

Johnny wondered how sensitive the man's work was, and what exactly he was involved in. "Maybe there's a connection between this and your client."

"You can't be serious," Joseph said, appearing baffled. "There can't be a connection." He unbuttoned the top button of his dress shirt and fanned himself. The air conditioning must not have been cooling him off very well.

"Who's your client?"

"Barry Genzer of Genzer Laboratories," Joseph said. "He's a computer chip developer."

Johnny did his best to hide his surprise. Barry Genzer was this man's client? Thinking back to his years in college, Johnny recalled graduating after Barry had already left the school. But his name had been everywhere, and all Johnny's classmates knew that Barry Genzer was destined for success. He just couldn't believe the irony, then recalled lunch with Mel. She'd acted as if everything was fine, but he'd known otherwise. Now it became clear to him. Without even having to wait for Joseph's explanation, Johnny knew something was going on with Genzer Labs, and Mel must know something about it. The laboratory and the offices were right down the street, so close to the dojo, so it didn't surprise him that everything had unfolded practically in his lap.

He shook his head, holding up a hand. "I know Barry Genzer. Well, not very personally, but we went to the same college."

"I really can't get into my arrangement with Barry until I clear it with him...you, I mean..." Joseph stammered again. "I mean, clear you with him...working for us...for me." He shook his head, running his hand through his light brown hair. "Shit." He wiped the back of his hand across his forehead. "You know Barry?"

"Yeah, but like I said, not really well. He was just a classmate, and he graduated before me anyway. I haven't seen him in a while, but I'm good friends with someone who works for him."

"I feel so relieved to be talking with you." Joseph exhaled heavily. "What should I do?"

"I think I can help you. But it sounds like Mr. Genzer could be the link in all of this."

"It's been a long day." He heaved a sigh. "You really think you can find out what's going on here, Mr. Macc...Mr....Johnny?"

"Yes. Why don't you call Mr. Genzer and set up a meeting? I'd like to ask him a few questions." Johnny rose from his seat.

"Okay." Joseph followed suit, trying to straighten his sweaty hair with his fingers. "Shit," he said again.

"What is it?"

"I...I have no car."

Johnny walked around the desk and placed a reassuring hand on the man's shoulder. "Come on. I'll give you a ride home."

\* \* \*

The drab stone apartment building was located on a street with other, similar old buildings, the bricks cracking and weeds poking up from the sidewalk. The day dragged on, and Joseph was surprised to discover it wasn't even four o'clock when he arrived home and climbed the concrete steps to the front door. Making his way inside to his apartment, he decided he'd have time to check on Matt at the hospital.

Matt had been his driver ever since Joseph had been promoted. Appearances were important to the clients, and when they saw Joseph roll up in the limo and climb out wearing a pristine Armani suit, they were always impressed. Today was supposed to be routine; it shouldn't have ended up with Matt in the hospital. Joseph realized with a sudden jolt of panic that he didn't even know the extent of his friend's injuries.

He showered and changed hurriedly, then emerged from the bathroom and into the tiny, sparsely furnished living room. He'd never felt so uncertain, so anxious and unsteady. The paramedics had wanted to take him to the hospital just to check him out, but he knew there was no point. He was just frantic, upset over the whole ordeal. There was nothing they could do for him. When he'd arrived home, he'd left his wallet on the coffee table. He picked it up now, and pulled the tiny computer chip out of an inside pocket. He studied it for a moment before placing it on his desk, then picked up his phone and dialed a number by heart.

"Hi, it's me," he said when his call was answered. "I think you were right." Scrubbing his hand over clean-shaven face, he huffed and slumped onto the sofa. "Well, before I was run off the road by some maniacs wielding guns, I found what looks like a bug in my car." He answered the question with a degree of irritation. At least he was home and in one piece. "I don't know," he said. "I just got home and haven't called the hospital yet. The paramedics said he was stable, though, before they took him from the accident."

He paused. "Yeah, I'll keep you posted." An ache rose in his chest as he thought of Matt, his longtime friend, whose only job was to drive him around in that goddamn limo. He didn't deserve this. "I would like to know one thing, Barry," Joseph continued into the phone. "How the hell did they know? I mean, I just left your office." He paused again, listening. "Yeah, well, I think I have a solution to the problem in the form of a P.I. I'll fill you in when I see you." Joseph fought the urge to fall asleep on the sofa. Instead, he took a deep breath and said, "Yeah, you be careful too. Bye."

When he hung up, he slipped the phone into his pocket and sighed heavily. All he could think was that, at the very least, God must've been looking out for him when he had those nuts chase him and Matt into the alley behind the martial arts school.

Someone was after him, or more accurately, after information. There must be a leak at Genzer Labs, and Barry Genzer had information that somebody wanted.

It was obvious to Joseph that this *somebody* wouldn't stop until they got what they were looking for.

He hoped he wouldn't become a casualty. Without Johnny Macchia, Joseph would've been done for.

# Chapter 4: Impersonators

Mass General Hospital was a massive building that overwhelmed Joseph's senses. He hated hospitals. He entered, carrying the bouquet of flowers he'd bought to brighten up Matt's room, and approached the information desk inside the main entrance.

"Excuse me," he said. The security guard glanced up at him from her paperwork.

"Yes, can I help you?"

"I'm lookin' for…for my driver," he explained, fumbling with his words.

"First, I need your I.D."

Joseph handed the security guard his license and watched as she typed something into her computer, then glanced up a moment later, handing him a printed guest pass with his picture on it. Joseph removed the backing and stuck it on the breast pocket of his shirt.

"Can you tell me what room he's in?"

"I sure can if you tell me what his name is."

Joseph felt his face heat. "Oh, sorry." He forced a chuckle, but it couldn't have sounded that amusing because the security guard's expression remained impassive. "His name is Matt. Matthew Crespo."

She typed on the keyboard again, finally offering him a compassionate smile. "He's in room 430," she said. "Take the elevator down the hall to the fourth floor."

"Thank you," Joseph said. As he started off down the hall, he halted, glancing down at the flowers in his hand. A moment of inspiration caused him to tug a flower from the bouquet and turn on his heel. He headed back to the security guard and handed her the flower. She blushed in reply, and he set off down the hall.

When he located room 430, he paused at the door, smoothing a hand down his shirt, and readjusting the bouquet in his hand. Then he pushed open the door. The sight of his friend in the bed, hooked up to an IV, made him hesitate. He was hooked up to oxygen, along with EKG wires to monitor his heart. How bad had the damage been?

"Hey, Matt," he started, having to clear his throat first. He wasn't certain his driver was awake. "I brought you some flowers. I wasn't sure what kind you liked...so I...I had the florist do a kind of a mishmash." He stared down at the flowers, feeling increasingly awkward. Then he stepped into the tiny bathroom, ran the water, and returned with the flowers arranged in a plastic pitcher he'd found. He placed them on the bedside table and shoved his hands into his pockets.

Matt still had his eyes closed. Joseph stared at him, then said, "I hope you don't mind, but I gave one away."

He startled when he heard the door open behind him. A doctor entered, appearing surprised to find Joseph there.

"Oh, hello," the doctor said. He extended his arm, and the two men shook hands. "I'm Doctor Mason." The doctor was a stocky man, his thin brown hair slicked back, a stethoscope hanging around his neck.

"Joseph, Joseph Holmes."

"Are you family?"

"You could say that," Joseph said, contemplating his answer. "His parents are deceased and I'm the closest thing he has to a brother. Besides that, we work together. He's my driver."

The doctor nodded in understanding, appearing fully aware of Matt's occupation and how he'd ended up in this mess.

"Uh…how is he?" Joseph asked.

"Well, the bullet hit the subclavian artery. He's been in and out of consciousness and he's lost a lot of blood, but he'll pull through."

Joseph realized he'd been holding his breath the entire time the doctor had been talking. He exhaled heavily. "Okay. Good." He reached into his pocket and pulled out his business card, handing it to the doctor. "Please, if there's any change, let me know. I also want the hospital bills sent to me. I feel this is all my fault. If we hadn't been going to see that client this morning…" He shook his head as if to clear it. "It was me they were after, I'm sure of it. Not him. Matt wouldn't hurt a fly. He didn't deserve this."

If the doctor was shocked at Joseph's willingness to handle all the bills, he didn't show it. Instead, he offered him a sympathetic smile. "You can let the financial office know about the billing issue, and they'll take care of it for you. I'm sure the police officers who were here earlier are diligently following this case. They were very anxious to talk to Mr. Crespo. The nurses told me they almost had to call security to make them leave. He needed his rest."

"The police? They were at the scene. They know how bad he is. Wouldn't they wait for him to wake? What did they look like?" Suddenly afraid to leave his friend alone, he waited for the doctor's reply.

"The nurses told me the police officers were three Asian gentlemen."

Joseph felt his face flush as anger brewed within him. How could the hospital staff let phony cops into Matt's room? "Those weren't cops," he said, gritting his teeth. The doctor, appearing shocked, started to say something, but Joseph cut him off. "Were they dressed like cops?"

"Well, yes, of course."

"Don't let those guys in here again. If they show up, call the *real* cops," he said, knowing they must have presented fake identification in order to get past the guards. "And I demand to speak with the hospital administrator."

"Sir, I can assure you, this won't happen again."

"I *still* want to speak with the hospital administrator. Now," he snapped.

"Yes, sir. I'll take you to him."

# Chapter 5: Yakuza Connection

Kazumi Tabata entered his plush office, catching his breath while wiping the sweat from his brow. The air conditioning felt good on his bare chest after a long exercise session. Two men were waiting for him in front of his massive desk; he'd made them wait. He liked being spontaneous because it kept his men on their toes. Both gentlemen appeared nervous as they stood there, since Kazumi himself had summoned them.

Akira and Kenzi, both in their mid-thirties, had been working for him for some time. They had yet to be told why they were there. He preferred it that way. Rounding his desk, he whipped the towel away from his neck, baring the Yakuza tattoo that filled most of his back. Wiping away the remainder of the sweat, he chuckled and said, "Workout. An interesting American word. It is not work, and it is not out. No wonder English is so difficult." Lowering himself into his chair, he looked across his desk at the two men. "There is much to discuss." He couldn't help but notice both underlings appeared terrified of him, yet respectful. *Good.*

When he gestured to the chairs across from his desk, both men sat down.

"Tobata-sama," Kenzi began, his voice steady. "There are whispers you are displeased with DeSantis-san. Does he jeopardize our operation?"

Akira leaned back, his hands firm on the leather arms of the chair. "It would be a simple matter to dispose of him."

Kazumi shook his head, frowning. "Not so simple, and there is too much at stake." He reached into the top drawer of his desk and retrieved a tiny electrical device, holding it between his thumb and index finger. "Behold," he said. "*Suzumebachi*...Hornet. The Hornet of the Yakuza. Only Japanese technological superiority could produce such a device. With this, we are the world's *real* superpower." He knew both men were impressed, but neither showed a flicker of emotion.

"There are those who would pay any price for it," Kenzi said.

Akira nodded. "Already we receive inquiries from the caves of Afghanistan and the deserts of Iran."

Kazumi allowed the corner of his lip to twitch upward in a sly smile; he couldn't conceal his pride. "The secrets of the Hornet are not for sale. Not just yet. A taste of its power will be shared...with the right people."

"And you have determined who these people are, Tobata-sama?" Kenzi inquired.

"Patience is a virtue among us, Kenzi. It won't be long until each of our partners learns his place."

Akira folded his hands in his lap. "DeSantis does not know his place, *Oyaji*?" he asked, referring to his leader as *Boss* in Japanese.

"DeSantis is of some concern, yes," Kazumi confirmed. "But not for the reason you believe. He is eager to tie his family to ours. The ways of...of...*La Cosa Nostra* are not the ways of the Yakuza."

"It is presumptuous of him to think he stands on equal footing with you, Tobata-sama," Kenzi said.

"Americans are often presumptuous. It has served them well."

"And how can we serve you now?" Akira asked.

"Follow DeSantis." Kazumi leaned forward, clasping his hands on the mahogany surface of his heavy desk. "Learn all you can. We must help him find his true place among us."

"We will not fail you, Tobata-sama."

Both men rose from their seats, but before they could leave, Kazumi stopped them. "I also want you to follow up on the man who came to Mr. Holmes's rescue," he ordered. "Find out who he is, what he does, and find out his place in all this. It could be nothing, but I suspect this man is more than he seems."

"Do you think he threatens the Hornet?" Kenzi asked, turning on his heel.

Kazumi lifted the device to eye level, scrutinizing it, pondering before he spoke. "To threaten the Hornet invites death by its sting." As the men left, Kazumi stood and stared out the large window, across the city.

No one would interfere with his plans. He would make sure of it.

# Chapter 6: The Twilight Zone

Johnny carefully navigated his Corvette through the narrow city streets. It was so hot, he spotted a bunch of kids in a nearby park playing in a fountain. Feeling glad for the air conditioning in his car, he sang along to the music singing on the oldies radio station. His cell phone rang, spurring him to turn the music down and hurriedly answer his phone.

"Hello?"

"Johnny, it's Anthony."

"Hey, man, what's up?"

Anthony DeLuca, a master of the martial arts, taught in Johnny's Dojo. They'd known each other since childhood.

"How did Jake do in his class this morning?" Anthony asked, mentioning one of their students.

"He didn't show up," Johnny said. "How's this kid gonna graduate to the next rank if he never shows up?"

"He promised he'd be there."

"Well, he wasn't. I know you want me to cut him a break, Anthony, but the bottom line is when my students perform, and master their techniques properly, they deserve to be promoted. Then and only then will the student be promoted to the next rank. There are no exceptions! I will not give ranks to students who do not deserve it and I will not deviate from my principles. No pain, no gain! Furthermore, there're kids in my class who are really dedicated and want to learn so—"

Before he could finish rattling off the many reasons why letting a kid slide in a martial arts class was a bad idea, Johnny felt his body jolt forward when someone slammed into his car from behind. Glancing in his rear-view mirror, he spotted a white van. He wondered if the driver was legally blind, or just an idiot, because the van hit him a second time.

His gut told him the driver wasn't stupid. Johnny was being targeted.

"I gotta call you back," he said into the phone, tossing it on the passenger seat before Anthony could reply.

Then he sped up, passing a slow moving Cadillac when he got a chance, and piloting the car to a somewhat wider city street where he might be able to lose his pursuers. He had the streets of Boston memorized. Dodging traffic and whipping around turns, he did his best to elude the tail. However, the van kept appearing behind him, whether it was a few cars back, or closer. The van passed a few vehicles to get closer, and someone hit their horn repeatedly.

Thinking quickly, Johnny took a turn down a narrow side street, listening to the crunch when the van collided with a line of parked cars. It would take them a second to back up and continue the chase, which was just enough time for Johnny to conceal himself. Recalling a narrow alley nearby, which connected to another street on the other side, he whipped his Corvette into the mouth of it and made sure all the lights were off. Flanked on both sides by brick apartment buildings, he waited a moment.

It had worked. While the driver of the van had been busy dislodging himself from the parked cars, he hadn't spotted Johnny slip into the alley. He watched the van speed past the mouth of the alley, and breathed a sigh of relief.

While his mind reeled with questions of who might've been after him, and why, Johnny drove the car down the one-way alley and slowed at the stop sign. The alley led to a wider, busier road. As he glanced both ways and prepared to turn, he spotted Joseph crossing the road, talking on his cell phone. He carried a gray herringbone sport jacket in the crook of his elbow, and wore a long-sleeved white shirt and gray trousers despite the heat—probably on his way to a business meeting.

The alley behind him was rarely traveled, so he knew his car would be safe for the length of time it would take him to say a quick hello to Joseph. He put his car in park and hopped out, walking toward the younger man. As Joseph crossed the street, he appeared not to notice the large truck barreling toward him. The truck horn blew, and Johnny knew the driver couldn't slow down fast enough, so he jolted forward and grabbed the oblivious man. Pulling them both out of the way, they hit the hood of a parked car and rolled onto the sidewalk.

Huffing, Johnny righted himself, feeling the ache in his back. The day had begun with a white van pursuing him, and now he'd saved the clueless Joseph from turning into road kill. What the hell kind of a day was this?

"Didn't your mother...ever teach you to look both ways before...crossing the street?" Johnny asked, catching his breath. When he didn't hear an answer, he glanced to his left and realized Joseph was crawling around on his hands and knees, looking for something.

"My glasses." Joseph gasped. "My glasses, I have to find my glasses!"

"Your glasses?" Johnny asked, incredulous. He'd just saved the guy's life, and he was worried about his glasses. He rose to his feet, watching Joseph scurry around on the cement. Finally, the man shot to his feet, but wavered unevenly. Johnny placed a hand on his shoulder, steadying him. He watched as Joseph searched his pockets.

"Have you seen my cell phone?"

"Your cell phone?" Johnny shook his head in disbelief. If he didn't know any better, he would've assumed he'd been pranked, or possibly slipped into *The Twilight Zone*. He glanced around the busy street for Rod Serling, but failed to spot him among the shoppers, teenager tapping away at iPhones, and smartly dressed executives stepping into air-conditioned buildings. Nearby, a bum yawned and sat down on a bench. Nope, he wasn't in The Twilight Zone after all. "How do I get myself mixed up in this stuff?"

"Oh, here it is," Joseph said, appearing relieved as he retrieved his cell phone from where he'd dropped it. "I'm so glad the screen isn't cracked!" He hurriedly tapped a button, and waited a moment. "Sorry, Barry," he began, shooting Johnny a glare that seemed extremely unwarranted, "I was just tackled in the middle of the street. Never mind. I'll explain later. See you in a bit." He hung up and tucked the phone into his pocket, slightly loosening his death grip on his blazer.

Johnny rubbed his temples. "Do you realize that you almost became imbedded in the grille of a Mack truck?"

Joseph glanced around, seeming puzzled. "Mack truck? Oh, yes…yes. Well, I suppose I owe you a debt of gratitude again, don't I? You always seem to be in the right place at the right time."

"Yeah, so I've been told." Johnny sighed, brushing some dirt off his clothes. As he headed back to his idling Corvette, he wondered what else the day had in store for him.

# Chapter 7: Genzer Labs

In a room at Genzer Labs, Inc., where computer chips were assembled, evening light permeated the room. As they entered, Joseph watched as Barry Genzer led the way, flicking on an overhead light. Most of the staff had left for the day, and Joseph knew that Barry wanted to minimize their chances of being overheard.

"I thought we were as secure as a space station," Barry said, lowering his heavy frame onto a lab stool. "Our cameras and sensors function all day, every day. No one gets in or out that we don't know about."

Joseph slipped his hands into his pockets. "None of this makes sense, then."

"We're a technology company, for Christ's sake," Barry said, running his hand over his head to straighten out his comb-over. "How can Itchito-Mori, Japan's leading applied technology firm, be developing designs that mirror our own? It's un-fuckin' real."

"Are you sure something's actually wrong?" Joseph took a seat across from him at the lab table. "Could it just be a glitch in the system?"

Barry shook his head. "I've been around computers and their inner workings my whole life. As a kid, I built my own version of a guided missile."

Joseph's eyes widened in appreciation. "Wow, that's impressive."

"You couldn't pry me out of the lab in college," Barry said, chuckling. "You already know I earned a master's degree in theoretical design at MIT. I worked for a number of small and large applied technology firms before striking out on my own. I think I know a glitch when I see one," he added, his tone morose.

"What about your staff? How well do you trust them?"

"Everyone here is someone I worked with before, and everyone has been checked out—thoroughly. There isn't a single spy among us," Barry assured him. "I'm absolutely certain."

Joseph leaned his arms on the table before him, frowning. "Look, you wouldn't be the first CEO to learn someone on his team worked for the competition. I'm not saying that's the problem, but there *is* a problem."

"Yes, you don't have to remind me of that."

"It's espionage," Joseph said. "Johnny Macchia is meeting me here. What happened to me the other day was more than a warning. I'd be dead if Johnny hadn't been there."

Barry seemed uncertain. "What makes you think we can trust him? I had him checked out. He teaches martial arts to neighborhood kids and has a private investigator's license. I'm not impressed by his client list."

"You don't have to be. I am. There's more to Johnny than meets the eye. I trusted him immediately. I liked the way he handled himself. He's professional and unconventional." Joseph clasped his hands before him. "It's what we need."

* * *

Johnny elected to bring his business associate, Ray Hachimoto, to his scheduled meeting with Joseph and his boss. Ray was a tall man, like Johnny. Both men were clad in business casual. They'd been friends for years, and Ray was also a Karate master. They worked closely at the dojo, and Ray had always been able to offer business knowledge that Johnny didn't know off-hand. He was an essential asset to the front that concealed Johnny's true position as an undercover FBI agent.

As the security guard led them toward the glassed-in lab, Johnny spotted the two men inside. "There's Joseph," he said. "The other guy with the graying hair must be Barry Genzer. I haven't seen him in ages."

When they were led inside, the security guard took up a post outside the room. Joseph rose to his feet, extending a hand. The two men shook warmly, and Johnny introduced his friend.

"Some set-up you got downstairs," Johnny said. "I don't usually let someone get so frisky with me unless she buys me a drink first, but in this case, I'll make an exception."

"My fault, Johnny." Joseph led them toward the table where two other chairs sat waiting for them. "I told the guards to expect you, but forgot to tell them to forgo the usual search procedures."

"No sweat! Actually, it lets me see just how serious you are about security." He gestured toward his old friend. "Ray knows some aspects of business that I'm not as familiar with, so I bring him along sometimes. I hope that's okay."

Both men nodded. "Thank you both for coming," Barry said, introducing himself. "Have a seat." Once they were seated, Barry continued, "We're dead serious about security, Mr. Macchia—"

"Everyone calls me Johnny."

"All right, Johnny. As I was saying, without security, this company dies and so do thousands of others who rely on the impenetrability of the codes and ciphers built into our applications."

"Very nice set-up you've got here," Ray interjected.

"What this nice set-up does is effect the outcome of conflicts around the world for the next hundred years. The U.S. is one of the few superpowers left. I won't deal with any foreign nations despite the money offered."

"Do you have an offer?" Joseph asked.

Barry shrugged. "I always get offers. There are a number of firms that would pay almost anything for a piece of Genzer Labs. They're like flies. I brush them off, and they circle and come back for more. Annoying, but no real threat."

"So what's different now?" Johnny wondered.

"Barry's design innovations are showing up in Asia and Central Europe," Joseph explained. "At a recent design symposium in Japan, a presentation was made hinting at the applications being developed here. Only, no mention of Genzer was made."

"Since the fall of the Soviet Union, strange alliances have formed around the world," Barry said. "Globalization takes on a new meaning when we're talking about industrial espionage."

Ray nodded, running his thick fingers over his neatly trimmed goatee. "Okay, let me see if I get it. Top secret computer application technology is getting out of this maximum security facility and showing up in places it shouldn't be. Your sensors, cameras, guards, and high-tech gizmos are no help? Maybe you need to adopt a low-tech approach."

The sound of the glass doors opening caused the men to turn and glance at the entrance. A beautiful woman in her forties who looked years younger than her age, clad in a tailored, light gray suit, stepped toward the table. Her simple gold earrings and necklace twinkled in the light, her neatly styled hair curving around her slender neck. The woman's poise and confidence was apparent. Johnny grinned when he saw her.

"I heard the tail end of that," she said. "Sorry I'm late. Very good, Mr.—"

"Ray Hachimoto," Johnny said. "Glad to see you again, Mel."

Barry rose from his seat and draped a protective arm around the woman's shoulder. Johnny's eyebrow quirked upward at the gesture. Why did it seem like every man was after her? He'd have to ask her about Barry during their next lunch date. She gave Johnny a wink.

"Mel and I met at MIT," Barry said.

"We were never in classes together, were we, Barry?" Johnny said. "You graduated the year before me."

"That's right. And while you were off doing whatever it was you do best, I convinced Mel to join me once the lab was open."

"I know. She's damn good at what she does."

"Her job is to use every means available to destroy, disable, deprogram, or in some way interfere with an application's performance. If Mel can't make it fail, no one can." Barry gently squeezed her shoulder and stepped back to his seat, indicating the empty chair beside him.

Joseph shook her hand. "It's a pleasure to meet you, Mel."

Once everyone was seated again, Johnny leaned forward, eyeing Mel with increasing curiosity. "You think Ray is on to something?"

She nodded. "Yes. Barry and I have been over this place a hundred times. All the equipment checked and re-checked. Staff, too. Nothing enters or leaves the building unless it's taken apart and put back together with us watching. Despite all we're doing, we can't seem to stop the leak. To me, that means we're looking in the wrong direction."

"I agree," Joseph said. "If high-tech prevents anything from getting in or out, then low-tech is the answer."

"Whatever this is, it's simple. So simple that we're overlooking it. That's why we need help."

"And whoever is behind it doesn't care if people get hurt," Johnny said, recalling the injured limo driver.

"Have any attempts been made on anyone other than Joseph?" Barry asked.

"Not that I know of," Johnny replied.

"Well, I do feel as if I'm being watched." Barry scratched his chin thoughtfully. "Maybe I'm just getting paranoid."

Ray shook his head. "Paranoia gets a bad rap. It keeps you alert and could keep you alive. Pay attention to it."

Just then, Johnny was distracted by the ringing of his cell phone. He listened to the woman on the other line for a moment, then said, "Damn it, Gina, I'll be there within the hour. If that's not good enough—" He paused, glancing at the screen on the phone. "She hung up on me."

Mel smirked. "Your girlfriend sounds pretty demanding. Should we discuss that later, Johnny?"

"Believe me," he said, rising from his seat, "that was no girlfriend."

# Chapter 8: Visitor From D.C.

Nunchucks Martial Arts Supply Store was located in the front area of Johnny's dojo on a busy street in an urban downtown area of Boston. He'd taken his son, J. J., on this outing. The kid didn't appear too thrilled. He was a thin young man, with a full head of chestnut brown hair and hazel eyes. He much resembled his father when Johnny was younger. He was quiet, and not very outgoing, but Johnny knew he had a couple girlfriends at school.

The two entered the store, which was loaded with every type of martial arts equipment imaginable. Items were stacked everywhere, appearing chaotic, but Johnny knew his store manager kept the place extremely organized. He knew where everything was located and could find something for a customer within a minute's notice. A man in his thirties with dark skin and nappy hair stood behind the counter, clad in a black t-shirt that advertised the name of the store. Avery was talking to Anthony DeLuca, who stood on the other side of the counter.

When the bell over the door chimed, Avery looked up and said, "Damn, I knew I shoulda got myself a guard dog." He chuckled. "Never know who's gonna come strolling in here."

Johnny led his son toward the front counter and greeted both men. While J. J. became distracted by some book on *Wing Chun*, Avery emerged from behind the counter and he and Johnny joked around for a while. They'd been good friends for a long time. Avery turned his attention to Johnny's son.

"Hey, J. J. How's it going?"

"Pretty good," J. J. said, paging through the book and placing it back on the shelf. "Just hangin' with the old man. You know how it is."

Anthony leaned against the counter and nodded toward Johnny. "Hey, boss, if you came by to pick up a new uniform for the Roth kid, don't bother. Beat you to it." He held up the stuff he'd just purchased, and handed it to Avery who placed it in a plastic bag.

Johnny smacked himself on the forehead. "Holy shit. I forgot all about him. That skinny kid turned out to be one hell of a fighter. Glad I ran into you, though. I have some business to attend to." He gave his son a pointed glance.

"No problem," J. J. said. "I'll just keep Avery company while you guys talk."

Johnny led Anthony away from the front of the store and into the back of the dojo, where they stood on the *tatami* mats talking.

"I just picked up a new job," Johnny explained. "Computer stuff. Interesting people. Ever heard of Genzer Labs?"

"No, should I?"

"Nah. They're into secretive government work. Work that's turning deadly." Johnny kept his voice low. "You still have buddies down on the dock, right? I want you to renew old acquaintances. See if any new players are setting up shop. Nose around a bit. Nothing turns up, leave it be. Don't push."

"Hell, there's always something going on down at the docks. *Re-vi-tal-i-zation*," Anthony said, sounding out the word. Cheap real estate brings in lots of new people. Anyone in particular I should be looking for?"

"Asian. Specifically Japanese."

Anthony frowned, chewing on his bottom lip. The effect made him look like a chubby pink beaver. Johnny maintained an impassive expression.

Thrusting his hands into the pockets of his blazer, Anthony quipped, "Like I'm supposed to know one from the other."

"Just get your ass down there," Johnny said.

Their conversation complete, the two men walked back to the front of the store. "One more thing," Johnny added in a low murmur, "Be careful. I mean it."

Anthony left the store, waving to Avery and J. J. on his way out. Johnny turned toward Avery and motioned for him to follow him toward the dressing rooms. J. J. was occupied by something on his cell phone. For the first time, Johnny felt grateful for the annoying gadget that seemed to suck up so much of his son's time.

"They here?" Johnny asked, once he and Avery were alone.

"Hell, they're always here."

"Lady G called me to a meeting," he said, referring to Gina. "Any idea what it's about?"

"I mind the store and my own business. It's safer that way," Avery reminded him.

"Right. Tell my kid I'll be right back. Don't let him give you a hard time."

"Sure, man."

As Avery headed back to the front counter, Johnny stepped toward the curtained area of the men's fitting room. There was more going on here than most people realized. Upon entering, he pulled the curtain shut, letting his eyes adjust to the darkness. Then he felt along the side of the mirror and located a hidden lever. Having pressed it, the mirror swung out, revealing a descending staircase. He'd done this so many times, he didn't need to see to know where things were.

After stepping inside, he hit a button on the wall and the mirror closed behind him. The two-way mirror revealed the dressing room beyond, but Johnny was part of another world now. He headed down the stairs, stepping into a spacious basement which was divided into several sections.

At a nearby computer station, two people sat. The man was busy monitoring cameras that displayed the interior of the store and the perimeter of the parking lot. In one of the monitors, Johnny saw his son at the front counter with Avery.

Near the man whose back was turned, a woman sat, reviewing what appeared to be GPS photos and satellite images. The slender woman, whose name was Skyler, was clothed in tight jeans and a black top, and had her sandaled feet propped up on the desktop. Her raven hair hung around her shoulders.

"Afternoon, Sky," he said, nudging her shoulder. "If you ever get tired of looking at those pictures, I've got some snapshots of my ass you might find entertaining." He grinned, having always enjoyed their crude, friendly banter.

She rolled her eyes. "This is high altitude surveillance, not pictures of Uranus." Despite her attempts, he could tell she had difficulty hiding her amusement. "Guess you heard?" she asked, nodding toward the office.

"Heard what?"

"We have a visitor from D.C. Mr. Gianni DiCenza has climbed down from his high horse to pay us a visit."

DiCenza was the assistant director of the FBI in Washington, D.C., working under the current director, Thomas O'Keefe.

"Richard's boss is here?"

"Mm-hmm, and he doesn't look happy," Sky added. "I suggest you get in there." She returned her focus to the monitor before her, and Johnny walked toward a rear office.

Feeling a little nervous, but refusing to show it, he glanced through the window in the closed door first. Two men sat by a large desk, deep in conversation. Johnny recognized Richard Brenner, chief of the FBI Organized Crime Strike Force for the area.

After knocking quietly, Johnny stepped into the room, which was full of heavy cigar smoke. "Didn't anyone ever tell you it's against the law to smoke inside a building? I could have you two arrested."

Richard slammed a ham fist on the desktop. "It's about fucking time you showed up." He popped the cigar out of his mouth, blowing smoke into the air. "You know Gianni DiCenza?"

Johnny nodded toward Gianni, shaking the man's hand. He had the olive skin of an Italian, and he was a big man but not overweight. The sleeves of his white dress shirt were rolled up, and he leaned back in his chair, fixing his dark eyes on Johnny.

"What brings you to town?" Johnny asked.

"Trouble," Gianni said simply. "Serious trouble. National security shit."

"And you need to be up close and personal?"

Gianni pointed a finger at Johnny, his voice loud as he spoke firmly. "Why I need to be here is none of your business, and when Lady G summons you—"

"Lady G can kiss my ass."

"Only in your dreams, dickhead," a female voice intoned.

Johnny hadn't noticed Gina seated close to the back wall, dressed casually in jeans, a work shirt, and laced up sneakers. Her dark brown hair was pulled back in a ponytail. The cigar smoke didn't seem to bother her.

"Okay kids, enough," Richard barked. "We have some serious business to discuss."

"What's so goddamn important that you had to pull me off a job?" Johnny asked.

Gianni put out his cigar. "We've intercepted communications coming into the Boston area from parts unknown. This puts us at a high alert, gentlemen…and lady," he added, glancing at Gina.

"From Genzer Labs?" Johnny crossed his big arms over his chest.

Gianni didn't hide his shock and apparent suspicion. "What the hell do you know about Genzer Labs?"

"It pays to discover these things."

"Cut the shit, Johnny," Richard said. "Genzer Labs and everything connected with it is highly classified."

"I ran into Joseph Holmes the other day—literally. He was run off the road and would have been killed if I hadn't stepped in. To show his gratitude, he hired me as an investigator for him and Barry Genzer. That's where I was when *she* called." He glanced at Gina. "They filled me in on Itchimoto Mori and the impossibility of design coincidences."

Everyone appeared somewhat surprised, even Johnny himself. It was just as Joseph had said; he always seemed to be in the right place at the right time.

Gina leaned against the wall, straightening her shirt. "We think your old friend DeSantis is involved."

Richard puffed on his cigar again. "His usual businesses aren't pulling in the cash they once did, thanks to you. We think he's looking to revamp his organization."

"I had the same thought," Johnny admitted. "I ran into Anthony upstairs. I sent him to do a little dock walking. If Sonny is tied into what's going on at Genzer, Anthony will find out."

"You always send your friends to do your fuckin' dirty work, Johnny?" Gina asked. The two had known each other a long time and often spoke to each other as if they were quarreling siblings.

"This work isn't nearly as dirty as your mouth—"

"Bite me."

"Enough!" Gianni growled. "If you two don't like each other, too fucking bad. I really don't give a shit, but you have to work together. Once this is over, you can kill each other, for all I care."

Richard rose from his seat and stepped between Gianni and Johnny, trying to defuse the situation. "Johnny, Genzer and Holmes fit right into our plans. This is exactly what we need. Just make sure you check in with me daily." He turned to the fiery young woman on the other side of the room. "We'll work up some cover to get you inside too, Gina."

"I hear there's an opening for lap dancers at Sonny's club," Johnny said, unable to stop himself.

"Go fuck yourself," she snapped back, but he saw the smirk on her lips.

Johnny's smart mouth often ran off without him.

# Chapter 9: The Docks

The sun set slowly, twilight making the water in Boston Harbor appear like glass. At the docks, workers continued to load some of the cargo ships, while others had been deserted for the day. The work day was over, for the most part. There were few people around, but Anthony knew he'd find the men he was looking for. He approached a heavyset guy in a hardhat, who wore torn, dirty jeans and a work shirt. The man squinted up at a huge crane that was being used to load a large metal pod onto a cargo ship.

"Hey, Bruno," Anthony said. "How's it hangin'?"

"Hey, Anthony!" Bruno beamed, his fat thumbs hooked into the belt loops of his jeans. He stepped toward him, and the two men embraced like old friends. Anthony clapped him on the back and they parted.

"What the hell brings you down here?" Bruno asked, looking up again to survey the crane as it continued to load freight.

"I need some information and I thought, 'Who knows everything about everything on these docks?' So, here I am."

Bruno nodded, then turned to the crane operator and yelled out, "Hey, Carlo, shut it down! I'm takin' five." Then he put his arm around Anthony's shoulder and led him toward a large door in a building behind them. He stopped just short of entering, and the two men faced each other. "What's on your mind?"

"I'm interested in anything you have on Asian activity down here," Anthony explained, getting straight to the point.

Bruno's curious expression turned wary, his brow furrowing. He took off his hardhat and scratched through his graying hair. "Anthony, what are you doin'? You shouldn't be asking questions that could get you hurt. You know what I mean?"

"No. Why don't you explain it to me?" Anthony remained resolute, standing tall, his arms hanging loosely at his sides.

Bruno glanced around to see if anyone was watching. Then he turned his attention back to his old friend. "Okay. About a month ago, I go over to pier twenty-eight to visit Mario. You remember Mario. He used to date that broad with the tits out to here—" Bruno demonstrated double D-sized breasts with his calloused hands, cupping his palms in front of his chest. "You know, the chick who lives over on 9th Street."

Anthony grinned, knowing that broad was somebody he wouldn't soon forget.

"Anyway," Bruno continued, "I go over there and it's all roped off with these big ropes. I go under the ropes, not thinkin' I'm violatin' anyone's space, and this Asian guy stops me by putting a gun to my temple. It seemed like he came outta nowhere. He starts yelling at me in Chinese or Japanese or 'Dirty Knees,' and I think I'm a goner! Then I hear this other guy say somethin' and the guy with the gun turns around, bows to this dude, and walks away, leaving me in a puddle of my own piss. I look up to explain I was just lookin' for my friend, and there was nobody there. I got outta there so fast, I think I left skid marks."

Anthony frowned. "And you said it was pier twenty-eight?"

"I'm tellin' ya, man, don't go pokin' around where you don't belong."

"Thanks, Bruno." The two men shook hands warmly. "Say hello to your wife and kids for me, okay?"

As he turned to walk away, Bruno called out, "She's gonna want to know when you're comin' to dinner."

Anthony chuckled, turning and walking backward as he spoke. "Hey, I'm only a phone call away." He turned on his heel and headed for pier twenty-eight, listening to the water in the harbor sloshing against the ships.

The walk was a short one from where he'd parked and met Bruno. Glancing around, Anthony felt the hairs on the back of his neck stand up, as if he sensed someone might be watching. But when he looked around, surveying the quickly darkening buildings, the docks, and the long stretches of concrete, he saw no one.

Just as Bruno promised, a large area at pier twenty-eight had been roped off. For a moment, Anthony debated investigating, wondering if he should report back to Johnny with the information he'd discovered so far. Weighing his options, he decided now was a good time to look around. The place seemed empty, and he was unlikely to get caught. Then he could return with even more information for Johnny.

Ducking under the ropes, he walked a few paces and examined his surroundings. It looked like all the rest of the work areas at the docks; nothing appeared amiss. Finding a warehouse door, he tried to peek in the window, but the glass had been covered with black paint.

*Strange.*

Trying the knob, he found the door was unlocked. Glancing in both directions once again, he was sure no one was there—even though the tingling sensation had returned to his neck, and he kept glancing behind as if expecting to find someone standing there. Inside the building, he found himself cloaked in near darkness. The door clicked shut behind him. He took a slow, quiet breath, and allowed his sight to adjust.

Taking a few steps around some piled boxes of freight, he saw a yellowish light emanating from what appeared to be an office on the other side of the warehouse. The silhouette of a man moved across the lit window, but Anthony couldn't make out his features.

Deciding it was time to leave, realizing he was no longer alone, Anthony took a step back and started to turn toward the exit. A sharp pain exploded in the back of his head, and he only had a moment to realize someone had struck him with a blunt object. Images of Johnny, and the martial arts store, flashed through his mind. Snippets of his day returned to him like scenes from an odd dream. He felt his body crumple to the ground, and looked up to see several Asian men before they began kicking and beating him relentlessly. He tried to escape, tried to shield his face from the blows, but it was too late.

He felt himself go limp, slipping into unconsciousness, and soon, he saw nothing but blackness.

# Chapter 10: Call 9-1-1

Despite the summer heat, Johnny loved that he could keep his house cool and curl up under the soft, cozy blankets. He slept comfortably, dreaming and lost in his own subconscious. When the alarm clock began its infernal screeching, he groaned and reached blindly to shut it off. Instead, he accidentally knocked it to the ground and it continued blaring. He swung his body over the side of the bed and opened his bleary eyes, glaring at the alarm. "Jesus! Do you know how early it is?" he asked, speaking to the device as if it could reply.

After turning off the clock, he placed it back on the nightstand, then stood and scrubbed his face with his hands. After going to the bathroom and then washing up, Johnny grabbed his phone and called Mel. He had a good arrangement with her; they were close friends, and they dated casually, sometimes sleeping together. Neither of them ever got attached, and they both preferred it that way. He sat down on the bed and leaned against his thighs.

"Hey, it's me," he said into the phone. After listening to her for a moment, he said, "How come you didn't stay last night after our little outing? Yeah, I know you had to work early. You coming over tonight?" After she told him she'd be too busy, they made small talk for a moment longer before hanging up.

He dressed in jeans and a clean dark blue t-shirt, slipped into his shoes. Then he heard screeching tires outside, and glanced out the window. He saw a white van pull up onto the sidewalk in front of his house, carelessly knocking over plastic trash cans. Refuse spilled across the street, and a woman walking her dog turned and hurriedly walked away as if frightened.

Johnny immediately noticed the Japanese *kanji* on the side of the van—some kind of logo for a flower shop—and wondered if this was the same van that had chased him the other day. Before he could consider it further, a door on the side of the van slid open and a body was thrown to the ground to join the trash scattered across the cracked cement.

Without missing a beat, Johnny shot out of his house and into the warmth of the early morning, rushing to the scene as the van sped off. A few people on the other side of the street had stopped, seeming frozen in fear and unsure what to do. Johnny turned the body over in his arms and knew who it was immediately. Tears stung the backs of his eyes as he shouted, "Somebody call 9-1-1! Hurry!"

He turned his attention to the man whose mouth was slack, his eyes shut, his body and face covered in bruises. A car had stopped and someone was calling an ambulance, but Johnny barely heard what was going on around him. All he could focus on was Anthony.

"Hang in there, buddy. I've known you too long. I can't lose you now. Help is on the way," he assured the unconscious man. Looking up, he realized a small crowd of bystanders had gathered. Some were on their phones.

A siren wailed in the distance. The police were on their way.

\* \* \*

It was Sunday, and the dojo was closed for the day, but Johnny was hanging out in front of the building with a few good buddies. He felt fortunate to have such a nice building for his martial arts studio. The place had a small yard in front, which was kept carefully landscaped, and now Johnny and his friends were talking and Johnny demonstrated a few kicks and jabs. The guys tossed fake punches at each other, laughing. They'd just had lunch together, and the morning had been much smoother than the days Johnny had experienced recently.

When a long black Lincoln pulled up, Johnny grimaced, feeling as if his luck might change. After recognizing the passenger in the car, he motioned for his buddies to leave and told them he'd see them later. The three guys headed to the back of the building where they'd parked their cars, and Johnny walked toward the Lincoln.

A man stepped out of the back of the car, dressed in a well-made tailored suit. He stood a bit shorter than Johnny, but remained an intimidating man. His dark hair was neatly slicked back and his sharp eyes surveyed his surroundings.

"*Buon giorno*, Johnny," he intoned, his accent thick. He tugged a handkerchief from his lapel and wiped his forehead. "What, you don't introduce me to your friends? You too good to be associated with me or somethin'?"

"Frankie." The two men shook hands. "Your driver get lost? Can't remember the last time I saw you in my neighborhood. You slummin' or just looking for my pretty face?"

"Both."

Johnny frowned, cocking his head to one side in disbelief.

"Hey, what? Old neighborhood has some good memories. Hell, great memories. We had some fuckin' good times here, didn't we, Johnny? Always in the right place at the right time."

Trying not to fidget where he stood, he tried to remember how many times that exact phrase had been spoken to him—too many to recall.

"Some good, some not so good," he said. "Too many people we knew are dead or in prison. But you didn't come all the way here to make small talk."

Frankie stepped toward Johnny, and the tension rose a notch. Something about this visit was making him increasingly uncomfortable. Frankie kept his hands at his sides, and began to raise an arm, only to have Johnny block it.

"*Whatza* matter? You don't trust me? We're family, Johnny."

"What the fuck you want, Frankie?"

"Sonny sent me to see you. He ain't happy. Ain't happy at all. He hears things. Things that make him wonder if you turn on your own. Family don't turn, Johnny. Family don't rat." Frankie turned and stepped back toward the car, motioning for Johnny to join him. Both men leaned against the hood, facing forward. Rather than look at Frankie, Johnny surveyed the street, the small trees planted along the sidewalks, and the benches which created shady canopies for anyone who went outdoors in the summer heat. A slight breeze rustled the leaves on the nearby trees.

"Too bad about Anthony," Frankie finally said, once again making Johnny uncomfortable. "I thought he was smart. Turns out, not the right kind of smart. *Un cacasenno*—smart ass. Mother fucker didn't know when to mind his own business. Could happen to you, too. But Sonny, he listens to me. I tell him your blood is our blood. He wants to make sure. Wants a sit-down at Guarro's. Him, you, a little wine, a little *scunguili*, and all will be well. We can put this mess behind us."

Johnny stewed in fury for a moment, choosing his words carefully. Then he grimaced, turning to the man beside him. "You tellin' me Sonny had Anthony hurt? Is that what you're tellin' me, Frankie? Sonny's the reason Anthony is in intensive care? I'll fuckin' kill him."

Frankie turned and moved nose-to-nose with Johnny, stared him down, and prodded him in the chest. "*Arruso!*" he snapped. "You meet with Sonny or *you* die."

# Chapter 11: Vital Information

The bright neon lights of Vixen's Gentlemen's Club beckoned to Johnny as he stepped inside, met by velour carpeting and a tiny front desk. A gorgeous half-dressed blonde leaned forward, her cleavage spilling invitingly from her top. "Hello, handsome. Nice to see you again." She winked. "Go on in."

"Thanks, babe." Johnny stepped into the club. The place was warm and inviting, lit dimly, and decorated by plush couches and comfortable chairs. Small round tables were close to the stage, where groups of men—and a few women—enjoyed cocktails and watched the strippers. The club had once been upscale, but had suffered some financial troubles. It was a nice place, but not as impressive as Johnny remembered it.

As he walked toward the bar, he glanced up at the stage as the seductive thumping beat of the music thrummed through his body. A brunette, her breasts bare, undulated and shimmied around a pole.

At the bar, Johnny nodded to the bartender and took a seat. "Hey, Nick."

"Hey, Johnny. Good to see you back."

"Good to be back, I think."

"Your usual?"

"Yeah. Hari in?"

Nick gestured toward the stage. A song had ended, and another stripper had stepped out onto the stage. Johnny turned to watch her dance, taking a sip of his lager. The woman on stage still had a sexy figure, a round bottom, and luscious breasts. Her auburn hair appeared silky as it cascaded down her back. Johnny had known her a long time, long enough to know she was thirty-five and a bit tired—worn out from being on stage. He grabbed his beer and moved toward one of the round tables by the stage, taking a seat. In the center of each table, the flame of a red candle flickered, adding a seductive ambiance to the club.

She noticed him, and once he sat down, she focused her gaze on him as if the dance was for Johnny alone. Dancing to the edge of the stage, she turned and bent down, moving her bottom invitingly, glancing over her shoulder at him. Johnny smirked. She sure knew how to put on a show. When her routine ended and the song changed, she grabbed her top and refastened the sheer piece of fabric, then stepped carefully off the stage and toward his table.

Placing a delicate hand on his shoulder, she spoke in a husky voice. "Run out of uptown playmates, Johnny Boy? I thought I was having a fuckin' hallucination."

"You still kiss your mother with that mouth?"

"*Vaffanculo!*" Hari snapped, and Johnny knew she meant *screw you.*

She started to turn and walk away, her irritation obvious, but Johnny grabbed her arm with a gentle squeeze. "I need to talk to you, Hari."

She swung around to face him. "Don't call me that! No one calls me that anymore, especially not here." She leaned toward him carefully, as if every move she made was intended to tempt him. "My name is *Satin*," she said firmly. "I kicked Hari to the curb a long time ago." She tried to pull away, but Johnny tightened his grip on her arm.

"It's about Anthony," he said, knowing this would get her attention. "If you want to hear what I have to say, put that uptight ass of yours in a chair before I do it for you."

They stared at each other for a long moment as if caught in a stalemate. Then, Johnny gestured to the chair across from him. Hari yanked her arm away from him and sat down. Johnny leaned in to speak as the firelight from the candle flickered off their faces. "Some *faccia di stronzo*—asshole—kicked the shit out of Anthony this afternoon. He's in Mass General. He's hurt real bad."

"How bad?" Hari said, her chest rising as she took a short breath.

Johnny closed his eyes and shook his head, then looked up to discover Hari holding her head in her hands. She was distraught; he'd expected this, but she needed to know.

"I warned him about running his mouth," she said, her voice trembling as she held back tears. "Would he listen to me? No!"

"Hari, before the paramedics put him in the ambulance, he kept saying your name and mumbling something about how *you* were the source. Do you know what he was talking about?" Johnny spoke in a low voice—loud enough that she could hear him over the blaring music, but quiet enough to keep others from overhearing their conversation.

Hari moved suddenly to rise from her chair, but again, Johnny stopped her. "I need to see him," she said.

"Soon. First, tell me what you know. Anthony is my best friend. You know that. The three of us grew up back in the old neighborhood—together. You know me, Hari. You know how I am." He paused, meeting her furtive gaze. "If they hurt him, *I hurt them.*"

As they stared into each other's eyes, Johnny still holding firmly to her smooth wrist, he thought about old times—growing up with little Hari and Anthony, hanging out, being kids together. They had to stick together. They had to help each other. He knew they still had an unbreakable bond, something that would never dissipate.

"Hari, I know there's a lot of history between us, and some unfinished business as well," Johnny said, taking a moment to gently stroke her wrist with his thumb. She noticed the affectionate gesture and bit her lower lip, glancing at his hand and then back into his eyes. "That's for another time," he continued. "I need you to tell me what you know now."

She said nothing, simply staring at him, her eyes moist with unshed tears.

"Damn it, Hari! Tell me."

She sunk into her seat, withdrawing her hand, and motioned to the bartender to fix her a drink. She glanced around, appearing to assess the patrons in the strip club, ensuring no one would overhear their conversation. After the bartender brought her drink, she took a sip, and leaned toward Johnny.

"Word on the street is that guys from the neighborhood are mixing with some pretty bad people, and I'm not just talking your average bad. Asian. Mean. Computer geeks. They talk 'mega' this and 'mega' that, encoded, embedded. What the hell do I know? It's all mumbo-jumbo to me. I ain't some rocket scientist!"

She rose from her seat, took a long gulp from her drink, and placed the glass delicately on the table. Then she leaned close to Johnny, pressing her lips to his ear. He could smell her hair, the perfume she wore. The heat of her body radiated from her breasts, and he resisted the urge to reach out and cup them in his palms.

"They're buying and selling information," she murmured, the timbre of her voice tempting him. It seemed as if she could make anything sound sexy. "That's all I know." She withdrew, her hand on his shoulder, and looked down at him.

"I need names."

In case anyone drew close enough to listen, Hari had to make their interactions appear natural, as if Johnny were just another patron of the strip club. She lowered herself onto his lap, crossing one leg over the other, and wrapped her arms around his shoulders. As he finally relented to a bit of his desires by placing one hand on her thigh, she whispered in his ear. "I don't know names," she said. "Just heard talk here at the club from some semi-regulars. You know the type, the kind who are free with their cash and their hands. They had me doing a private lap dance and kept talking while I did my thing. Kept saying the word 'Yakuza,' whatever that means."

Johnny tensed, trying not to react to Hari's use of the term.

Moving away from his ear, she stared into his eyes again. "You don't think this has anything to do with what happened to Anthony, do you?"

"I don't know," Johnny admitted. "But I can promise you I'm going to find out." He coaxed her off his lap, even though it was the last thing he wanted to do, and finished off the rest of his beer. Just as he was about to leave, Hari tugged on his hand.

"One more thing," she said.

He turned to face her, and the expression on her face told him she was trying to find the right words. "One of them Asian guys was real excited about something," she said. "Something to do with insects."

"Insects?" Johnny asked, pressing close to her.

"Yeah. Bees, wasps…" Suddenly she remembered something, and her eyes widened. "That's what it was. *Hornets!* He was real excited about hornets…"

# Chapter 12: Sonny's Trust

Sonny DeSantis thought Guarro's was one of the best Italian restaurants in the city. Part café, part gourmet dining, it had something for everyone. Sonny liked the place at lunchtime because it was virtually empty on some days. It was tucked away from the majority of the big corporations, on a narrow, quaint street. During the week, many of the business people went to lunch at local sandwich places, saving Guarro's for dinnertime.

Sonny preferred the lack of distraction. The privacy. He smoothed his thin, white hair back with one hand, then eyed the men around him. They looked uncomfortable. Luis was twiddling his thumbs on the table, his carefully styled black hair shining in the low light. He took a moment to adjust his collared shirt.

Beside him, Paul—a heavyset guy in casual business attire—took one of the cloth napkins off the table and blew his nose on it, loudly.

*Some guys have no class*, Sonny thought.

"*Mangiare!*" he exclaimed, raising his hands, palms up. Plates of food sat before them, and Sonny was the only one eating. He gave them a scathing look. "What's za matta? You're not hungry?"

Dominic sighed, picking up his fork and gesturing with it. "It's not that, Sonny. It's all this fuckin' waitin'. I don't like waitin'. It makes me nervous."

"I say eat, you eat!" Sonny retorted, tightening his hands into fists on the table. His own food smelled mouth-watering. What the hell was wrong with these guys? "I don't want you to faint from hunger, you bein' so little and all." When Sonny let out a hearty guffaw, the other guys joined in, and Paul started eating first—after he'd dropped the soiled napkin onto his lap.

Luis took a bite, then asked, "Yeah, Sonny, where the fuck is this guy?"

"He'll be here. After all, what choice does he have? Now settle down, you're gonna give me *agita*."

The tiny bell sounded on the front door of the establishment, on the far side of the room.

"Well, it's about fuckin' time," Paul said. "Hey, Sonny…" He jabbed Sonny with his elbow and motioned toward the front door.

Sonny dropped his napkin on the table and signaled for the waitress to clear their dishes. "Dominic. Luis. Go greet the *mamaluke*. Make sure he understands I don't like to be kept waiting."

Dominic grinned, standing. "Luis, let's have a little fun with the *fottuto idiota*—fucking idiot."

Though Sonny couldn't quite see the front entryway from where he sat, he listened as the two men went up front. His remarkable hearing picked up the conversation.

"Luis, you smell somethin'?" Dominic asked. "Check the bottom of your shoe. I think I gonna gag."

Sonny listened to Luis's reply. "I should have known. It's Johnny Macchia. That must account for the stink, eh, Dominic?"

"Where's Sonny?" Johnny's loud voice boomed.

"You mean Mr. DeSantis, asshole!" Luis retorted.

"Look, I don't have time for your shit."

Listening to a slight scuffle, Sonny followed the grunts and groans with his ears, envisioning what might be taking place. A *thwunk* followed a loud shout told him that Johnny had bested at least one of his men, and the shout following the noises confirmed it.

"What are you gonna do now, asshole?" Johnny yelled.

Sonny chuckled and rose from his seat. When Johnny rounded the corner, he clapped his hands. "Bravo, Johnny, good show," he said. "Next time you sell tickets, huh? *Venuto qui.*" He waved him over and gestured for him to take a seat. Johnny did so without a word. "Look, Johnny, why you have to break my balls? You were supposed to be here over a half an hour ago. If I didn't know any better, I'd think you didn't have any respect."

Johnny looked him in the eye. "Sonny, you know I have nothing but respect." Then he turned and eyed the other men at the table, some of whom had arrived through the back entrance while Johnny was up front. Luis and Dominic remained in the foyer.

"Been so long, Johnny," Sonny said. "Maybe you no longer remember my business associates." He nodded to each man in turn. "You know Frankie, to my right."

Frankie straightened his brown suit jacket and offered a smile that looked more like a grimace.

"Paul Barone, my consigliere," Sonny said, then nodded to the man beside him. "That's Mousy DeVito. Mousy handles our finance division. Peter Bianchini. He handles our accounting. And Cesare Mesopolitti heads our entertainment operations."

"Hey, Johnny," Cesare said.

"Hey, Cesare. How's the whore business?"

"You should know. I hear you're one of my best payin' customers," Cesare quipped.

Johnny laughed lightly, and the other men joined in. The only man who did not laugh was a tall, beefy fellow with thinning brown hair. Sonny nodded to him. "Finally, this is Slavic Androposky, our security expert."

Slavic offered a glare in Johnny's direction. "You makin' a joke of our business? You find something funny?" he snapped.

"Hey, Slavic," Frankie said, "you're outta place. You're only a guest here. Johnny's family. He's one of us."

Everyone gestured in agreement. Sonny stared directly at Johnny, but spoke to the security expert. "Slavic, Johnny sees things differently. I'm gonna help him see things our way. The rest of you...clear out."

Without a word, the men rose and began to leave.

* * *

Johnny relaxed in his seat, expert at projecting whichever façade he wanted people to see. He perked up, overhearing Mousy whispering to Peter as they walked past him.

"Why does Sonny bring this Russian *piscione* to the table?"

"He does what he wants," Peter replied quietly, as if concerned he would be overheard. "You don't have to like it."

Soon, Johnny and Sonny were alone at the table. The waitress approached and asked, "Can I bring you anything else, Mr. DeSantis? The canoli is fresh."

He smiled at her, but shook his head. When she was gone, he turned to Johnny and said, "Too bad about Anthony. But I hear he's gonna live."

Beneath the table, Johnny dug his nails into his blue jeans. "I wouldn't want to be the person who did this to him," he said. "Hope you had nothin' to do with it, Sonny."

"You accusin' me, Johnny? I didn't have nothin' to do with Anthony getting hurt. I heard about it after. Fuckin' shame."

"If you didn't order it, who did?" Johnny asked.

Sonny leaned back in his chair. "That's not your concern. Learn from Anthony's mistake. Don't go pokin' around where you don't belong. *Capisce?*"

"Who did it?" Johnny pressed. "I need to know."

He watched Sonny's face redden, his brow crinkling in annoyance. When Sonny rose to his feet and slammed his fist on the table, the silverware clattered and the vibration upset a glass of water, which spilled across the tablecloth and dripped on the floor. The waitress had the good sense to ignore the mess for now.

"You question me?" Sonny shouted. "You want to know. Who the fuck are you? I tell you what you need to know. *Cocciuto!*" He leaned over Johnny, seeming a bit unsteady on his feet, yet his anger made his skin burn red. "*Stronzo!*" His voice was even louder now. "You should be answerin' my questions, not the other way around. Are you a rat, Johnny? Did you turn on your blood, Johnny? I hear things, too. Whispers that you're working for the Feds now. The fuckin' Feds! I could kill you right now, and it would be my right."

Internally, Johnny felt anxious, knowing he was alone with this guy and anyone else in the restaurant—the waitress, the dish washer—would protect Sonny if he carried out his threat. He was in a dangerous position, but he couldn't let it show. Keeping his expression calm, his body language relaxed, he locked eyes with the older man. "Sonny. You know better," he said in a low tone. "What's with you?"

Sonny reached into his pocket. The move made Johnny uncomfortable for a brief second, until he realized the older man was just pulling out a monogrammed handkerchief. He wiped his runny nose, and in the process, accidentally dropped a small brown vial. It fell to the ground, and Johnny scooped it up.

"Part of Cesare's entertainment empire?" Johnny asked. "You do know cocaine is bad for you, don't you? Fucks with your head. Makes you think crazy things."

Sonny swiped the vial out of his hand and shoved it back in his pocket along with his handkerchief. "How do I know you're bein' straight with me?"

"Sonny, you know me. I think the drugs are making you paranoid. What the hell you fucking with that shit for?"

Sonny sat down and let out a ragged breath. "Everything's changing, Johnny. Nothin's the way it was. Used to be a guy could make a buck…broads, a little gambling, some loan sharking. A respected way to earn a living. The old way. Cops were on the payroll. The Feds were too busy going after the dirty cops to bother too much with us. But that's all changed." He had a weathered expression on his face, as if he'd seen too much and felt tired. "Did you change it, Johnny?"

"Sonny, it's the twenty-first century. Old ways don't cut it anymore. It's all this computer crap." Johnny shrugged, as if to admit he didn't fully understand it either. "There're eyes and ears everywhere. You can't take a piss without someone counting the drops."

Sonny laughed, appearing to relax, but he said nothing.

"I run my dojo, do a little P.I. work, and look after my friends," Johnny said. "I don't have time to do favors for the Feds."

Sonny looked directly at him, as if trying to ascertain whether or not he was being honest. When he spoke, his tone was almost fatherly—before it turned threatening. "If it ain't you, then who is it, Johnny? Can't have my business interrupted no more." He learned forward, his gaze as piercing as a sharpened throwing knife. "Not by the Feds," he added, "not by Anthony. Not by anyone."

# Chapter 13: Sudden Impact

Kenzi crouched low in the drab gray car, knowing the vehicle didn't stand out. It was why he used it—so he could watch without being seen and report back to Kazumi. The tinted windows helped, and when he saw Sonny DeSantis emerge from the restaurant along with another man, he raised his hand to Akira, who sat beside him, and pointed across the street without saying a word. Akira lowered the sandwich he'd been munching on and watched, quietly.

Sonny and the other man embraced like old friends, then walked in opposite directions. Both seemed oblivious to the fact they were being watched. When both men departed, Kenzi started the engine of the little car and drove toward the tall office building that housed Kazumi's office. After parking, they climbed out in silence and Akira trailed behind Kenzi. They rode the elevator up, then walked to Kazumi's office. Kenzi rapped on the door and then entered without waiting for a reply.

Inside, Kazumi looked up from some paperwork and interlocked his fingers over the shining mahogany surface. He wore a tuxedo and his hair was slicked back. "This better be important," he said. "You pulled me away from a crucial social function that I did not want to miss."

Kenzi and Akira both bowed in respect.

"We thought you would like a report on the surveillance we have on Sonny DeSantis," Kenzi said.

Kazumi rose from his chair, glaring. When he spoke, his voice was tinged with fury. "You pulled me away from my daughter's birthday party for a status report?"

Both men bowed their heads. In a hurried voice, Akira said, "He met with the man we encountered when we were chasing Mr. Holmes. We thought you would like to know right away."

Kazumi's expression relaxed and he slowly sat down in his leather office chair. "Continue," he said calmly.

"We got a tip that DeSantis was having a meeting at a restaurant in midtown," Akira began. "We were there waiting for him to leave, and we saw the man who helped Mr. Holmes come out with him. They hugged like good friends."

"We know this man's name is Johnny Macchia," Kenzi added. "He is a private investigator and also teaches martial arts. It was behind his martial arts school that we inadvertently cornered Holmes and his driver."

"I recall," Kazumi said between gritted teeth.

"He has many friends here in Boston and he is well liked," Kenzi said. "We thought you should know immediately, Tabata-sama."

Kazumi stared at them, causing Kenzi to quiver where he stood. He rose from his seat and walked to the side of his desk, his gaze trained at the floor as he spoke, his hands clasped behind him. "First it was Mr. Holmes and now Sonny DeSantis. Who is this man who seems to be getting in our way, and what does he know?"

"Should we send him an invitation to our party, Tabata-sama?" Akira asked.

Kazumi's expression remained hard, and Kenzi could not guess what he might be thinking. Every moment spent in this man's presence was nerve-wracking. Finally, Kazumi turned and said, "No. Keep a close eye on Sonny. I want to know who he meets with, who he sleeps with…if he wipes his ass wrong, I want to know about it. I have special plans for our Mr. Macchia. We have come too far to be bothered by some nobody who thinks he's Dick Tracy. Go. I will be in touch soon."

Kenzi and Akira both bowed, then turned and left the room. Once the elevator doors had slid shut, Kenzi released the breath he'd been holding.

*Back to work.*

\* \* \*

As he emerged from the back entrance of the dojo, Johnny acknowledged a strange feeling he'd been having lately. It reminded him of the last time he'd gone to a party, and he'd been standing by the buffet table sipping whiskey on the rocks when the sensation of being watched had come over him. He'd turned and met the sultry gaze of a woman he hadn't seen in a long time. A redheaded knockout in a shimmering gray cocktail dress. *Gingers*—they were dangerous. Even though the night had ended well, Johnny recalled the drama she'd brought into his life. The strange feeling he'd been getting lately had nothing to do with women. Instead, it was the sensation of being watched that reminded him of the seductive redhead from the party.

Johnny could always tell when someone was watching. This time, it wasn't a woman. Who? Did Sonny have him tailed? He doubted it. Sonny DeSantis trusted him, and that was exactly how he wanted it. The door shut behind him, and he shoved his hands into the pockets of his jeans. He was dressed casually in the heat of the day, the white t-shirt keeping him cool. He looked around the empty parking lot, spotting his car, but nobody else was around.

He headed for his car, tugging his keys out of his pocket. His phone rang, and he saw the caller I.D. clearly displayed before he answered.

"Hello, Joseph, what's up?"

"Johnny, you wouldn't believe what I just discovered."

"What's that?"

"A woman from our staff was watering the plants and on close inspection, she found something. We discovered someone had hidden an exotic electronic device in one of the flower pots. I had a theory that some kind of bugging device was used to steal information without anyone from our staff being involved, and this confirms it. After I analyzed the device, it appears that somehow it steals information from the computer and then transmits it outside the office to a nearby listening post."

Johnny frowned. "I think the listening device is probably hidden in that service van, which I always see parked in front of your office complex. It's the same white van that rear-ended my vehicle, and there was the name of some flower shop on the side of the van. I'll head over there now and investigate. Talk to you later." Without waiting for a reply, he hung up.

Turning, he saw the white van parked in the alley, at the side of the road, almost completely concealed by the trees at the edge of the sidewalk and the wooden fencing that separated Johnny's property from the business next door.

He shoved his keys back in his pocket and headed for the van, his long legs taking him quickly across the lot. As he drew closer, he saw the flower shop logo on the side of the van, which appeared to be empty. Without waiting another second, he rounded the van and yanked open the driver's side door. Glancing in the back, it was just as he suspected—no one was there.

He pulled open the glove compartment and looked inside, only to find it empty. Reaching under the seat, he located what felt like wiring. A wiring harness under the seat? It didn't make sense.

Hopping down from the seat, Johnny dug around and followed the wires until he spotted a black box that displayed a timer.

*A timer...*

It read ten seconds. Then nine, then—

"Holy shit!" Johnny shouted. Without waiting another moment, he raced away from the van and ran toward the back of the dojo. Before he could reach the back door, an explosion rocked the ground and he threw himself forward, pressing his body to the cement with his hands over the back of his head. The sound of metal and glass crashing against the ground followed, and Johnny didn't move until all he could hear was the raging inferno of the vehicle burning, flames jumping from the wreckage.

He rolled to a seated position, listening. A few moments later, sirens wailed. Someone must've seen the flames and called the fire department. His phone rang, and he tugged it out of his pocket to answer.

"This better be good," he said, in lieu of a greeting.

"Johnny, it's Joseph again. What's the matter? You sound stressed."

"Stressed? Naw." Johnny shook his head as he watched the vehicle burn. Some of the flames jumped to the nearest tree, and he hoped to God the fence wouldn't burn, too, and send the inferno to his dojo. Thankfully, the sirens sounded closer, and he was sure they'd put the fire out before that could happen. "Almost burned out is more like it," he muttered, his tone tinged with irritation. He rose to his feet and brushed the dirt off his front.

"What's going on?" Joseph asked. "Did you learn something?"

"Shit, yeah," Johnny grumbled. "I learned I'm getting too fuckin' close and someone doesn't like it."

"What the hell are you talking about?"

"I'll explain when I get to your office." He hung up the phone and shoved it back in his pocket, then crossed his arms over his chest and watched the spectacle before him, listening as the sirens grew louder and louder.

The sensation of being observed continued to linger.

At Genzer Labs, he found Joseph Holmes sitting at a desk in the lab and described the trap that had been set for him. He sat down at a metal table, leaning tiredly against it.

"You okay?" Joseph asked, looking him up and down.

"Yeah, I'm fine. Just tell me about this thing you found in the flower pot."

He showed him the tiny device, sliding it across the table. "Well, it picks up impulses in electrical wiring in computers, then stores the data. I figure it takes a sizeable computer facility to decode and interpret the information the bug steals." He turned and began typing quickly on a keyboard. "I searched to find out who in Boston ordered a certain type of sophisticated computer equipment. The name of the shipping company that turned up was Marine Shipping Incorporated, and they have an office on the docks in Boston." He turned the screen so Johnny could see the address.

"That's why my friend Anthony was beaten into a coma. He was investigating down at the docks and must have stumbled on their operation," Johnny said, his heart beating fast with rage. He rose from the seat and stalked toward the door when his phone began to ring. "I'll see you later, Joseph, I've got things to do but I'll be in touch. I'll look into this flower shop."

The little man appeared in awe of Johnny, perhaps impressed by his resilience. "Okay, Johnny, sure, sure. See you later. Be careful."

# Chapter 14: Errand Boy

The city park was busy with skateboarders, kids playing, and people walking their dogs. The sun shone brightly while tufts of white clouds hung in the blue sky. Johnny remembered when his son was little and he used to take him to the park. Little J. J. would point up to the sky and say, "Daddy, Daddy, look! Happy little clouds."

Johnny smiled at the memory as he walked along the path, beneath the verdant foliage of the trees. The lake stretched out to his left, the water calm and inviting. A few small boats floated nearby, and fishermen cast their lines out over the gentle surface. Johnny approached the stern looking man who stood staring across the water, his hands in the pockets of his trousers. Johnny stopped beside him and mimicked his stance.

"You're late," Frankie finally said.

"Yeah, well…I stopped by the hospital to see Anthony. He's still in a coma."

"Fuckin' guy. I told you before, he should've minded his own business. You should learn from this."

Johnny gritted his teeth, having heard all this before. He was sick of Frankie. The man came on too strong. Sonny's underboss or not, he'd really love to punch him in the face. "What the hell is that supposed to mean?"

"I was coming to your place to have a word with you," Frankie said. "I saw the fireworks. You makin' new enemies, Johnny?"

He glared at him. "How do I know it's not my old friends who want me dead?"

"Because if it was, you'd be dead already. If that van would have gotten you, I would have called the guys and had a fuckin' weenie roast."

The comment was disconcerting, but it made Johnny laugh. Frankie shook off his mood and suddenly became sincere, his tone edged with concern. "Listen. Sonny wants to talk to you. He likes you, Johnny. He doesn't know you like I do, you dumb shit. He wants to make sure you have his best interests at heart."

"Well, no offense, but I don't think Sonny has his own interests at heart lately."

"Naw, Sonny's okay, and he's still the boss. You just show up for the meeting. I'll meet ya at Sonny's office bright and early, and you better not keep him waiting."

The two shook hands and embraced briefly before Frankie turned and walked away, leaving Johnny to stand by the water and stare out at the boats.

* * *

The next morning, Johnny was on time as promised. He wore his regular street clothes, and parked his Corvette behind the building. He sat in one of the comfortable leather chairs across from Sonny's desk, and clasped his hands in his lap. The old man hadn't stepped into the office yet. For once, Johnny was relieved he was on time and the boss was late. He smirked at the irony.

"Sonny feelin' better?" he asked, glancing at Frankie.

"He's better. You'll see." The other man had dressed in business attire and crossed one leg over the other when he sat beside Johnny.

"Sure as hell hope so. Never thought he'd use the shit."

"Just watch your mouth," Frankie warned. "He don't like talkin' about it."

Behind them, the door opened, and Sonny crossed the room. He seemed to be in a jovial mood, and he was well dressed. He ran his hand over the classy tie he wore, and his cuff links gleamed in the daylight that streamed in behind him from the wide windows.

"Hey, Sonny," Frankie said, rising to greet him. "Thought you forgot about us."

Johnny stood and shook hands with Sonny, who said, "Not a chance." He shook hands with Frankie, too, before sitting down behind his desk. "Johnny, I'm glad you came. I wasn't sure you would."

"Sonny, have I ever let you down?" Johnny replied, sitting back down again.

"Funny you should mention that. I have a job for the two of you."

"What kind of job?"

"It don't fuckin' matter," Frankie said. "What you need, Sonny?"

"I've been doin' a lot of thinking and I figured out who's playing footsy with the Feds. Once my head cleared, it was obvious."

Johnny remained impassive, true to the part he was playing. "You sure?" he asked.

"As sure as I need to be." Sonny paused, then said, "Bennie Napolitano and Ralphie Carter."

"Never heard of either of them," Johnny said, feeling relieved.

"Doesn't matter who you know or don't know. It's what I know that counts. I want you two to talk to them. A serious talk, so there's no misunderstanding regarding my concern in this area."

"Bennie's your cousin, right?" Frankie said.

"*Non me ne frega niente di lui*—I don't give a damn about him. *Capisce?* Just let me know when the job's done."

Both Johnny and Frankie agreed as Sonny rose and left the room. The men stood, heading for the exit, and Frankie tapped Johnny lightly on the chest with the back of his hand. "Come on. Let's go."

"I have to pick up Mikey and J. J. and drop them off at school." It was now the beginning of September, after Labor Day, which meant his sons were headed back to classes for the new school year. He wanted to see them off. "Tell me where to meet you and I'll be there," Johnny added.

"Pick me up on the corner by your place in an hour," Frankie said.

Johnny nodded. "Got it. See you then."

# Chapter 15: Clipped

Johnny was proud of both his sons. J. J. was usually the quiet one and Mikey tended to be more outspoken. Both of the boys enjoyed practicing martial arts with their father. Mikey was twelve, and had brown eyes and short, dark brown hair, spiked on top. He was very inquisitive about everything, enjoyed sports and had started playing hockey recently. He glanced at the screen of his smartphone and scowled as Johnny pulled the SUV up in front of the school. Kids crossed the street and a school bus passed by.

"Damn it, Dad, I'm late," he snapped.

"Hey, watch your mouth," Johnny said, glaring at him. "It couldn't be helped. I'll write you a note. When you see your brother, tell him I said thanks for waitin'."

"He went with some friends. What's the big deal? You should have let Aunt Kate bring me instead, like always."

Johnny leaned back and sighed heavily. He appreciated Kate's help. Ever since his wife Kimberly died, Kim's sister Kate had always been willing to help. But Johnny wanted to see more of his sons. "Mikey, we haven't gotten together much lately. I just wanted to spend a little time with you two."

"Whose fault is that?" Mikey said, tugging his backpack up onto his lap. "You missed our last two weekends together."

"It couldn't be helped," Johnny replied, knowing how demanding his work had been lately. Sometimes he wished he could explain it to his kids, but that was impossible. Some things had to stay a secret. There would be no explaining. He had no excuses to give. "That's why I picked you up this morning," he continued. "Gonna come by tonight about dinner time and take you and your brother out. We can grab a pizza or burgers. Your choice. Okay?"

"Steak," Mikey decided, narrowing his eyes at his father.

"Steak?" Johnny shrugged. "If that's what you want, it's okay by me." Johnny tugged a notebook out of the glove compartment and wrote a note for Mikey, explaining his lateness, and signed at the bottom. "Here you go. So you don't get in trouble."

"Thanks, Dad." Mikey folded the note and tucked it into his backpack.

"I have a little business to get out of the way, and then I'll be over tonight, okay?"

"I'll be waiting," Mikey said as he climbed out of the SUV.

"Good. See you later, son."

Once Mikey had shut the door, Johnny drove off, deciding there was no way he'd disappoint his kids today. He'd been doing enough of that lately.

He pulled up in front of his house. As expected, he saw Frankie standing there, waiting. Bennie stood beside him, a gold cross earring dangling from his left lobe. He didn't seem uncomfortable, suggesting he probably didn't realize what was going on.

"Sorry I'm late," Johnny said, after lowering the window.

"No problem," Frankie said, indicating the man beside him. "You know Bennie?"

"No. How's it going?" Johnny said. "Hop in."

Bennie made his way to the back passenger door of the SUV and pulled it open. Before he could climb in, Frankie shook his head and said, "Bennie, take the front seat. My leg is acting up and I wanna stretch it out."

Bennie shrugged and did as suggested. Frankie climbed in the back and sat behind him. "Sonny got an errand for us outside of town," he said. "You don't mind going for a little ride, do you, Bennie?"

"Nah, as long as I'm not going swimmin' wit the fishes."

The men chuckled, and Johnny drove the SUV back into traffic.

"Johnny, head out toward Middleboro," Frankie instructed. "I'll tell you where to get off."

"Hope this won't take long," Johnny said. "I've got dinner plans with my boys tonight." It was still hours away, but he didn't know what Sonny had planned. Whatever it was, Frankie knew more about it than he did, and he just hoped it wouldn't take all day.

After a substantial drive, Johnny pulled the Escalade into an empty lot inside a wooded area. If the situation had been different, he might have taken time to admire the beauty of the area, the sunlight streaming through the leafy trees, and the way the breeze rustled the foliage. Instead, all three men climbed out of the vehicle and Johnny shut the driver's side door, leaning against it.

Bennie glanced around at the woods, still oblivious. "Who's this fuckin' guy we're meeting?"

Frankie pulled out a gun with a silencer on it and aimed it at Bennie's forehead. "Your Maker," he said, and without waiting for a reply, he shot Bennie between the eyes. The body crumpled to the ground with a *thunk*, and Frankie spat on the corpse.

Johnny hid his surprise; he'd expected him to beat the shit out of Bennie, teach him a lesson. But kill him? "What the fuck you doin', Frankie? It's broad daylight."

"Nobody saw nothin'," Frankie said, tucking the weapon away.

"Sonny said 'talk to him.' I didn't know that meant kill him."

Frankie shrugged. "I did talk to him…'den I killed him. It's what Sonny wants. You're gonna do the same to Ralphie Carter."

"This is crazy," Johnny said. "He never said anything about killing anyone."

"Yeah, he did. You just don't listen. He said *serious*…dead is as serious as it gets. Johnny, you take care of Ralphie for Sonny, and he knows you're loyal. You don't and he might get *serious* with you." Frankie reached into his pocket and withdrew a knife. He bent down and cut off Bennie's ear, making sure he removed the ear with the earring on it, and slipped it into a plastic bag he'd pulled out of his other pocket. Johnny watched with subdued horror, refusing to let Frankie see his disgust. Instead, he maintained his calm, nonchalant body language.

"What the hell are you doin'?" he asked.

"Sonny likes proof, a little memento of a job well done."

"Yeah, well, I just wish you didn't enjoy your work so much."

Frankie chuckled as he climbed into the passenger seat of the SUV. When Johnny opened the driver's side and climbed in, he watched Frankie place the bag into the glove compartment.

"Just remember to do the same with Ralphie, huh?" Frankie said, before he called to have someone go and dispose of the body.

As they drove, Johnny tried not to think about the dead man's ear in the glove compartment. And most of all, he tried not to think about what he would have to do next.

# Chapter 16: Ralphie Boy

Late in the afternoon, Johnny had finished his business and was headed for Kate's house to pick up the boys. As he drove, he finished up a call on his cell phone. A call he hated having to make.

"Sonny wants me to kill some *mamaluke* named Ralphie Carter," he said, then paused a moment. "Yeah, check him out. Then set up a meeting for tomorrow morning."

He pulled up in front of a modest brick home. Before he could park, he saw Mikey rush outside, the breeze tousling his dark hair. "You made it!" he called out.

Johnny climbed out of the SUV, about to head inside the house to look for J. J. "Yeah, where's your brother?"

"He didn't want to come," Mikey explained. "So don't worry about looking for him. He's with his girlfriend."

"Oh." Johnny gestured for his son to climb into the passenger side. "Hungry?"

"Always."

They both got in, and Johnny started the engine again. "I know where there's a steak with your name on it," he said.

"Awesome!"

The vehicle sped away from the curb, and Johnny tried to forget about everything else for a while.

\* \* \*

In a drab, gray conference room, four FBI agents sat around a table drinking coffee and discussing recent developments. Saul sat at the head of the table, dressed in a suit, complete with a colorful tie his wife had bought him for Christmas. He sipped his coffee, then absently ran his hand through his graying hair. A silence had fallen in the room.

Now, Saul cleared his throat and said, "This is serious shit. Johnny's getting himself in too deep."

"He doesn't have much choice," one of the other agents, Larry, commented. "If he backs out now, Sonny will have him killed."

The other agents nodded in agreement.

"How do we know Johnny's not taking us for a ride?" Saul wondered. "He gets a little too close to the edge for my taste."

One of the women, Abby, snorted in annoyance. "What the hell does that mean? He's nowhere near the edge."

"Johnny's been undercover a long time," Larry said. "He knows how to protect himself."

Saul stared into his coffee. "He's never had to kill anyone before. Maybe he'll forget which side he's on."

They all looked up when the door to the conference room opened and Johnny stepped inside. Saul sized him up—street clothes, black jeans, t-shirt, dark brown hair neatly combed, about fifty years old. *Could this guy turn on us?* He watched Johnny step over to the coffee pot and fill a mug. The man didn't say hello, just brought his coffee to the table and sat down.

"What did you learn about Ralphie?" Johnny asked, looking directly at Saul.

"Sheila?" Saul looked to the woman nearest him, who opened a folder and began to review its contents.

"He's a low level soldier and member of Peter Bianchini's crew," she said. "Loan sharking, mostly. Not known for brains. Doesn't mind helping himself to a little extra cash every once in a while. Until now, not a problem."

"What about personal ties?" Johnny asked.

"No family. Grew up on the street. Lives alone."

Johnny nodded. "That explains it."

"Explains what?" Larry asked.

"Why Ralphie? He's expendable. No one will miss him."

One of the other agents, Abby, shook her head in disgust. "Sonny DeSantis is one sick son of a bitch. How are you going to get rid of Ralphie?"

"Don't know yet," Johnny admitted. "But it ain't going to be easy."

"How so?" Saul asked.

"Sonny wants proof. Frankie killed Bennie Napolitano yesterday. Took his ear as a souvenir for Sonny. I can give you directions to where they took the body."

Saul was enraged, appalled. "You just let it happen? I don't believe this."

"Wasn't a fuckin' thing I could do," Johnny exclaimed. "Thought Frankie was going to talk to him, maybe rough him up a bit. I didn't see it comin'. He shot him before I even knew what happened."

Saul caught Larry glaring at him. When he looked at the other agent for explanation, Larry said, "What did you want him to do, blow his cover?"

"There's got to be some way of satisfying Sonny and keeping Ralphie alive," Sheila said. "Unless you're planning on killing him?"

"Shit, no!" Johnny retorted. "I'm not planning on killing Ralphie. I just wanna make him disappear. Figure I can be seen snatching him, then hand him over to you."

Abby nodded. "We can stash him at the nearby base. No one will question our coming and going."

"Fine," Johnny said. "But what in God's name am I going to take to Sonny to prove I offed the guy?"

"Don't know if this is any help, but says here Ralphie Boy is nuts about soccer," Sheila said. "Likes to be called Kicker. Even had himself tattooed."

The agents exchanged knowing glances. Meanwhile, Saul stared across the table at Johnny, hoping this guy wasn't hiding anything from him.

# Chapter 17: Tattoo Kicker

The next day, Johnny drove through a vast residential area in Boston, in between rows and rows of homes, until he reached the house he was looking for. He counted seven men sitting or standing on the stoop of an old brownstone, talking amongst themselves. Pulling up to the curb, he leaned against the open window of his car and called out to them.

"Anyone know where I can find Ralphie Carter?" He was already aware the burly man sitting on the stoop and smoking a cigar was Ralphie, but he didn't let on that he knew.

Instead of standing, Ralphie puffed on the cigar and handed it to one of his buddies. "Who wants to know?"

"Sonny sent me," Johnny said. "Are you Ralphie?"

The man rose from his seat and walked slowly over to the car. He wore jeans and a blue, button-up short-sleeved shirt. His dark hair was on the messy side. "Could be," he said.

"If you're Ralphie, get in. I have a matter of importance to discuss with you." He made eye contact with the man, adding in a low tone, "You could say it's a matter of life or death."

Ralphie glanced around to look at the men gathered on the stoop, but none of them were paying attention to him. He waited a few seconds before walking around the car and climbing in the passenger side. Once the door was shut firmly, Johnny pulled away from the curb and drove down the street.

"Lift your pant leg," Johnny said without hesitation. He glanced at Ralphie and saw the man watching him with a peculiar expression on his face.

"What?"

"You heard me. Lift your pant leg. I have a message for Ralphie and I want to make sure I'm talking to the right guy."

Ralphie finally did as instructed, lifting his pant leg to reveal a tattoo above his ankle which read *Kicker*. "This what you're looking for?"

"Yeah," Johnny said. Then, without warning, he slowed the car, reached out his right arm, and punched Ralphie in the jaw, knocking him unconscious.

\* \* \*

The tinted windows of Johnny's Corvette concealed the slack-jawed man whose head hung forward and bobbed from side to side whenever the car took a turn. With calm efficiency, Johnny drove to a predetermined location, an upscale neighborhood in Boston where he'd agreed to meet the other agents. He turned into a narrow driveway flanked by neatly trimmed shrubs and trees. Gardens stretched into the back of the property, which was surrounded by tall hedges. The large brick house hid the car from the road as Johnny parked close to the back entrance.

After turning off the car and climbing out, he went to the passenger side and unloaded the baggage. Ralphie's limp body was awkward to lift, but he managed it, maneuvering him out of the car and onto the pavement. Grunting with the effort, he hefted Ralphie over his shoulder, closed the car door, and carried him toward the house. The door opened before he reached it, and he was ushered inside by one of the Feds—Sheila. She stepped to the side as Johnny carried Ralphie inside and deposited him on a tan suede sofa.

Johnny released a heavy breath and looked around the room. The drapes were drawn, though the daylight still seeped through. Larry was sitting in an armchair, dressed in a gray suit. He motioned toward the man on the couch, who had yet to wake up.

"I have a feeling we'd be better off letting Johnny carry out Sonny's orders," he said.

Saul stepped into the room from a wide, sun-lit kitchen, his arms crossed over his chest. "I second that."

Sheila frowned. "Well, as much as we'd all like to save the tax payers a lot of money, we have a job to do. Let's move Sleeping Beauty into the basement."

Larry nodded and rose from his chair. He and Saul grabbed Ralphie's arms, and Johnny wrapped his hands around the bulky man's feet. He was relieved to not have to carry him by himself. Johnny was a big man, capable of lifting heavy weights, but carrying a full-grown unconscious man was awkward at best. It was good to have help this time.

They got him down the steps and into the basement easily enough, with Sheila following closely behind. The large room was nearly empty, except for a single chair. They placed Ralphie in the chair, then bound his legs with duct tape. Sheila then taped his hands. Once they were finished, all four of them stepped back to admire their handiwork. Saul checked on the captive, examining his eyes and checking his pulse.

Sheila slipped her iPhone out of her pocket. "One thing left to do," she said, turning to Johnny. "Care to show me some skin?"

He chuckled, then lifted Ralphie's pant leg to reveal his tattoo. Sheila took a few pictures with her phone. "This is for the boss. You make sure to take your own pictures." She watched as he got out his phone and snapped a few photos of the tattoo.

"Thanks, Sheila. I'm sure Richard wants you to check in," he said. "I'll leave you to your guest. No wild parties, now."

"We'll see about that," Sheila replied, smirking.

As Johnny ascended the steps, he overheard Larry, talking into his cell phone. "Yeah, it's Lar. Tell Richard his package has arrived and we wrapped it for him."

# Chapter 18: Foot Replacement

The following morning, Johnny headed to the city morgue. At the end of a long hallway, he spotted his destination: the office of Doctor Margaret Mitchell, Chief Medical Examiner. He knocked lightly under the golden nameplate, then entered.

Margaret looked up from her desk and smiled. Laugh lines crinkled at the corners of her deep blue eyes. Her familiar face was framed by blonde hair which hung around her shoulders, and she wore a smart business suit with a pretty white blouse. It took Johnny a moment to realize someone else was in the room.

"Sorry I'm late." He glanced at the man who sat opposite her desk. "Gianni..."

Margaret had risen from her seat and rounded the desk. "Hello, Johnny." They shook hands, and for another brief moment, Johnny forgot about the other visitor in the room.

"Margaret, it's been a long time." They'd dated casually some years back, but he hadn't forgotten her.

"Yes, it has," she said, her eyes betraying a playful curiosity he couldn't quite define. Suddenly he realized her small, warm hand remained enclosed in his, and was unable to draw his gaze away from her captivating eyes.

"You look great," he said.

"You don't look too bad yourself," Margaret replied in low tone, almost a whisper.

Johnny felt startled when someone cleared their throat to his right. It was Gianni, who'd risen from his chair, and stared in their direction. Johnny drew his hand away from Margaret and looked at Gianni.

"Well," Gianni began, "I hate to break up this happy reunion, but we have work to do. I've been filling Doctor Mitchell in on why we're here. She assures me we have her office's full cooperation."

Margaret then led both men out of her office and down the hall, stopping outside a room. Beside the door stood a table providing surgical gloves and some folded disposable scrub gowns and hats. She handed each man a hat, gown, and a pair of gloves, then pulled her own gloves on, donning the hat and gown.

"I hope we have what you're looking for, gentlemen," Margaret said. Giving Johnny a pointed look, she pushed the door open, leading them into a room that was much colder than the hallway they'd come from. Rows of metal tables lined the bright room, but only one table was occupied by a body. She turned to Gianni as they approached the table. "You gave me a very generic description. Male, Caucasian, in his early thirties…I hope this John Doe fits your needs."

With that, she revealed the corpse by drawing the sheet down.

Johnny nodded, his face set in a grim frown. "We need to see his feet to make sure there's no damage to the ankles."

Without a word, Margaret moved to the other end of the table and uncovered the dead man's feet. Johnny and Gianni both peered at the man's limbs.

"He'll do," Gianni said. "When can you have it for us?"

"I have someone waiting for my call as we speak," Margaret said. She stepped over to a table covered in surgical instruments, and chose a small circular saw.

"Are you sure your contact can be trusted?" Gianni asked.

The question seemed to irritate Margaret. "Of course," she said. "He's my son-in-law, and he's the best tattoo artist in Boston."

She turned and focused on her work. Removing John Doe's ankle was the first step in making Ralphie disappear. Johnny was sure the scheme would be believable enough. They'd hide the real Ralphie, and Sonny would be appeased by the dead man's freshly tattooed ankle.

*This will save my ass, for sure.*

* * *

Sonny reclined in his desk chair, placing his hands behind his head and frowning. Two days had passed, and he'd gotten word the job was complete. "So, he did it, then?" he asked, glancing at Frankie who sat across from him. He still hadn't seen the proof, and that irked him.

"Told you not to worry," Frankie said. "No one's seen that asshole Ralphie in almost two days."

"Seein' is believin'," Sonny reminded him. "When I have proof Ralphie is dead, then I'll believe Johnny is one of us."

"You'll have your proof. I'd stake my life on it."

Sonny eyed him curiously. "I still think you shoulda gone along."

Frankie shrugged. "I had to make a condolence call to Bennie's family. It would've looked bad if I didn't show." He turned when someone knocked on the door. "This could be what you're waitin' for."

"Come in," Sonny called out.

Johnny stepped inside, shutting the door behind him. He had a shoebox under his left arm. *This better be what I'm lookin' for,* Sonny thought. He didn't want to have to kill Johnny. He liked the guy.

Johnny placed the box on his desk. "As ordered," he said.

"What the fuck is this?" Sonny asked, glaring at the emblem on the side of the box. "You bring me a pair of Nikes? Where's my proof that Ralphie's dead?"

Without speaking, Johnny took the lid off the box and dropped it on the desk. He watched him, waiting. Sonny peered into the box, then nodded. He'd done as he'd been told. Instead of a pair of shoes, the box held a severed human foot, still in a sneaker. And above the ankle, in blue ink, was a tattoo that read *Kicker.*

Leaning back in his chair, Sonny was satisfied. "Now 'dat's proof!"

# Chapter 19: Russian Balls

The old stone church had been the perfect place for a wedding—
and not just any wedding. The bride was Peter Bianchini's daughter.
Now that Johnny had proved his loyalty, Sonny seemed unconcerned
about him, and satisfied that the deaths of two men had supposedly
sealed the leak that had funneled information to the Feds. Johnny
made an extra effort to be more cautious than usual, using all his
instincts and skills to remain under the radar.

His invitation to the wedding was a good sign.

It meant they trusted him. He had become one of them.
Sometimes it made him nervous, because he was playing two sides
and had to pretend to be someone he wasn't. How long could it last?

After the ceremony, Johnny entered the reception hall and
glanced around at the gathering, almost forgetting the presence of his
date, Gina. She had a part to play, too. Behind them, the receiving
line of family, bridesmaids, and ushers filed in, followed by the bride
and groom. The bar had opened, and people were lining up for
drinks. Johnny smoothed his hand down the front of his shirt and tie,
then spotted Mousey Devito talking with Paul Barone and Cesare
Mesopolitti. He sensed Gina taking in the surroundings, as well,
probably filing each detail away in her mind.

Through the crowd, Johnny made eye contact with Frankie, who
stepped toward them.

"Hey, Johnny, good to see you," Frankie said, and the two men
embraced.

"Good to see you too, Frankie," Johnny replied, clapping him on the back and withdrawing to put his arm around Gina. She was dressed in a conservative navy blue dress, and even Johnny felt surprised at how quiet this firecracker of a woman had become in anticipation of the wedding. She could switch gears faster than his Corvette.

"Not every day Peter's daughter gets married," Frankie said, glancing around at the gathering crowd. "Lucky for him he stepped up to the plate and did the right thing. These kids nowadays…who can keep their eyes on them every minute, ya know?" Frankie eyed Gina curiously, adding, "So Johnny, you gonna introduce me to this lovely lady, or am I gonna have to try to get to know her myself?"

"I'm sorry, Frankie. This is Gina. Gina, this is Frankie Novello."

Gina reached out delicately to shake his hand, but instead he lifted her fingers to his lips and placed a gentle kiss on her knuckles. True to the character she played, Gina allowed a rosy hue to color her cheeks. "It's a pleasure to meet you, Mr. Novello."

Frankie winked. "Please, call me Frankie. And the pleasure is all mine."

Johnny noticed how he stared at her, taking in her curves in the tight dress, as if undressing her with his eyes. It seemed to make her uncomfortable, and she glanced away nervously.

"Hey, sweetie," Frankie said, sounding much too friendly. "Why don't you get yourself a drink, huh?"

Gina glanced at Johnny, and only he could see the irritation in her eyes. She stepped away without a word, and Frankie watched her, ogling her every step without a shred of shame.

"Nice piece of ass, Johnny," he said, once she'd gone. "You takin' Viagra to keep up with her?"

Johnny chuckled, shaking his head.

"Come on." Frankie nudged him. "Sonny wants to talk."

"Now?"

"Yeah, now." He took Johnny by the arm and led him through the crowd.

"Why do I feel like I'm going to the principal's office?"

Frankie ignored his comment. They reached the corner of the room, where Sonny stood with a few other men, gathered around one of the round tables. Each table was covered in white linen, and the flames of candles flickered in the reception hall. Sonny had placed his tailor-made dark silk suit jacket on the back of a chair, and he was clad in a designer dress shirt and tie. As soon as he saw Johnny, he gave him a hug.

"Nice to see you, Johnny," he said, stepping back and leaning on a chair. "Did Frankie fill you in?"

"Nah, he just told me you wanted to talk."

"Let's move to a more quiet setting," Sonny said.

"What about my date?" Johnny asked, glancing in the direction of the bar. He spotted Gina sitting at a stool and ordering a drink.

"She'll be fine. Come on."

Frankie trailed behind them as Sonny led Johnny out a side door and into a deserted hallway. Then, Sonny glanced around to ensure they were alone. His cobalt glare met Johnny's gaze before he spoke.

"There's somethin' big goin' down," he said. "Frankie and I have been in contact with the heads of the other big families around the country. We have a meet set up in Miami. You interested in taggin' along?"

Johnny tilted his head, thinking. "Sounds serious."

"Serious don't even begin to touch this thing," Sonny said in a hushed voice. "This could change everything about *this thing of ours*. I don't want to get too verbal in a place like this because the walls have eyes and ears, ya know? Can I count on you, Johnny?"

"For you, anything," he replied without hesitation. "You just tell me where and when, and I'll be there."

"I'll let Frankie give you the details," Sonny said. "I'll see ya back inside. I need a drink." He turned and went back through the side entrance, headed for the bar.

Frankie shook his head in seeming disapproval. "I don't know if I like this thing, Johnny, but who the hell am I, right? I'll be in touch with all the details in the next few days."

"I'll be waiting."

Back in the reception hall, the music was starting and family and friends were celebrating. Frankie joined Mousey, Peter, Cesare, and Paul, while Johnny weaved his way through the crowd and toward the bar.

He found Gina sipping a mojito, and doing her best to slap Slavic's hands away from her ass. The man had a lot of gall, and seemed to think Gina was interested.

"Is this man bothering you, darling?" Johnny asked, slipping his arm around her waist.

"It's nothing I can't handle, sweetie," she replied in a singsong voice, smiling yet sending him a look that made it clear she wasn't interested in Johnny, either, despite the charade.

Slavic took a long gulp from what looked like a rum and Coke and sidled close to her despite Johnny's presence. "I'm just trying to get laid," he said, slurring. "What do you say, honey? We can go out to my car and be back here in an hour."

Johnny used his arm around her waist to tug her away from the man, effectively separating them. "You're drunk," he said. "I think you owe this lady an apology." He stepped in front of her, standing nose to nose with Slavic.

Instead of stepping back, Slavic spoke loudly, almost shouting. It was loud enough to get the attention of the people surrounding them, who all turned to see what was going on. "Well, isn't she one of Cesare's whores?" he snapped. "Come on, baby, pucker up and blow." He guffawed, spilling some of his drink, and then tipped the glass back and swallowed the rest. Then he slammed the glass on the bar and glared at Johnny.

Although Johnny and Gina had something of a love-hate relationship, he didn't like the idea of this drunk messing with her. He reached into his jacket and retrieved the weapon before Slavic realized what had happened. He only noticed when he felt it—the barrel of the gun pressing into his flabby gut, just above his groin. He looked down in shock.

"Now," Johnny began, holding the gun firmly in place, "we can do this quietly and like gentlemen, or we can have the waitresses picking your balls up from the floor along with all this confetti," he finished, indicating the colorful decorations around them.

After a long moment of heavy silence between them, in which some of the people around the bar had backed up uncomfortably, Slavic grinned and threw his hands up in the air. "What, don't you have a sense of humor?" he said, as if he'd been joking all along. "Can't a guy have a little fun? This is a party, right?"

Johnny slipped his gun back in its holster as Slavic backed up and walked away. Before he left the bar, he stopped by Gina. She leaned back in disgust when he pressed his face into her hair.

"I'm sure we'll meet again," he said, sticking out his tongue and licking her cheek.

She recoiled, wiping away his spittle with the back of her hand, as Slavic retreated into the crowd. There wasn't much Johnny could do right now, with all these people around. He shook his head in disgust.

"Thanks for the help," Gina said.

"Well, I guess he knows a hooker when he sees one," Johnny replied, inviting their usual banter.

"Very funny. That guy's a pig!"

Johnny couldn't deny that. "I'd love to stay and chat about your future boyfriend, but we have something big unfolding here," he said, whispering. "And we have to make contact with our associates."

He took her by the arm, and led her from the reception hall.

# Chapter 20: Meeting Of The Minds

The deserted highway had a perfect meeting place—an old gas station beside a diner. The parking lot was mostly empty when Johnny pulled in and climbed out of his car. He locked the vehicle and went inside, where a middle-aged, tired looking waitress toyed with the curls in her hair and stared at a copy of *People* magazine. She glanced up at Johnny as if annoyed by his presence. Behind her, a window to the kitchen revealed a chef with a stained apron who was frying eggs.

Johnny glanced around the diner, and saw Gianni sitting in a corner booth. He was the only customer.

"Great place, huh?" Gianni DiCenza asked sarcastically. "Not a soul around." He sipped from a mug of coffee and said, "Want some?" Without asking for a reply, he waved to the waitress, who shuffled slowly across the room and tugged a notepad out of her apron.

"Coffee, darlin'?"

"Sure, and a piece of the apple pie I saw in the display case," Johnny said.

She nodded, and walked away to retrieve the coffee and pie. When she brought the steaming mug, and the small dish with a large piece of pie hanging over the chipped edge of the plate, Johnny took a bite of the pie and washed it down with a sip of coffee.

"This better be good," Gianni said, waiting.

"Oh, you'll love this one." Johnny wiped his mouth with a napkin. "Sonny called a meeting."

Gianni seemed to crumple against the dull laminate of the wobbly table. "You got me out of bed on a Sunday morning to meet you in this God-forsaken place to tell me that Sonny's called a meeting? Well, hot damn!"

"Hear me out, Gianni. Not only has Sonny summoned the heads of the families in Boston, but he's also called Chicago, New York, New Jersey, Detroit, Atlanta, Miami, Providence, Cleveland, Los Angeles, New Orleans, Vegas…the list goes on and on."

Gianni's eyes widened. "Holy shit."

"I went to Peter Bianchini's daughter's wedding yesterday and Sonny asked if I was interested in attending."

"I hope you agreed."

"Of course." Johnny took another big bite of the pie. "I told him I'd be by his side every step of the way."

"Where and when?"

"All I know is that it's in Miami. I don't have the when yet. Frankie said he'd be in touch. I just thought this news justified you meeting me in East Bumfuck," Johnny added, nodding to the empty parking lot and barren street.

"Let me know as soon as possible. For Sonny to call in the *Big Cheeses* from across the country, there must be some heavy shit going down."

"You'll know as soon as I know," Johnny assured him, finishing the pie and sliding the plate away from him.

Gianni took out his wallet and tossed some cash on the table. Both men slid out of the booth seats and exited the diner. "I'll fill Richard in when I get back," Gianni said as he walked Johnny to his car.

"Sounds good."

"Be careful." Gianni leaned close. "It sounds like you stepped in something big and it ain't no bed of roses."

"I'll watch my ass," Johnny said. He shook the man's hand, then climbed into his car, and drove off. In his rearview mirror, he saw Gianni climb into his own car and leave the diner.

Johnny arrived home with a fresh pizza for dinner that evening. He ate alone, then showered and read for a little while. After he'd started dozing on the couch, his phone began to ring. It startled him and he sat up, reaching for the cell phone he'd left on the end table.

"Hello?" he said.

A distorted voice came across the line. "Tomorrow out of Logan, seven in the morning, a ticket will be waiting at the ticket counter at American Airlines," the voice said.

"Where do I—"

"No questions," the voice barked. "Be there. Don't look for us. We'll find you."

There was an audible click, and the phone hung up. Johnny leaned back on the couch, staring at his cell for a moment. Then he dialed a number and waited.

"Hello? Yeah. Gianni DiCenza, please."

\* \* \*

Johnny made his way through the Miami Airport, not looking forward to the sticky heat of Florida. He made his way through the bustling building, sidestepping people who were rushing to their respective planes, and almost dropped his carry-on when a woman bumped into him carelessly in the hallway.

Shaking his head, he finally found the exit and stepped outside.

Lines of cars came and went. Vehicles pulled up, and people climbed in or hugged friends and relatives. Johnny wasn't quite sure where he was supposed to go. He'd only been told someone would be here, and that he shouldn't ask questions. He wondered what it would be like if he were here to visit family, or go on vacation. Instead, he was on a mission he couldn't really define, playing two sides. Essentially being two different people.

Finally, a limo pulled up to the curb in front of him, and a smartly dressed driver climbed out. He scanned the area, then stared at Johnny for a moment. He seemed to recognize him, as if he'd seen his photograph.

"Mr. Macchia?"

"That's me," Johnny said.

"Come with me, please." The driver stepped to the rear of the limo and opened the door for Johnny, then took his bag and placed it in the trunk. With the doors securely shut, and the driver back behind the wheel, the limo moved quietly away from the airport and into midday traffic.

The divider was open between the back of the car and the front. For a moment, Johnny watched the driver through the rearview mirror. Then, he said, "So…where are we headed?"

"The pier," the driver said vaguely.

"Why the cloak and dagger routine?"

"Just sit tight. Everything will be explained to you soon."

Before Johnny could reply, the driver closed the partition between them, effectively ending their communication. Johnny had no choice but to sit back, relax, and wait.

Soon, the limo pulled off the main road and headed toward the pier. As the car drove in between a couple of drab looking concrete buildings, Johnny spotted luxury cars parked in the lot—Lexus, Mercedes, even a Lincoln town car. One of the chauffeurs was standing in front of the Lincoln trying to light a cigarette. Johnny watched him light it and take a long puff as he stared up into the sky.

The limo came to a stop beside the Lincoln, and Johnny climbed out after the driver opened the door for him. "I'll hold your bag for you, sir," the driver said.

"Thanks." Johnny nodded to the chauffer who was smoking a cigarette and said, "Hello."

The chauffer only nodded curtly and took another drag of his cig. Johnny surveyed the area and finally saw Frankie and Sonny climbing out of one of the other cars. They had been waiting.

"Johnny," Sonny said, approaching him and shaking his hand. "Glad to see you could make it."

"Hey, Sonny. Where else did I have to go?" Johnny said, shrugging.

The older man laughed and led him toward one of the squat buildings nearby.

# Chapter 21: Flight Of The Hornet

The stuffy heat followed them inside the building. Johnny could smell hints of mold in the air. Not a single window brought in the daylight, and the room was lit only by bare bulbs that hung from the ceiling. The yellow glow illuminated the many tables in the room, which were arranged end to end. Two computers sat in the middle of one table. Johnny noticed one of the monitors was turned off, while the other glowed.

When he entered with Sonny and Frankie, several men turned and scrutinized them. A few stood, some were sitting at the tables. One man, who was a bit heavier and balding, rose to his feet and extended his hand to greet Sonny.

"Nice of you to make it, Sonny. Rocco here was just saying you were gonna be a no-show." He grinned, baring yellowing teeth. "But I reaffirmed that how could our gracious host be a no-show? As my wife would say, you was just fashionably late."

"Don Carlo," Sonny began, squeezing the man's shoulder in a friendly gesture, "It's been a few antipastos since I saw you last, huh?"

The other men chuckled, and Don Carlo stepped back, spreading his hands as he spoke. "Now, what could be so important that you had to call a meeting of the minds here?"

Sonny turned and addressed everyone in the room. "We have a monumental opportunity here, gentlemen. An opportunity to make money, and I mean lots of it. As soon as the guest of honor arrives, we can get started."

A door creaked, and footsteps sounded in the cavernous room. "I'll take that as my cue, Mr. DeSantis," a voice said.

Johnny, listening closely, glanced to the origin of the voice and saw an Asian man descending the metal steps from the warehouse room on the second floor.

He was slim, dressed in a neat suit, his hair slicked back. He approached the table and stood in front of the glowing computer screen, where two other Asian gentlemen rose to their feet to acknowledge his presence.

"Mr. DeSantis is correct, gentlemen," the middle-aged man began. "You have an opportunity to make a lot more money here today. But instead of me explaining, let me show you what I'm talking about."

Johnny remained behind some of the other men, hoping he wouldn't be seen directly. The room was dark enough that perhaps he could blend into the background. He knew this man to be Kazumi, and he certainly recognized the other two.

There was no way they could connect him to the Feds, but after he'd saved Joseph, and complicated their plans in other ways, they would still see him as a threat. He stayed quiet, listening.

Kazumi snapped his fingers and one of the men beside him immediately extended his hand, holding a wooden box. Kazumi opened it and extracted a device. Johnny knew right away what it was. "This, gentlemen, is the future," Kazumi said. "In this age of information, we have the technology to do almost everything by computer. We bank, shop, book trips, and even pay our bills with this technology. This is just what simple folks do from…what they *think* is the privacy of their own homes, as well as on their tablets and smartphones wherever they are. Then you have the smalltime hackers who can steal your identity and use it for a trip to the Bahamas for themselves and their mistresses." Kazumi grinned. "What they don't know is that this is what you Americans call…small potatoes. This, my friends, will change all of that."

Everyone in the room was quiet as he placed the device by the computer screen. Immediately, it seemed to come to life. A light buzzing sound began, and the device—the Hornet—rose and hovered above Kazumi's hand. The other men in the room began to mumble quietly amongst themselves, a few gasping in surprise. The Hornet moved toward the computer and landed on it, then sunk into it like a piece of ice on a hot sidewalk. The low mumblings turned into heated conversation as the men watched. Johnny did his best to blend in.

Kazumi typed a command on the computer, and then turned the screen so the men could watch the steady flow of information the Hornet was gathering.

"So what you're showing us is a sophisticated way of stealing, is that right?" Sonny asked.

Kazumi gave a half-nod. "In a sense, yes. Just imagine your wives trying to purchase something with their credit cards, and finding them maxed out…or imagine the bank foreclosing because you defaulted on your mortgage…your children failing college, your accounts closing. But let's not stop there, Sonny. Just imagine what this can do with the world banks and satellites."

Sonny raised his bushy eyebrow. "You mean…spy satellites?"

"Just imagine letting this loose in your CIA headquarters. Within minutes, anyone can have the names and operations of hundreds of men and woman. Information your country, or any other country, will be willing to pay billions for. Russia, Iraq, China…the possibilities are endless."

Johnny ran his tongue over his dry lips. This new knowledge made him nervous, but he wouldn't show it. Everyone in the room was silent for a long moment, still staring at the stream of information on the screen until it finally stopped, indicating the Hornet had gathered everything in the computer's memory.

"If this is true," Don Carlo said, breaking the silence, "why do you need us? Why haven't you let this loose already?"

"Simple. I have a meeting next week in Russia and the week after that in China." Kazumi smirked. "So on, and so forth. So, you see, it is not definite that this technology will be yours. You Americans always think you deserve everything without having to pay for it."

Sonny frowned. "Then you're not here to solicit, you're here to extort?"

"Such ugly words," Kazumi replied, shaking his head.

"Why us?" Don Carlo asked. "Why not our government?"

"I would think that would be obvious. Whoever prospered from blackmailing a government? To do so would be suicide. Your families, on the other hand, have money. And just think of the power you'll have at your fingertips."

Again, all was silent as the men considered this.

"I don't think you understand the magnitude of what the Hornet is capable of," Kazumi said. "Not only can it destroy a nation's economy, but just think what it can do with the computers that control all your nations' nuclear warheads."

He turned and typed another command on the keyboard, causing the Hornet to reappear as easily as it had seemingly disappeared. Kazumi picked it up and placed it back in the wooden box, closing it. "The price is fifty million dollars," he continued. "I leave for Russia next week. This is a first come, first served basis. So, don't keep me waiting. Gentlemen." He bowed his head to the men, then stepped away, his two cohorts following closely.

Johnny exhaled slowly.

"We hafta talk," Don Carlo said, breaking the silence. He gestured to Sonny and Frankie, who indicated for Johnny to follow them as they walked across the room and headed for a side door.

Johnny squinted when they stepped out into the bright sunlight, slipping his sunglasses out of his shirt pocket and putting them on. Just as the door shut behind them, Don Carlo whirled around, glaring at Sonny.

"You call a meeting which is unheard of and dangerous in this day and age, with the notion that we can make a ton of money," he accused, "and we walk into a James Bond movie starring Jackie Chan! What the fuck is goin' on, Sonny?"

Sonny raised his hands in surrender. "Hey, I'm just as surprised by this slant-eyed cock sucker as you are. Do you really think I would help this maggot slip it to ya? We were all ass-fucked by this, Don Carlo. The question is, what the hell are we gonna do about it?"

# Chapter 22: Uninvited Guests

The trip to Miami and back was a fast one. While he'd waited in the airport for his next flight, Mikey had called and wanted to know how close his father was to Disney World. Johnny recalled rolling his eyes as he sipped the overly expensive coffee he'd bought from an airport shop.

"Kid, you know Miami ain't nowhere near Orlando," he'd said.

Mikey, sounding sheepish, changed the subject. Johnny had made a mental note to check the kid's report cards and see how he was doing in geography class.

As he trudged up the few steps to his front door, he felt weary. Flying always exhausted him. It wasn't the airplane that bothered him, so much as the entire experience of getting in line at security, taking off his shoes, raising his arms and being felt up by the TSA. Fully prepared to make a snide remark to the male attendant about expecting dinner and a show before he got fondled, Johnny had kept his mouth shut. After all, he just wanted to go home, and messing with the TSA wasn't advisable.

He tugged his keys out of his pocket and unlocked his door, thinking about taking a nap and ordering takeout. As he shut the door behind him, he pulled out his cell phone and dialed a number, simultaneously placing his bag on the table in the small foyer.

"We need to meet," he said, without bothering to say hello. "Yeah, I remember where that is." He paused, then added, "I'll be there in forty minutes." He hung up the phone and stepped out of the foyer and into the living room.

Even Johnny, despite his calm and calculating personality, couldn't stop himself from startling when he saw Kazumi Tabata sitting in an easy chair in the living room. Two henchmen stood on either side of him with their hands behind their backs.

It appeared as if Johnny hadn't gotten away without being noticed, after all. The fuckers had followed him home from Miami.

"How the hell did you get in here?" Johnny snapped.

"Let us not ponder on such trivial things, Mr. Macchia," Kazumi replied, steepling his fingers before him.

Johnny said nothing, bothered by the fact that Kazumi knew his name. He was so careful, always covering his tracks. He hoped his name was *all* that Kazumi knew.

"Yes," Kazumi said, as if sensing Johnny's confusion. "I know who you are, and I know Genzer Labs hired you to find out who was leaking secrets from their lab. They are just my puppets, Mr. Macchia, nothing more. Everything worked according to my plans. They didn't even know the technology they were giving me was going to destroy them. The question that should be before us, Mr. Macchia, is *why* can't I get rid of you? You do not take hints very well."

The middle-aged man rose to his feet and wandered around the living room. He picked up a framed photo of Johnny with his two sons, J. J. and Mikey, and tilted his head as he examined the picture. It made Johnny increasingly nervous. He didn't want this man to know what his kids looked like. If he even dared to go near them—

"As you are well aware by now," Kazumi began, "I cannot afford to have someone interrupting my plans."

"You mean your blackmail scheme? It's laughable."

Kazumi turned on his heel and glared at him, setting the framed photo back down on the table. "How simple-minded some of us tend to be, Mr. Macchia. Do you really think I thought your so-called Mafia would foot the bill for your whole country? You see, the Hornet has already been sold to the highest bidder. I had to keep your CIA and your FBI busy while the negotiations were being ironed out. You should have seen them running to figure out why the country's mob bosses were having a secret meeting."

He chuckled. "The Hornet is ready to go on a plane to Iraq as we speak. Now it's my turn to laugh, Mr. Macchia. You see, since you have been a good puppet also, I am going to give you the courtesy of dying a quick death, not like your friend Anthony. I'm sure you're well aware of the fact that Anthony was putting his nose somewhere it didn't belong. Look where it got him. Dead!"

Johnny gritted his teeth as a cold sweat enveloped him. Dead?

"You didn't know?" Kazumi said, appearing to notice. "Well, I'm sorry to have to break it to you, but your friend crossed over about an hour ago. He must have been in a lot of pain before he died. Needless pain, to say the least."

Johnny squeezed his fists so tightly he felt his nails biting into his palms.

"Well," Kazumi continued, "I'll leave you here to have fun with my friends." He turned, nodding to his henchmen. "Don't take too long." He headed for the door, adding, "Sorry to leave your children fatherless, Mr. Macchia, but it must be done. I am sure they will be fine."

Johnny felt his stomach flip. "I just want to know one thing," he snapped. "Who was leaking the secrets from Genzer Labs? Since I'm gonna die anyway, I figure it won't hurt if you tell me."

Kazumi smiled wanly and stepped out, not saying a word. As the door shut behind him, Johnny faced the two intruders. Both men had revealed Samurai swords which gleamed in the light, and Johnny wondered how many people they'd killed with those razor-sharp weapons.

Knowing he couldn't escape, Johnny went on the offensive. He had to think quickly, so he grabbed a nearby bowl of pistachio nuts and threw them to distract the attackers. A vase proved a useful tool to knock out one of the men, who crumpled to the floor easily. Johnny executed a Jujutsu roll across the carpeting and grabbed a bar stool from the kitchen island, slammed it against the wall, and used two legs of the stool as if they were Filipino Arnis sticks.

They battled vigorously until the assailant cut Johnny's sticks in half with his sword. He dropped his cut sticks and charged the attacker, but the man lunged toward him with the sword pointed at his face. Johnny slammed the palm of his hands in front of his own face, utilizing the Iron Palm Kung Fu technique, and locked the sword between the palms of his hands. Taking control of the weapon, he cut off the man's hands, then beheaded him.

The man on the floor awoke, coming at Johnny with his sword. They battled and Johnny slipped and fell on his back. His attacker jumped high into the air and came down aiming for his chest. Johnny used another Jujutsu roll to escape just in time, as the sword became imbedded in the wooden floor. The assailant was unable to free it, so he charged at his opponent's waist. Johnny thought quickly, flinging the sword across the room, and fell back onto the floor, catching him in a *Tomoe nage* Judo Circle Throw, tossing the assailant through the window of his house where he bled to death, having severed his carotid artery on the glass. Out on the street, a dog barked and a woman shrieked. Johnny heard the brakes of a car squealing, a man shouting. The cops would arrive soon.

When the house was quiet, and his attackers were both dead, Johnny made a phone call while he ran outside. He didn't have much time left. His friend Ray could clean up for him, but he had to notify the FBI, too.

"Hey, O'Keefe?" He huffed, catching his breath. "I've got a scene for you to investigate. My place. Hurry!"

# Chapter 23: Traitor

The Corvette kicked up dust as Johnny swung it into the parking lot at the diner, which was almost as empty as he remembered it. This time, an old couple sat near the entrance in a booth, slurping from bowls of soup. Johnny nodded to the waitress, who appeared less than enthused to see him, and headed to the back of the diner in search of Gianni.

Walking into the back of the restaurant, farther into the room than they'd sat the first time, Johnny stopped in his tracks. Gianni wasn't there.

He slid into the booth across from the other man, just as the waitress brought him a coffee. This time, he declined the apple pie. He was too shaken up to eat anything.

"What are you doing here?" Johnny asked when the waitress walked away. "I expected to meet Gianni. Where is he?"

Richard smoothed his hand over his dark hair and sipped his water. "Something came up and he asked me to meet you here. What did you find out?"

"We have to move fast," Johnny said, whispering hoarsely across the table. "Get the team together. Right now there is a device that can bring this country to its knees, and it's about to be put on a plane to Iraq."

"What the hell are you talking about? What device?"

"I don't have time to explain." He rose from his seat and dropped a couple bucks on the table for the coffee he'd barely touched. "Just call Gianni and have him meet us at the airport. You drive."

Outside, Richard led him toward a car parked on the other side of the lot and climbed into the driver's side. Johnny got in the passenger side, noticing the heavy plastic beneath him when he sat down.

"What's this?" Johnny asked, fingering the plastic. Something about the car seemed familiar to him—the worn sticker of the American flag on the glove compartment, the broken radio dials, the gold cross hanging from the rearview mirror. "Hey, isn't this Gianni's car?" he asked, realizing sinking slowly over him. Before he could put the pieces together, he heard a click.

Richard was pointing a gun at him. "I'm sorry, Johnny, but you brought this on yourself."

"What the fuck are you doin'?"

"Kazumi pays a lot more than our government," Richard explained.

"Where's Gianni?" Johnny demanded. He'd figure out what the hell happened later on; first, he needed to know what had happened to his friend.

"Let's just say he won't need his car anymore. Now we're gonna switch places, and *you're* gonna drive. Got it?"

Wordlessly, Johnny did as he was told and switched seats with Richard. Then he put the car in gear and started out of the parking lot, leaving his own vehicle behind. He hoped he'd be alive later, so he could come back and get it. It didn't take him long to notice the other car behind them—a gray sedan. It remained close, but not close enough to pique Richard's interest. Johnny had a feeling about it. *Who the hell is that?*

He'd grown tired of surprises. "Is it worth it, Richard? Betraying your best friend and your country for money? There's a word for people like you."

"Yeah," Richard said, laughing. "Rich!" He kept the gun trained on Johnny while they continued down the road, but it was low enough that no one they passed would be able to see it.

"No." Johnny tightened his hands on the steering wheel. "The word is traitor. Do you really think Kazumi is gonna keep you alive with everything you know?"

"What the hell do you know about anything?"

"Tell me something: how the hell are you getting anything over to Iraq? I mean, there are no American passenger planes heading there anymore. And why Iraq? Surely there must be other countries that want the Hornet."

"But they aren't the ones willing to pay for it. Frankly, I don't care what happens after they get it," Richard said. "I'll be living in some neutral country, like Sweden or Norway. Turn here," he added.

Johnny took a right, piloting the car down a narrow side street that took them into a wooded area. Richard instructed him to stop at the side of a river. From there, they could see the city, buildings reaching for the sky. No one over there knew what was going on. No one knew the world was at the brink of insanity, and the man seated beside Johnny had given everything away just for the promise of cash. It disgusted him.

"Turn the car off and get out."

Doing as he was told, Johnny climbed out of the car and thought he saw a flash of gray farther down the road. They'd been followed, all right. Whether the tail was friend or foe remained to be seen.

Richard held out his hand. "Give me the keys."

He started to hand them over, but at the last second, he decided to make a risky move despite the fact the other man had a gun pointed at him.

He tossed the keys in the river. "Oops. My mistake. Looks like you're walking home."

"Smart ass until the end, huh, Johnny? It's gonna be a pleasure poppin' one into you. Well, it's been a pleasure knowing ya. Say hi to Gianni for me."

The gunshot rang out, and Johnny waited for the pain. When a moment passed and he didn't feel anything, he ran his hands over his gut and chest, looking for a bullet wound. That was when he saw a red stain begin to appear on Richard's white shirt. The man's eyes widened as he fell, crumpling to his knees before his face hit the ground.

Dead.

Johnny remembered the gray car and wasn't perplexed for long. Turning around, he saw Gina walking toward him, clad in tight jeans and a black tank top, a gun in her hand. "Thought you could use a little help."

"How'd you know…" He shook his head as if to clear it. "Never mind. You can tell me while you drive. Head out toward the highway. I'll get my car later on."

Gina had parked at the side of the road, and the thick trees concealed the gray car. She pulled the car closer, and they loaded Richard's body into the trunk. Johnny climbed in, and she drove back toward the diner and into town.

Johnny exhaled heavily. "Jeez. That guy is heavier than he looks."

"Tell me about it. Gianni called me and told me he was meeting you," Gina said. "He wanted backup, and told me to meet him at his place. When I got there, the door was open and he was lying on the floor in a puddle of his own blood. I figured whoever shot him knew how to cover up their tracks. Or knew people in the right places…"

Johnny started to say something, but Gina held up her hand to stop him. "Don't worry, he's gonna make it," she said. "He was actually alive. I guess Richard left him for dead, but he's real damn lucky. He's at Mass General. Oh, speaking of the hospital…" She glanced at him, her thin lips turning down at the corners. "Sorry to hear about Anthony. I know he was a good friend of yours."

"Thanks," Johnny said.

"Anyway, Gianni was semi-conscious when I got there, and he tried to talk to me, believe it or not. I could just make out something about Richard shooting him and how you were in danger, so here I am." She offered a small smile. "I've always known about your secret rendezvous. Where are we headed?"

"The airport. I think I figured out how they're getting this thing overseas."

\* \* \*

Parking proved difficult, and by the time Johnny and Gina entered the airport and rushed toward an office marked *security*, he was worried the flight might've already taken off. Johnny slipped his badge out of his pocket, showing it to the TSA agents. Gina flashed her own badge, and the agents appeared to scrutinize them.

"What can we do for you?" a young, uniformed woman asked.

"We need to know how many flights you have going to Iraq."

"I'll have to look it up. Hang on a minute." The agent stepped into the office. In a second, she returned and said, "We only have one flight a day. It's leaving from terminal four in about fifty-five minutes."

Without saying another word, Johnny pointed toward the sign that directed travelers toward terminal four. He and Gina ran through the airport, dodging families with small children, and people dragging wheeled luggage. Johnny sidestepped a guy carrying a hot coffee, and the man cried out in surprise, almost spilling his drink.

"This way!" He led Gina through the airport, and where needed, they showed security guards their FBI clearances in order to gain entrance. Without their identification, they never would have made it this far.

Going out the back, and finding themselves in a security-only area, Johnny and Gina rushed onto the tarmac. Johnny caught his breath as a guard approached, but when he tried to explain the situation, he quickly discovered the guard was Iraqi and couldn't speak English.

"Damn. Now what?" he said to Gina.

She shook her head. "Got any more bright ideas?" She nodded toward the approaching guards, several of them, and they all looked as if they meant business. The language barrier was a major issue, but Johnny figured they must—at the very least—recognize the FBI emblem on his identification.

Deciding on a different tactic, he grabbed Gina by the arm and led her back inside. She bitched at him along the way, yanking her arm back, but followed closely on his heel. Amidst the crowds, Johnny pulled out his phone and dialed a number.

"Johnny," Frankie said when he answered the phone. "What's goin' on?"

"Listen," Johnny said, stepping into a more secluded area and lowering his voice, "does Sonny still have those surface-to-air missiles?"

Gina raised an eyebrow when she heard this, frowning.

"Sure, Johnny," Frankie said after a pause. "But why?"

"I'm gonna explain to him. Tell him I need him to meet me with one at the entrance of the airport."

Gina was still staring at him in disbelief when he hung up the phone.

"What?" he said. "Can you think of anything else we can do?"

# Chapter 24: Missile Defense

Just outside the parking lot where they'd left Gina's car, they stood at a curb and watched as a sleek black car pulled up. Frankie emerged, along with another man, and they retrieved a box from the back of the car and brought it to Johnny. On the dark side street, they were concealed where no one could see them.

"What the fuck do you want with one of these things, *pizano?*" Frankie asked. "And at the airport, of all places."

"Just get in your car and drive away," Johnny said. "Do it now. Please don't ask any questions. And tell Sonny I solved the problem for him and Don Carlo."

Frankie frowned, but said nothing. "Okay. You're on your own. Whatever it is you're up to, I don't wanna know." He rounded the vehicle, and he and the other man got back in and drove off.

"Now what, Johnny?" Gina asked. "Are you really going to do what I think you're going to do?"

"Of course," Johnny said. "And fast, because that plane's about to take off."

Concealing himself behind a parked car, Johnny opened the box and hurriedly assembled the weapon. Then he rose to his feet and watched as the airplane rose into the sky, taking off. He recognized the emblem on the side; it was the plane headed for Iraq. Aiming, he fired the weapon, and the missile shot through the air and found its target. The explosion burned bright in the sky, gray smoke spreading over the airport. Within moments, Johnny and Gina were running for the car.

"Get in!" Johnny threw himself into the vehicle, and peeled out of the parking lot, leaving behind them the sounds of sirens as Iraqi security guards poured out onto the tarmac and burst into action.

Johnny didn't want to see the aftermath. All that mattered was that he'd destroyed the Hornet. Hitting the gas pedal, the car sped off, away from the airport and the ensuing chaos.

At the hospital, Johnny paused at the open door to Gianni's room. Inside, a number of agents were gathered—all friends of Gianni's— and the television was relaying a news broadcast.

"*On the national scene, a massive explosion rocked Logan Airport this afternoon. It seems an Iraqi airliner burst into flames on takeoff,*" the anchorman was saying. "*Here's our own Maggie McDermott with more. Maggie...*"

Johnny and Gina exchanged a glance, and continued to listen. Gianni saw them, beckoning them inside. He looked like he was recovering well, though his arm remained in a sling.

"*Thanks, Ron,*" Maggie said to the news anchor. "*As you can see behind me, there was total chaos here this afternoon when an Iraqi airliner seemed to explode in midair with five crew members and one unknown passenger on board. The White House is scheduling a press conference later today, but sources tell us that it takes no responsibility for the earlier accident and wouldn't comment on whether it was an act of terrorism against the Iraqi people on American soil. The White House is, however, offering any help in the investigation to find out—*"

Gianni turned off the television set. "Johnny, come on in." Everyone else in the room smiled or nodded in greeting as he and Gina entered.

Gina surveyed the tired looking man in the hospital bed. "Thank God for Kevlar," she said, eyeing his injuries.

"You said it," Gianni agreed. "Lucky for me, I only have this hole in my shoulder instead of the other three Richard wanted in my chest. Thanks, Gina. I owe you one."

"One?" She laughed. "Honey, you owe me more than that. But you can start with a raise. A big one! I brought you what you asked for." She tugged a laptop computer out of her bag and placed it on the bedside table.

"Thanks," Gianni said. "I appreciate it."

"No worries."

He smiled crookedly. "Hey, I have to work or I'll go crazy just lying in this bed." He nodded toward the computer. "Gotta do something while I'm here." Then he turned and looked at Johnny, his smile dissipating. "Where the hell did you get that missile?"

Johnny shrugged, playing dumb.

"Don't ask," Gina warned.

"I know it was you, you know," Gianni said. "And I want a full report on my desk by Monday morning." With Gina's help, he got the laptop turned on and sitting in front of him on the bed. Johnny couldn't help but admire his hard-working boss.

A nurse walked in, getting everyone's attention by clearing her throat. "Mr. DiCenza needs to rest now," she announced. "You'll all have to come back tomorrow." She stepped over to the IV to check a few readings, while the agents began to leave, each wishing Gianni a quick recovery.

Johnny and Gina waited until everyone else had left.

"Nurse, is it all right if we speak to him alone for a moment?" Johnny asked.

The nurse frowned and said, "Well, okay. But make it quick." She stepped out of the room, shutting the door behind her.

Johnny turned to Gianni and asked, "What do the guys at the Pentagon have to say about all this?"

"Look, we have our ways," Gianni replied. "Those who need to know, know. Otherwise, it stays within our little family. Certain people wouldn't be too happy knowing you were involved with any of this, knowing who your childhood friends are."

It was true, Johnny had always walked a fine line, having grown up admiring his friend Sonny, who was ten years older than him. Working against him and with him, at the same time, was an uncomfortable experience that often left him feeling guilty.

"Too bad," Johnny said, shaking his head. "This country owes my childhood friends a debt of gratitude. No telling what could have happened if that insect was let loose on the unsuspecting public."

"I know. But what can you do?"

"Well, all I know is, those guys may not walk on the right side of the law, but they're bigger patriots than most politicians I've met. Come on, Gina. Let's go." He gave Gianni a small wave. "We'll see ya tomorrow, boss." As he stepped out of the room, Gianni had turned to his laptop and was typing away.

Johnny and Gina barely made it to the end of the hall before they heard Gianni calling out for them. Johnny ran back, hurrying into the room, where he found him staring at the computer screen. He looked pale.

"What the hell is wrong with you?" Johnny asked, looking at the medical equipment, thinking something must have gone wrong. He started to call a nurse, but Gianni stopped him.

"No, Johnny, it's not that." He shook his head, turning the laptop around. "You need to see this."

A picture of a hornet had appeared on the screen. Johnny felt his throat dry and tighten. His phone rang in his pocket, and he answered it quickly.

"Hello?"

The voice on the other end was eerily familiar. Johnny's stomach twisted as he listened, dread rushing through him in waves. "I just wanted to tell you a little bit about insects, Mr. Macchia." Kazumi spoke slowly, enunciating each awful syllable. "Hornets are seldom alone. They travel in swarms."

There was a loud click, and then a dial tone. Johnny slipped his phone back into his pocket, stunned, as he exchanged glances with both Gianni and Gina.

It wasn't over, yet.

# Chapter 25: Land Of The Rising Sun

The call from Thomas O'Keefe the next day was unexpected, summoning Johnny for a meeting. Due to Richard's death, the director of the FBI Headquarters in Washington, D.C., had come to the Boston FBI Headquarters to take charge of the industrial espionage investigation.

"Bring your full report," he ordered. "It's important."

At the office, Johnny sat back in the visitor chair—more than a little concerned that he might get in trouble for the missile incident at the airport—and reported everything that had happened.

"Well, Johnny, you stopped the Hornet from going to Iraq, but our work is not done. As you know, Kazumi will keep searching for buyers. We need to prevent them from selling their Hornet device to other countries and stop them from stealing U.S. government secrets which will destroy our national security and our economy." He folded his hands on his desk. "You're going to take a little trip. Your client, Mr. Holmes, will be watched by the FBI to ensure he isn't attacked again. Of course, he won't know this." He paused. "I think what happened to Joseph outside your dojo, as well as the explosion of the van and when you were attacked in your home by the Asian assailants, are connected to the Yakuza. They were after Genzer Labs because of their government contract and you and Holmes got in the way."

"What do you want me to do?" Johnny narrowed his eyes. "And what'd you mean by 'a little trip'?"

O'Keefe rose to his feet and walked to the window, looking out over the parking lot. It was a bright, clear day. "Remember how many times you spoke to me about going back to Japan and studying with your old master, Mr. Yanagi?"

"Yes, I do, but Japan is a long way from here."

"Well, you are going to take a trip to Tokyo."

Johnny wasn't sure what to say. As much as he wanted to study with Mr. Yanagi again, and increase his skills in martial arts, he had a lot to do here in the States. His kids needed to be looked after, not to mention the fact that Joseph Holmes seemed so grateful just to have Johnny around for his muscle alone. "Okay, boss, but what am I really going there for?" Johnny asked, exasperated. It was clear he wasn't getting out of this one. At least Kate could look after J. J. and Mikey for him while he went away. She was always there for him when he had to take sudden business trips.

"I want you to have a talk with your old Master Yanagi," O'Keefe said. "Ask him if he could give you information about where the Yakuza frequent. I know he has knowledge of this."

"I see where this is going." Johnny frowned, smoothing his hand down his button-up shirt. "Now it all makes sense. I knew there had to be a secret agenda for the FBI to pay for my trip."

O'Keefe ignored his last remark, and handed Johnny an envelope with his airline tickets and a passport with his new identity.

"What's with the new identity?" Johnny asked, eyeing the passport suspiciously.

"We do not want to tip off the Yakuza that you are going to Japan." He glared at him. "Got it?"

"Got it."

"Your flight leaves on Monday. Here's your new driver's license and credit cards."

"What's my credit limit on the cards?" He'd traveled courtesy of the FBI before; this was nothing new to him. Another assignment, far from home.

"Twenty-five thousand a piece and don't spend it all at once. You will be there for a month and by the way, no one in our group or anyone else is to know where you are going."

"What's my cover story?"

"Just tell people you are going to Canada to research another case."

When he left the office, Johnny made sure to call Master Yanagi and let him know he would be coming. It had been a long time since they'd seen each other.

He had to leave in three days. That gave him enough time to notify Joseph, and have dinner with his family to let them know he would be gone for a while.

Once again, his plans to spend time with his kids were put to the side. Johnny let out a heavy breath, knowing his late wife wouldn't have liked that one bit. As he climbed into his Cadillac Escalade, he dialed a familiar number on his cell phone and waited.

A cheery voice answered. "Hello, stranger."

"Hi, Kate," he said, unable to stop the smile that crossed his face. His sister-in-law, Kate, always had a delightful disposition that could drag him out of any foul mood. "What are you doing tonight?"

"Need me to the watch the kids?"

"Well, yeah, but that's not what I meant. I was hoping we could all have dinner together at your place. Anything you guys want. If you wanna get takeout, we can do that too."

"What's the occasion?" Kate asked, sounding surprised. She was well aware how hard Johnny worked, and how busy he always was. What she didn't know were the details of his work, but she never pried and accepted the fact that he had secrets—much the same way Kimberly had.

"On Monday, I have to go to Canada on business. Research for a client," he explained. "I'll be gone a month, so I'd like to spend some time with you and the boys before I go."

"Wow. A month, huh?" She paused. "Well, no biggie. You know they always have bedrooms here at my place, and we live close enough to the school that I can drive them."

"You're a doll, Kate."

"Anything for my brother," she replied. When her sister had died, she'd taken to calling Johnny her brother, and they were as close as any true siblings could get. He was grateful for her, especially since she was so willing to be around for her nephews.

"Thanks. So, I'll see you this afternoon around four, then? I will pick the kids up from school and bring them over."

"Sounds good. See you then, Johnny."

Once he hung up, he put the SUV in gear and drove back to the dojo to get some work done, all while looking forward to dinner with J. J., Mikey, and Kate.

# Chapter 26: Reunion

His sons each had their own bedroom in the one-story home he'd once shared with his wife, but both J. J. and Mikey tended to spend more time at their Aunt Kate's house than at home. Later that day, Johnny picked the kids up from school, and brought them home to get whatever they needed to bring with them to their aunt's house.

"How long are you gonna be gone, Dad?" Mikey asked, shoving clothing into a bag. "We can come back here sometime, right?"

"Of course, kiddo," Johnny said, grabbing a bottle of water from the fridge. "I'll be gone a month. Your Aunt Kate has the house key, so if you guys need anything, she can bring you over. I'm sure you'll have fun at her place while I'm gone." As he took a long drink of water, he reminded himself to call Joseph before the man called him first. Johnny felt confident Joseph would be safe while he was in Japan. He had a suspicion Joseph's attackers would realize they were being watched, and would back off until they were able to orchestrate something. The attack on Joseph and his limo driver certainly hadn't gone the way the attackers had planned.

"Lemme make a quick phone call," Johnny said, but Mikey had already rushed out of his room and was digging through a closet for something. J. J. was sitting at the kitchen table with his backpack, engrossed in something on his iPhone. He was sure Kate wouldn't mind if they were a little later than four p.m.; it was three-thirty now. He found Joseph in his contacts list, and tapped his name, then waited.

"Hello?" the man answered.

"Joseph, it's Johnny Macchia. Listen, I gotta go out of town for a month, so we'll have to resume our investigation when I return. Or, I can give you a few numbers—"

"I don't trust anyone else, Johnny," he interrupted. "I'll wait until you come back. Where are you headed?"

"Canada, for a client. Business trip. I want you to lay low and call me if you have any problems. If something happens, let me know, and I'll send someone to look after you."

"You can do that, Johnny?"

"Sure."

"I really appreciate this."

"Of course. Can I give you a call when I'm back?"

"Yes, yes of course."

"Thanks. I'll talk to you soon." Without waiting for a reply, Johnny ended the call and slipped the phone back into his pocket. "You kids ready to go?"

A month in Japan—he wasn't sure how he felt about it. Johnny regretted the fact that he worked so much he didn't usually have time to have dinner with his kids, or with Kate. When he'd been younger, just entering MIT, and even when he'd graduated, he'd looked forward to getting older. Maybe he'd thought life would be easier, simpler, that he'd be a married man with kids, a life he enjoyed— things winding down toward a pleasant retirement. Instead, the Feds were sending him off to Japan to gather intelligence, and he'd be gone for a month. He was already looking forward to returning home, but at the same time, he knew he'd enjoy his visit.

He had a good feeling about it, though he wasn't sure why. *It'll all work out*, he thought to himself, as he drove the SUV toward Kate's house. When they arrived, the kids jumped out of the Escalade and hurried inside.

Johnny stepped into the house and hugged Kate.

"I ordered subs," she said. "Hope you don't mind. It's been a long day."

"Oh, that's okay," Johnny said. "It's the time we spend together that's more important. I'll see you all again when I get home from Canada." The omission—or rather, the lie—was firmly in place.

"So, boys, Friday you will take off from school for a sick day, giving us a three-day weekend to spend together," Johnny said, taking a seat at the table. Kate busied herself with setting out plates and bringing the sandwiches into the dining area. "We can catch up for lost time, see a movie, go to a football game."

"Great!" Mikey exclaimed, taking a big bite of his roast beef sub.

* * *

Their time together passed much too quickly. When Monday morning came around, Johnny arrived at the Logan airport to board his flight to Japan. The lines at security were long, leaving Johnny with a lot of time to think as he stood there, waiting. Getting through all the lines took some time, and finally he was seated in the airplane.

After many long hours of traveling, he arrived at the Tokyo terminal. After making his way through the crowded Narita Airport, he was greeted warmly by Master Yanagi. Yanagi had always been like family to him—like a father. His wrinkled, tanned skin and white hair was a familiar sight. He hugged Johnny tightly.

"So good to see you, Johnny Son."

"You as well, Master Yanagi."

"Do you remember my daughter, Meiko?" He stepped aside, indicating the beautiful woman beside him.

Her long, raven hair hung straight down her back, and her wide brown eyes brightened when she saw Johnny. "Hello, again. It has been a long time," she said, extending her hand. He took her smaller hand in his, squeezing it gently. The warmth and the slight jolt that passed through him gave him pause.

"Yes, it has been a very long time," Johnny said, realizing it had been about twenty years. Johnny had been in his early thirties when he'd last been training with his Master. Meiko, at age twenty, had been the Master's untouchable virgin daughter, a sweet young thing whom Johnny had only talked with briefly. Though he'd been attracted to her then, he hadn't pursued her as a matter of honor. Master Yanagi had become his friend, his teacher, and his father figure; he would not have done anything to jeopardize that relationship. Now, things were different, and as Meiko smiled at him, he saw her for the gorgeous woman she'd become, and his heart jolted in appreciation of her.

Both Johnny and his Master had tears of joy trickling down their faces at seeing each other again, but Meiko gave Johnny an entirely different feeling. Something about her drew him in, and he couldn't explain the intense attraction. It stymied him to the point that he almost forgot where he was.

"Johnny Son, we will now get your luggage and head to my humble home," Master Yanagi said, jolting Johnny back to the present. He broke eye contact with the lovely creature before him, and noticed the rosy hue flushing her cheeks.

"Is…is your wife, Toshi, at home waiting for us?" Johnny asked, stammering slightly. *What the hell is wrong with me?*

The sorrowful expression on Master Yanagi's face caught him by surprise. "Johnny Son…my wife has passed just a few months ago."

Johnny's stomach flipped at the news. He recalled the Master's wonderful wife, and was sad to discover he would not get to see her again. "I…I am so sorry," Johnny said. It was as if all the crowds, the strangers in the airport, had disappeared, and all that existed was the three of them together.

"Come, let's go," Master Yanagi said. "I am sure you have missed our good Japanese food." He smiled warmly as they walked through the airport, causing Johnny to relax somewhat.

"You can say that again." He began to realize how hungry he was; it had been a long time since he'd eaten last. He glanced toward Meiko, who walked beside him, radiating an intense warmth he couldn't ignore. "Meiko, how old are you now?" he asked.

"I am forty years old now." She smiled again, and he swallowed the lump in his throat.

"Are you married?"

"No. My father doesn't think anyone is good enough for me," she joked, chuckling.

"Well, in that case…you and I have a lot to talk about," Johnny murmured brazenly. Meiko laughed, looking into his eyes. The affection he saw there couldn't be missed. He hadn't expected this turn of events. When they arrived at the house, Johnny slid out of his shoes before stepping onto the immaculate tatami floor covering.

# Chapter 27: Reminiscing

Meiko showed Johnny to the guest room where he'd be staying, and she took a moment to remind him of where everything was. It had been a long time since he'd been there last. Hanging on the wall behind the bed was a folding screen featuring Japanese art of a landscape with flowering dogwood trees boasting lovely white petals. The adjoining bathroom was small, but functional.

His cell phone rang. "I've got to take this," he said, glancing at the caller I.D.

"Take your time," Meiko said. "Dinner will be ready in one hour." She closed the *shoji*, the sliding door, to give him privacy, and he sunk down onto the soft mattress in the small bedroom.

"Hello, Joseph," he said, answering the call, glad he had an international phone plan. "Everything all right?" He glanced at his watch; it was around six in the morning in Boston right now. He kept his watch on the time zone he was most familiar with, so that when he received phone calls from America, he could keep up the pretense of being in Canada.

"Everything's fine." Joseph sounded entirely too chipper. "Jeez, what's with your cell signal? You sound like you're on the moon or something."

"Just bad signal in this area," Johnny replied. "What's up? Just getting to work?"

"Yeah. And don't worry about me. Mel's keeping an eye on me. What a nice gal. We had drinks last night."

"She's keeping an eye on you?" Johnny raised an eyebrow. "She's a computer analyst. How's she supposed to help you protect yourself?"

A nervous chuckle came across the line. "Oh, she's just been so nice, we're going to have dinner this evening."

"You asked her out?"

"Well, yes."

Johnny quirked his eyebrow upward, frowning. His unexpected attraction to Meiko battled for dominance over the affection between him and Mel, a long-standing friendship in which Johnny had always felt protective over her. The idea of Joseph—a nice, if not nerdy and somewhat annoying little man—dating Mel somewhat bothered him, though he couldn't put his finger on why. *Am I jealous?*

Maybe it bothered him because he knew there was no way Mel would go for somebody like Joseph.

"Hey, you have fun," Johnny said, not sure he meant it. "I've gotta go. I'll talk to you later. You let me know if anything comes up that I need to be aware of." *What the hell do I mean by that?*

"Sure, sure, Johnny. I'll keep you posted."

"About the case," he added.

"Right, sure, Johnny. Talk to you soon." Joseph cut the call, and Johnny shook his head in amazement.

He laughed off his own discomfort. *Mel and Joseph? Not a chance.*

\* \* \*

The quaint little bedroom, with its light blue walls, reminded Johnny of his last stay in Japan when he'd slept here. The house was much the same as he remembered it. Ink paintings and calligraphy on silk and paper were displayed on the walls throughout the quaint home. Drawings on folding panels of cypress trees and Japanese gardens decorated the larger rooms, and some images showed women holding their parasols and walking through Zen gardens. Other paintings showed the Kabuki Theater of Performing Arts, and impressive renditions of Mount Fuji. Johnny had always been impressed by Master Yanagi's fine taste in art.

He cleaned up and showered in the adjoining bathroom, grateful to relax after his long flight. After dressing, he went into the kitchen where delicious scents met his nostrils. His stomach grumbled.

When Johnny entered the dining area, Yanagi, dressed in casual slacks and a white polo shirt, gestured for him to follow. He tugged on his collar with his thin fingers, and smoothed out the fabric.

"I have a surprise for you." Master Yanagi opened up a large *shoji*—a sliding door—revealing a new dojo. "I recently had this addition built. It is three thousand square feet. What do you think?"

"It is beautiful, Master Yanagi." Johnny gasped in amazement. "I have never seen a dojo like this before."

Red and blue tatami Judo and Jujutsu mats covered the floors, and there were shoji doors, windows, and room dividers consisting of translucent *washi* paper over wood frames, which held together a lattice of bamboo. White lanterns hung from the ceiling, and Johnny gazed upon a mural of Japanese Judokas practicing *Ronduki*—two Judo experts engaged in a match. Displayed the walls of the dojo were Japanese weapons such as *Nunchaku, Bokuto, Haka, Shinken, Kabuto wari*, decorative *Jutte*, a sword with a red tassel as well as *Tessen* fans. Also attached to the lower part of the wall were wooden racks of bows and staffs used in training the students in martial arts.

Statues of warriors dressed in armor and a pagoda with a tiered tower of worship with multiple eaves were displayed on the floor against the side of the wall. The dojo was an inside attachment to Yanagi's house, with a beautiful waterfall indoors, the sound of the flowing water creating a meditative atmosphere. Johnny was stunned by the beauty around him.

"Johnny Son, we will spend many hours here, refining your martial art technique." He turned from the room, shutting the doors behind him. "Let's go and eat, for we have much to talk about."

The kitchen was contemporary and modern, with natural stone countertops, cabinets, a large sink, dishwasher, refrigerator and freezer, gas stove with grill and broiler, and a microwave oven. Paintings of ancient pottery and sculptures were displayed on the walls of both the kitchen and the dining area.

Meiko had prepared Tempura seafood and vegetables by deep-frying in a light batter. Mackerel and vegetables were cooked on the stove grill, and she also made rice in the electric cooker. Miso soup simmered on the stove and oolong tea brewed in the kettle. Sashinabe, a small pot with a long handle, warmed the sake in a bottle.

The table had been set with white square plates, soup and rice bowls, tea cups, sake wine cups, *hashi*—chop sticks—and a bottle of soy sauce.

While sitting on Japanese calligraphy painted cushions at the low dinner table, Johnny asked how Master Yanagi lost his wife. "I hope you don't mind me bringing it up," Johnny added.

Yanagi appeared sorrowful, lost in memories, but not offended by the question. "Of course not," he said. "While visiting her sister in Kyoto, there was an earthquake which destroyed her sister's home. Her sister survived, but my wife, Toshi did not make it."

"My deepest sympathies."

"It only happened three months ago, Johnny Son." He shook his head sadly. "I would have let you know, but I did not wish to discuss it. My father told me three years ago that your wife died also. May I ask how?"

"It's a long story," he replied. "I guess you and me are on the same page. It's hard to talk about." He felt a chill pass through him as he recalled the hostage situation that occurred shortly after he'd graduated from the FBI Academy. He told Yanagi, while he stared down at his plate. "It happened at a bank in Chicago, where my wife Kimberly happened to be at the time. The police arrived at the bank first, accompanied by SWAT teams."

Meiko, sitting beside him, seemed to be watching him closely as he relayed the tale. Yanagi's eyes filled with tears as he listened.

"The bank robbers tied up fifteen people and held them hostage," Johnny explained. "Kimberly was one of the hostages. Shots were fired and two dead bodies were thrown out the front door." He remembered it so clearly, as though it had just happened. "After hours of negotiating, one of the robbers came out the front door holding a woman…" He hung his head. "That woman was my wife. A member of the SWAT team decided to shoot the bank robber, and accidently shot her."

"Johnny, this is terrible," Yanagi murmured.

"I know. I have thought so many times how it could've gone differently, how I could've saved her."

"What happened then?"

"The robber threw my wife down and ran back inside the bank," Johnny explained. "The FBI and the SWAT team charged into the bank and a lot of shots were fired. We were able to save the rest of the hostages. Losing her…it's been very difficult for me."

Yanagi nodded, saying nothing. They ate quietly, except for both Johnny and Yanagi reminiscing about their wives, remembering small things, wishing the past had been different. The discussion cast sorrow over their dinner, but Meiko seemed sympathetic. She squeezed Johnny's hand in reassurance, murmuring her own condolences for his loss.

Johnny still struggled with the loss of his wife. Though he dated women frequently, and enjoyed their company, he still missed Kim and thought of her often. Mikey had been nine at the time, and J. J. had been ten. They often talked about their mom and how much they missed her. If it hadn't been for Kate opening up her house to them, giving the boys a second home, Johnny didn't know what he would've done. Kate had no husband, no family of her own, so looking after the boys was something she cherished and enjoyed.

"I never really got over losing her. I don't think that's possible," Johnny said. "But I have learned to accept it."

"I understand this," Yanagi said. "I miss my wife, but I do accept she is gone. We cannot change this."

"That's right," Johnny said, finishing off the last few bites on his plate.

Meiko patted him on the hand again, smiling. The compassion he felt from her seemed endless. "I would like to visit America someday and meet your children," she said. "Maybe I can help them also." She refilled Johnny's plate, and they continued to eat.

"Thank you, Meiko," Johnny said. "That's very kind of you." He felt a connection between them, unlike what he'd felt with Mel and other women he'd dated. *Dated? Am I considering asking her out?* He wondered if that was a possibility, and if Master Yanagi would approve.

"Let's finish our dinner," Yanagi said, interrupting his thoughts. "Johnny Son will need his energy and strength, because tomorrow we will start our intensive training." He looked at him, grinning. "I will then find out the *real* reason Johnny is here."

# Chapter 28: The Dream

Early the next morning, Johnny and Master Yanagi started training while Meiko watched. Johnny was acutely aware of her observing him, and wondered what it meant. Since they'd last seen each other, Meiko had made great strides in her own martial arts career. Like him, she had studied hard, and had trained in the martial arts with her father since she was a little girl. Johnny wasn't sure what she did for a living, however.

Before going into the dojo that morning to train with Master Yanagi, Johnny had seen Meiko outside practicing Zen archery. Yanagi had praised his daughter and spoken highly of her expertise. With each passing moment, Johnny became more impressed with her and wanted to ask her about her background.

As she watched him train, she seemed to admire him and his technique, and he wondered how mutual their attraction was. He thought back to his youth. Could it work between them, now?

All of a sudden, Master Yanagi swiftly threw Johnny to the mat and placed him in an arm bar while Johnny tapped out vigorously. Master Yanagi laughed while applying severe pain to his elbow.

Johnny gasped, wishing Meiko hadn't been around to see that. Out of the corner of his eye, he saw her step out to answer her phone.

"See, Johnny Son, I did not teach you everything on purpose," Master Yanagi said. "This way, I will always have the upper hand over you." He snickered, letting him up and helping him to his feet.

Johnny stretched out his arms and legs, then ran his hand through his hair. "So when are you going to show me the rest of these techniques?" he asked.

Yanagi's expression turned serious. "When you level with me and tell me the real reason why you are here," he answered sternly.

"Okay, Master Yanagi," Johnny said, knowing there was no way he'd get out of this one. "Let's take a walk in the garden and I will discuss the reason for my visit."

They stepped outside, walking slowly among the beautiful plants and the Zen garden Yanagi often spent time in. The arrangements of rocks, water, moss, and pruned trees surrounded sand that had been carefully raked, resembling ripples in water.

A koi pond with lily pads and ornamental carp was in the center, water flowing down the rocks into the pond. A pagoda statue alongside a colorful slate walkway was surrounded by lavender wisteria, bamboos, grasses, and Japanese quince plants with red flowers. Yellow leaf Japanese maples adorned the garden as well as Japanese cherries, *niwaki* cloud pruned bonsai trees in pots and weeping green cedar with branches of blue-green pine needles. Today, the temperature was a pleasant seventy-eight degrees as the late summer sun shined down.

"Now we are alone," Yanagi said, glancing about to ensure Meiko wasn't nearby. "You can tell me everything. It is just between us."

"Well, the bottom line is there are Japanese firms stealing secrets from American computer designers by computerized means," Johnny explained. "I was sent here by the Feds to gather intelligence."

Yanagi raised an eyebrow. "Hm. Continue."

"We know the Yakuza is forcing this Japanese firm into industrial espionage. This endangers the relationship between Japan and the United States, as well as other countries." Johnny stopped walking for a moment, frowning. "The incident could very easily trigger another World War. If there is anything you are aware of about the Yakuza, something that could help me—"

Yanagi raised a hand, nodding emphatically. He placed his hand on Johnny's shoulder and stepped near. "Johnny Son, under the circumstances, I will teach you everything I know and provide information to help you infiltrate the Yakuza."

"You've got something else in mind, I can tell. What are you thinking, Master?"

"Come with me tonight to one of Tokyo's largest gentlemen's clubs, which is owned by the Yakuza. They own many gentlemen's clubs throughout Japan."

"Oh? That sounds promising." Johnny began to consider how he could collect intelligence by visiting businesses owned by the Yakuza.

"Yes, this can work in your favor," Yanagi confirmed. "This club is where the more prominent members of the Yakuza conduct their illegal activities, such as drug trafficking, prostitution, money laundering…and murder."

"That would be a good place to start." Johnny wondered how Master Yanagi knew this, but he didn't ask. He had a feeling he would find out soon enough.

"Yes. I will introduce you under your assumed name as one of my long-time students," Yanagi said. "Once I do this, you will need to return by yourself, and from that point on you will be on your own. One other thing, Johnny…do not ask questions or volunteer information about yourself. It may take a few visits, but let them come to you first, and under no circumstances deviate from the plan."

"That sounds good, Master," Johnny agreed, wiping the sweat from his brow with the back of his hand. "You are very knowledgeable."

"We will talk about that another time. Let's rest now from our vigorous workout, so we will be refreshed and have energy to handle the beautiful women with their voluptuous breasts and nice firm asses," Yanagi said, smirking.

"You sound like a dirty old man, Master Yanagi."

The Master guffawed loudly as they walked back toward the dojo.

"You know something, Master Yanagi, while I have been gone all this time, I also have learned much about women's breasts and asses."

"How is that?" Yanagi asked, catching his breath from laughing so hard.

"I have had the opportunity to study Tai Chi from a Chinese Master. That's why I know how to excite a woman by touching her breasts with the Tai Chi flowing through the movements of my hands and fingers."

Both men laughed.

"Now I know I had better not leave you alone with my daughter," Yanagi teased, jabbing him in the chest with a bony finger.

Johnny went to his room to lie down, and fell into a deep sleep. He dreamed he had already entered the gentleman's club. The lights were low, and a wide circular stage dominated the room. The silvery poles almost glimmered under the glow of blue tinted lamps. At first, he thought he was alone, except for the gorgeous woman walking seductively toward him. She was completely naked, her voluptuous body inviting his stare. It was then that he realized she was not just *any* woman. This was Meiko. Her body language invited him closer, her smile widening at his nearness.

Suddenly, Johnny turned and saw Master Yanagi standing there, waving his bony finger back and forth, his head moving side to side. "No, not my daughter!" he said firmly.

Johnny looked back at Meiko as she moved closer to him. He sat down, and she lowered herself onto his lap while draping her arms around him. Before Master Yanagi could attack him and tear them apart, Johnny startled when he heard a knocking sound.

The dream faded, and he awoke to the sound of Meiko's voice on the other side of the bedroom door.

"Johnny, it is time for you to get ready to go out with my father," she called out.

He gasped, realizing his breathing had become labored from the dream. When he rose from the mattress, it occurred to him that the sound of her voice had only increased his erection. Exhaling heavily, he called out, "Yes, thank you, Meiko," and hoped she wouldn't notice the fact his voice was tinged with excitement.

*I'd better take a cold shower.*

# Chapter 29: Protecting Mel

After his shower, he took out a fresh pair of jeans and a matching black button-up shirt to wear with a sleek new blazer. As he dressed, his phone rang, and he saw Mel's name appear on the screen of his cell phone. For a brief moment, still lost in the seductiveness of his dream, he wondered if she knew that he'd met someone he was interested in, but then dismissed the idea. *How could she possibly know about Meiko?*

He picked up the phone, happy to talk to an old friend, a woman he sometimes shared his bed with so they could both enjoy carnal pleasures. "Mel. What's up?"

There was a pause. "Johnny? Jeez, you sound like you're a million miles away."

"Bad cell phone reception," he said, using the same excuse he'd given Joseph.

"I wanted to give you a call and see how you're doing. I got your text message the other day, that you had to head to Canada. I'll miss our usual lunch date this week."

"Everything's fine," Johnny said. "Nothing too exciting."

"No worries. I don't expect details," Mel said. She, of all people, knew how secretive Johnny could be.

"How are things at Genzer Labs?" Johnny asked while pulling on his jeans.

"Everything's been okay, actually. For now. After Joseph discovered the electronic device in the office plants, nothing else bizarre has happened since the van explosion and the attack on Joseph outside your dojo."

"Well, that's good to hear," Johnny said.

"Except for one thing, I guess." Mel sounded dejected. Or was that annoyance he'd picked up in the tone of her voice?

"Mel, everything all right over there?" He finished tugging on his pants, and sat down on the edge of the bed.

"Well, sort of."

"What's going on? Is this about Joseph?"

"How'd you guess?"

"He told me you were keeping an eye on him." Johnny chuckled. "Said you had drinks the other night, that you were going out for dinner."

"Oh, God," Mel retorted, drawing out the word and huffing loudly. "This man is driving me nuts, Johnny!"

"What do you mean?"

"He won't leave me alone. He's got the hots for me."

Johnny laughed. "I don't know what to say, Mel. I'm so sorry." Mel was just as much of a player as Johnny, but he knew she'd never go for a guy like Joseph.

"Can you get him off my back?"

He thought back to all the times he'd protected Mel, when she had some creep after her. She was a gorgeous, talented woman, and the two of them had a history. Their friendship—with benefits—had always been deeper than the sexual attraction between them, and Mel frequently turned to Johnny for help when it came to rejecting her male suitors.

"I'll do my best, babe, but there's not a whole lot I can do from Canada. If he calls me, I'll try to talk him out of it. You know, let him down gently."

"I flat out told him to leave me alone," Mel grunted. "He seemed to think it was a joke, that I was really into him."

"I'm real sorry, Mel," Johnny said, but he was grinning nonetheless.

"He wants to take me out for lunch on the same day that you and I normally go."

That irked him. His grin dissipated. "Hey, even though we're just friends and we only date casually, I can still be jealous," Johnny quipped.

"That's my guy," Mel said, chuckling. "Little help here?"

"Tell him if he doesn't back off, he'll have to answer to me. Hey, if you have to, tell him we're together. I may be working for him, and I'll probably end up working for Barry Genzer on this case, but you're important to me, too."

"Oh, don't get me started on Barry."

"Have you two been dating?" Johnny was a little surprised, even though he knew they worked together.

"No, but Barry does entertain ideas about us being together."

"Wow, you've got more man troubles than I thought."

"Tell me about it."

"Well, I'll play boyfriend if I have to, to get Joseph off your back. Just don't tie me up in anything, Mel. You know I don't want to be attached to anyone."

"I know, I know," she said, laughing. "Playboy Johnny Macchia. I wouldn't dare attempt to take away the title."

"That's right," Johnny said, smiling. "All right, I gotta go. You take care of yourself."

"You too, Johnny. See you when you get back."

He ended the call, slipping the phone into his pocket. Then he finished dressing and carried his shoes into the living room to meet Master Yanagi for their evening out.

# Chapter 30: Yakuza Gentlemen's Club

When Johnny emerged, Master Yanagi whistled and said, "Wow, you clean up well. You look like a Mafia hitman."

"In that case, you better be careful tonight. You might have to worry more about me than the Yakuza." Johnny laughed. "How do you know what a Mafia hitman looks like, anyway?"

"Don't worry. I watch many American gangster movies. Such as Scarface, The Godfather, and Good Fellows.

Johnny smiled. "All good movies. Ready to go?"

Master Yanagi nodded and led Johnny out to the car, a sedan parked at the side of the house. The warm, darkening evening embraced them.

When they got on the road, Johnny asked, "Has Meiko been taking care of you since your wife died?"

"Yes, she takes good care of me," he said with pride. "However, it is difficult for her because it is like a second job."

"What type of work does she do for a living?"

"My daughter is an agent for the Japanese government. Something like your FBI!" While Johnny gaped, Yanagi added, "She trains new recruits at the MPD Academy in combat martial arts, Jujutsu and Judo, as well as police tactics."

"Are you kidding me?" Johnny asked, shocked.

"No, why would I kid you?" Speaking with great pride, he added, "Meiko is going to help you, Johnny Son."

"Really?" Johnny shook his head in amazement. He knew Meiko trained in martial arts, and he knew about her seemingly unnatural obsession with archery, but he never would have guessed she was an agent like him. They had a lot in common, and his interest in her continued to grow. Shaking his head as if to clear it, he listened as Yanagi told him more about Meiko's involvement in the case.

"I believe your boss, Thomas O'Keefe, has made arrangements with my government," he said. "She is going undercover as a stripper at the same gentlemen's club starting tomorrow night." He shot Johnny a glare as he drove the car, then returned his focus to the road. "Don't get any wrong ideas about her undercover. Because I don't mean under the covers in bed!"

Johnny's eyes widened. "I wouldn't dream of it." The truth was, he already had. He thought of the dream he'd had earlier, then tried to expel it from his mind. Now was not the time to be thinking about Master Yanagi's daughter in an intimate way. In fact, he wasn't certain there would ever be a time for that.

When they arrived, Master Yanagi parked the car and turned to Johnny. "What is your undercover name?" he asked.

"My undercover name is Johnny Rizzo. The FBI has developed a whole new identity for me which has been established in case someone decides to do a background check."

"Good. Okay, let's go inside, Johnny Rizzo," Yanagi said with a wink.

* * *

Two doormen who were the size of Sumo wrestlers met them at the entrance. "Welcome to Tabata's Gentlemen's Club," one of the men said, his voice reminding Johnny of gravel crunching under heavy tires. The huge men stepped aside, ushering Johnny and Yanagi into the foyer. The smell of incense met his nostrils, and the plush carpet felt like air beneath his feet.

While walking inside, Johnny asked Yanagi about the man who owned the club. The name sounded familiar to him. When the answer came to him, he realized why Yanagi had chosen this particular club. "Does this Tabata have a brother by the name of Kazumi?" Johnny asked.

Yanagi nodded as they made their way to a small table. "He does." The older man lowered himself into a chair, and Johnny sat beside him as they watched the show.

"Kazumi Tabata is the guy I was investigating back in Boston," Johnny said. The music was loud enough that they could talk privately without being overheard. "That bothers me." More than anything, he didn't want to be found out. But he didn't think that would happen, especially because he was Johnny Rizzo now, and his tracks had been carefully covered by the Feds.

"Don't worry too much," Yanagi said, patting him on the hand in a fatherly gesture. "Kazumi is not scheduled to come back to Tokyo for two months, and you will be long gone by then." Thanks to Meiko's involvement, and Yanagi's own knowledge of local goings-on, Johnny felt confident that he was right. He was still amazed at what Meiko did for a living, and hoped to discuss it with her later.

"Let's have a drink," Johnny said, glancing up as a buxom waitress approached. Her dark hair fell over her tanned shoulders as she leaned close, her breasts overflowing from the tiny silver top she wore.

"What can I get you gentlemen?" she asked, her voice husky. Though her accent was heavy, her English was very good.

"Whiskey on the rocks," Johnny replied, knowing he had to fit in. Johnny Rizzo wouldn't be here for the same reasons as Johnny Macchia.

Yanagi ordered a dark beer, and the two men enjoyed their drinks, sipping slowly and surveying their dimly lit surroundings.

While drinking, Johnny glanced up and saw a large, well dressed man walking toward their table. Despite his girth, he had handsome features, and dark hair that had been styled and slicked back. He wore a black suit with a crisp white shirt, and carried a glass in one hand. As he approached them, he held his arms out and exclaimed, "Master Yanagi, my old friend!" He leaned over the table and said, "How are you? Long time no see."

Yanagi rose from his seat and embraced the man, then stepped back and surveyed him, shaking his head. "Oshi, it has been a long time. You look the same."

"You look much older!" Oshi laughed, his voice booming as he clapped him on his slender shoulder.

"Thank you for sending the flowers for my wife's funeral," Yanagi said. The bigger man immediately sobered, his expression solemn. "It was very thoughtful of you," Yanagi added. "The flowers were very beautiful."

"That's the least I could do for an old friend," Oshi said, his tone sincere.

Yanagi nodded toward where Johnny sat, and said, "This is Johnny Rizzo, my student for many years and my future son-in-law." He winked at Johnny. "This is Oshi Tabata."

Johnny greeted the man, bowing his head, and thought to himself that if his cover as Rizzo included being engaged to Meiko, he definitely didn't mind. The woman had begun to get under his skin.

"Your daughter will start working here tomorrow night," Oshi said to Yanagi. "Do you have any reservations about Meiko dancing here?"

"I don't like it, but what can I say? She's a grown woman with a mind of her own."

"What about you, Johnny?" Oshi asked.

"I don't like it either," Johnny said, playing his part. "Just like her father said, she has a mind of her own. But she promised me she would stop when we get married." It made sense that his future wife should stop stripping for money when the time came to tie the knot. This seemed to appease Oshi, who gestured in understanding.

"So, Johnny, what do you do for a living?"

"I am a computer analyst for a large firm." Johnny imagined his alter-ego as a somewhat boring man who worked in a cubicle all day and traded gossip at the water cooler. He was glad the identity was a fake one.

"That's great," Oshi said, appearing impressed. "We will have to talk sometime. My family is also involved with computer research and microchips."

"Oh, really?" Johnny said, innocently sipping his drink. "That's interesting. It seems we have a lot in common, then."

"Indeed, we do. And now, we must celebrate my reunion with my old friend, Yanagi, and my new friend Johnny Rizzo." Oshi turned and signaled for four of his dancers to come over to their table to entertain them. The buxom waitress turned when he called out to her. "Drinks on the house for my two friends, and bring out a bottle of our best champagne."

Oshi sat down, his large frame taking up space in the corner seat. Their table was in a comfortable, private area, within view of the stage. Yet, they were able to sit and talk comfortably without the intrusion of other patrons, who mingled, sat at tables, and flirted with the strippers. The club was welcoming and comfortable.

"Johnny, I am intrigued about what you do for a living," Oshi said. He sipped from a tumbler of dark liquid, glancing to the stripper nearest him, whose breasts were bare and nipples hardened in the cool air. He looked back at Johnny and said, "You must come back to see me so we can talk more."

He hadn't expected to make progress so quickly, but he was glad for Yanagi's introduction. Because Oshi knew Yanagi, he now trusted Johnny. "Sure, when is it convenient for you?" he asked.

"How about tomorrow night. Are you free?"

"I'll make myself free for you, Mr. Tabata."

"Please, call me Oshi," the man said. "How about seven o'clock, Johnny?"

"You're on," he replied, offering a warm smile.

"We will meet in my office where it will be easier to talk." Oshi glanced to the approaching waitress, who carried the champagne. She opened the bottle and poured glasses for all three men. "A toast to my friends for a prosperous future together," Oshi said, raising his glass.

Yanagi and Johnny both raised their glasses, the bubbles sparkling and rising to the surface of the expensive champagne, catching the sensuous light of the club in the glimmering liquid.

"To the future, my friends," Yanagi said.

"To the future," Johnny echoed.

They sat and talked for a short time, enjoying their champagne, before Oshi rose to his feet. Once again, his enormous stature seemed to dominate the room.

"Now, I must go," he said. "I have many things to attend to. Johnny, I will see you tomorrow at seven."

"See you then."

"Enjoy your evening. The drinks and the entertainment are on me."

"You are too kind, Oshi," Yanagi said, shaking the man's hand warmly.

"It is the least I can do."

"Thank you," Johnny echoed, raising his glass.

He watched as Oshi left, walking through the dark recesses of the club and into a secluded hallway, disappearing into the shadows.

Now that Johnny had accomplished his goal for the evening, he and Yanagi enjoyed the drinks and entertainment, chatting with the strippers, making small talk, and watching the show.

On the drive home, Yanagi was silent for a long time. Finally, he said, "I want you to know I am out of this. You and my daughter are on your own."

"Understood," Johnny said, fully expecting the declaration. He was grateful to Yanagi for helping him get in. Now he just had to accomplish his mission—with Meiko's help.

# Chapter 31: Johnny's New Boss

The very next morning, Yanagi put Johnny through an intense training that lasted four hours. Johnny was glad he hadn't had too much to drink last night. Even with the amount of alcohol he'd ingested, he felt somewhat more tired than usual. By the time the training session was over, he was exhausted and ready for lunch.

The warm sunlight spilled into the garden and through the wide windows in the dojo. Johnny took a shower and dressed in casual pants and a t-shirt. The smell of food wafting from the kitchen made his stomach grumble. After lunch, Yanagi yawned.

"I will take a nap now," he said, trudging out of the kitchen.

"Sleep well," Johnny replied, waiting until he heard the bedroom door shut. Now, he had his chance. He had been hoping to speak with Meiko alone since he'd discovered her part in this.

Sitting across the table from her, he placed his hand over hers before she could walk away to start cleaning up the dishes. "Hold on," he said. "I'd like to talk to you." His heart pounded when he saw the slight blush creep into her cheeks. What did she think he meant?

"Yes, Johnny?"

"Look, to be blunt, what exactly is your position in all of this?"

She glanced down at his hand over hers. "I—"

Withdrawing his touch, he cleared his throat and said, "I mean, with the job. The work you do."

She exhaled slowly, placing her hands in her lap. "Ah, yes. My father told you about my work, then." Her gaze hardened and she straightened where she sat. "Then, to be blunt as you say, I am the head agent for the Organized Crime Control Bureau in the Tokyo Metropolitan Police. I am in charge of this case, not you."

The tone of her voice startled him. He started to speak, but she cut him off.

"You are a guest in my country and I am your boss, and that's the way it is going to be."

While Johnny had become entranced by her beauty and skill on a level bordering intimacy, he'd nearly forgotten that fact. It was true: she was his boss on this case, and not only did they have to work together, but he had to answer to her. It explained why he'd been sent here. Yanagi and his daughter were deep in the field of intelligence, deeper than he'd imagined.

"Your father introduced me to Oshi Tabata last night," Johnny said. "He approached me since I am a computer analyst."

She shook her head, her raven hair catching the light and shining like silk. "Johnny, don't get confused and too wrapped up with the computer end of his business. That is your cover. You are not really a computer analyst. Although, you do know a lot about computers. He may trip you up and you could find yourself in a compromising situation." The hard stare she'd given him a moment ago had faded, to be replaced by something close to concern. Was she worried about him?

He tried to disregard his feelings. He couldn't get distracted by anything; he had to work on this case and focus on nothing else.

"Mr. Tabata is also heavily involved in the heroin trade," Meiko said. "Maybe you should stick with that part of his business. It seems as though the FBI and the DEA have arrested you in the past for smuggling drugs. They set up a good cover for you."

"This is true," Johnny said. "My alter-ego, Rizzo, was not exactly a model citizen. His past will be appealing to Oshi Tabata."

"I will work more on the computer end of this investigation," Meiko stated with the firm tone of a focused business woman. "When Oshi approaches you to do some dealings with the computer end of it, why don't you suggest that I get involved with you in both the computer and heroin trade? This way I can cover for you on computer details." She gave him a sly smile. "After all, we're engaged, right? What better cover can you get—a soon-to-be married couple working together in the underground."

Johnny ignored the heaviness that settled in his stomach when she said *engaged*. "It's a deal," he said.

"Now let's rest for our big night ahead," Meiko said, collecting the dishes and putting away the leftover food. "By the way, I need to be there earlier than you for the change of shift. And don't forget, you aren't supposed to completely approve of my *job choice*. Be natural, Rizzo."

Johnny chuckled. "Okay, I'll see you tonight at the club."

# Chapter 32: Chemical Formula

Johnny arrived at the club ten minutes early for his seven o'clock appointment with Oshi Tabata. The Sumo goons he recalled from his last visit, dressed in crisp suits, greeted him at the door and ushered him inside.

"We have been expecting you, Mr. Rizzo," one of the men intoned. "Come inside, please."

As they walked through the club, stepping easily through the crowd, Johnny paused at the stage. His gaze was drawn to Meiko, who danced nude, undulating around the pole and leaning back, her shining dark hair hanging loose behind her. She straightened, then turned, and when she saw him staring at her, she quickly covered her breasts with her forearm, and took off the hat she'd been wearing to hold it over her pussy.

Hurriedly trying to act the part of the embarrassed girlfriend, Meiko leaned over to Johnny and whispered harshly. "You fucking asshole, you are standing there gawking at me like you never saw a woman nude before. I am supposed to be your fiancée, remember?"

Her words surprised him. She'd come a long way from being the sweet, demure virgin he'd met twenty years ago.

"No, your the one being an asshole," he replied in a low tone. "If you're my fiancée, you shouldn't be covering yourself up. It will make them suspicious of us." Grinning wickedly, he added, "So, uncover yourself immediately and rub your tits in my face and I'll stuff some money between your breasts. Sound good?" It certainly sounded good to Johnny. Meiko had no choice but to comply. If she concealed herself from him, it would certainly make Oshi and his men suspicious.

Dropping her hat, she leaned her body toward him, crouching on the stage, and rubbed her breasts against his clean shaven face. Hanging a twenty dollar bill between his lips, he passed it to her, and when she took it, her lips met his for a passionate kiss. Although he could tell she was annoyed with him, he sensed something in the way she touched him—affection, perhaps. He wasn't certain, but he thought the kiss held more promise than she'd intended it to.

"You really are an asshole," she snapped, withdrawing. "I'll take care of you tonight!"

"I can't wait," Johnny said, grinning.

Nearby, the two Sumo goons stood against the wall, their arms crossed over their chests, waiting for Johnny to finish. They were snickering, watching the show, and Johnny knew they must be aware of his *engagement* to Meiko.

Apparently, their act had been convincing enough. Even to Johnny, because he wasn't certain the kiss had been an act. As Meiko continued dancing, he joined the men and they escorted him to Oshi Tabata's office, which was located in a narrow hallway in which the lights were a bit brighter than the dim lamps in the main area of the club.

One of the goons rang a doorbell, and Oshi buzzed them in. The larger of the two men remained outside the door as a guard. Johnny was immediately patted down and an electronic wand was used to check for weapons and devices.

The goon turned to Oshi, who sat behind a large, imposing desk, leaning back in his chair. He held a glass filled with amber liquid in one hand.

"He's clean, boss," the big man announced.

"Okay," Oshi replied, nodding. "Now wait outside." Once the door had shut behind the guard, Oshi turned to Johnny and said, "Have a seat. Would you like a drink?

"Yes, please." He sat down in a soft, leather visitor's chair. "I'll have scotch on the rocks."

Oshi went to a large bar area on one side of the spacious office. He topped off his glass, then grabbed a tumbler and dropped a few ice cubes in it. He poured scotch from a slim bottle, then placed the bottle back on the shelf. "Top quality," he said. "Nothing but the best for my friends." He handed it to Johnny, then returned to sit behind his desk.

"Oshi, do you always pad down your guests like that?" Johnny asked, sniffing the delicious drink and enjoying the taste as it slid down his throat and warmed his belly.

"One must never be too careful," Oshi replied, his expression solemn. "You never know what can happen, true?"

"That's right."

"You know, Johnny, I checked you out and you have an extensive police record. Money laundering, counterfeit bills, and hijacking. I'm not so concerned about what you did, but I am concerned about how many times you got caught." Oshi leaned against the desk, swirling the liquid in his glass. A frown deepened the dimples on his tanned skin. "You need to cover your tracks and know who you are dealing with. Look at me: I haven't had one charge brought against me. Do you know why that is?"

"No." Johnny sipped his scotch, listening with interest.

"I'll tell you why, because I'm smart. I am smarter than anyone else. I am very careful with who I am dealing with. I want to deal with you, Johnny, but this extensive police record of yours makes me a little leery. You even have a narcotics charge against you. At least you did your time and never rolled over on anyone. This is honorable. That is why I like you and that is why I am going to do business with you."

Having made his decision, Oshi rose from his chair and stepped around his desk. Johnny stood and shook his hand, and the two men embraced.

"Thank you, Oshi. I am looking forward to working with you."

"Johnny, this is what we are going to do." Leaning against the desk, Oshi folded his hands in front of him, and Johnny listened closely. "Remember, I told you I have a big computer firm."

"Yes, I remember."

"I also own car and tire manufacturing plants. I need to find a new way to send the microchips."

"Well, I have an idea on how we can kill two birds with one stone."

"How do you plan to do that?" Oshi inquired, intrigued.

"I will be glad to tell you." He swallowed the rest of his drink and placed the empty glass on the desk. "First, tell me…what other items do you want to conceal and send to the United States?"

Oshi smirked. "Heroin, tons of heroin!"

"Then here is your answer. You can take the heroin and put the microchips inside the bags of heroin. Then, place the bags of heroin within the lining of the tires. Before the tires are sealed, there is a special chemical they can be dipped in to prevent the K-9 dogs from sniffing the drugs."

Oshi's thin eyebrows rose, his eyes widening. He appeared impressed. "What prevents them from detecting my electronic microchips?"

"I am glad you asked me that. I have an answer for that, too. You can place several microchips inside these very small plastic cases, and the same chemical can be used for coating the plastic cases."

"Are you sure?" Oshi asked, frowning.

"Of course, I'm sure. As sure as my name is Johnny Rizzo."

"You know something, Johnny, you are a smart motherfucker." The two men laughed before Oshi asked, "How can you get this chemical?"

"Introduce me to the chemist who runs your meth lab," Johnny said. "He can cook it up for you and then give it to your people at the tire factory."

"Wait here. I'll be right back," Oshi said, seeming excited at the prospect of solving his problems with one simple chemical. "The chemist and the foreman from my tire factory happen to be right downstairs in the club, probably having a lap dance." Having risen from his chair, he started toward the door. "Meanwhile, why don't you write down the chemical formula they will need," he added. "Here's a pen and pad." He moved out the door as quickly as a man of his size could manage, and Johnny thought for a moment, jotting down notes on the pad.

Ten minutes passed before Oshi returned, two well-dressed men on his heel. Johnny stood to greet them.

"Johnny, this is my top chemist, Naka," Oshi said, introducing the slim, bony man beside him. "And this is my foreman, Soke."

He bowed politely to both men. "Gentlemen, it is a pleasure to meet both of you."

"Do you have the list for the chemical formula?" Oshi asked, gesturing toward the notepad.

Johnny nodded, handing him the pad with his notes. "Here it is."

Oshi handed it to Naka, who read the list, his brow crinkling as he pondered the ingredients. "No problem. It will be a piece of cake."

"Soke, when Naka finishes mixing the chemical formula, then it's up to you to see that the heroin and microchips are properly placed in the lining of the tires," Oshi instructed. "Make sure you test it. Ensure it is foolproof by using the K-9 dogs. Also, make sure you have the correct electronic equipment to scan the tires."

"Okay, boss. Is there anything else?"

"That's all for now. You can return to the club for some fun. After all, it's Friday night."

Both men thanked him, and stepped out.

Oshi, grinning at the progress they'd made, shook Johnny's hand warmly. "Okay, Johnny, I want you to be my partner and my official representative in the U.S."

"With all due respect, that's a lot of risk and a great deal of responsibility on my part."

"I know, Johnny. That is why I am offering you five percent of all my profits made in the U.S."

Johnny cocked his head, thinking, before he finally nodded. "That is very generous of you, Mr. Tabata. You have a deal."

They shook hands again, and Mr. Tabata smiled, revealing his pearly white teeth. "Didn't I tell you to call me Oshi?"

Johnny chuckled. "Of course. Thank you, Oshi."

"Before you leave, I have a gift for you." Stepping across the room, he opened his safe and pulled out an envelope. "This is twenty-five thousand dollars in cash—a small token of my appreciation for solving my problem. You will make a hundred times more than that on a monthly basis working for me."

"Thank you, Oshi." Johnny slipped the envelope into the pocket of his suit jacket. "I look forward to doing business with you."

Downstairs, amongst the crowd of club patrons, Johnny pulled Meiko to the side to speak to her. "Everything went great with my meeting," he whispered in her ear, slipping his arm around her to make it look like nothing more than a lover's affectionate embrace. "I need to drive back to your father's house and get some sleep for another day of training. I'll fill you in tomorrow."

"Okay, sounds good. I'll be home late."

"Yeah, I know," he said, adding disapproval to his voice. After all, he had to appear like an irritated fiancé.

An amused yet teasing expression on her pretty face told him that she'd seen through his act; he truly was bothered by the fact she'd be out late. Why? It wasn't as if they were *really* engaged. He had no claim on Meiko.

Heading back to the house, Johnny dismissed the thoughts that crowded his mind. He just needed rest, that was all.

*I'll feel different after a good night's sleep—maybe.*

# Chapter 33: Watching Joseph

Joseph's paranoia often got the better of him. He wished Johnny hadn't gone to Canada. His friend Matt—the man who normally drove him—was in the hospital in intensive care after the attack on his life. The situation had frightened Joseph enough that he was having nightmares and startling at the slightest sound. He talked to an associate of Johnny's—a big guy by the name of Ray Hachimoto—who hung out at the dojo and was looking after things while Johnny was away. Ray had taken over for him when it came to teaching martial arts, and Joseph figured the two men were pretty close friends. They had a good arrangement, so the dojo could keep operating whenever Johnny went away on business.

"Are you a private eye, too?" Joseph asked, fidgeting in Johnny's office, where Ray sat with his feet propped up on the scratched surface of the desk.

"Nope, but I do look into things…from time to time." The man's voice was low, but his hard, dark eyes commanded respect. "You know, for Johnny."

"Right. Of course."

"Why'd you want to meet me today, Mr. Holmes?"

"I'm just scared," he blurted out. "Ever since they came after me and my driver, I'm just on edge. Was kinda wondering if you could keep an eye on things. Drive by my place from time to time, make sure…make sure…"

"Make sure you're still alive?" Ray suggested.

"Yeah, yeah," Joseph mumbled. He suddenly wondered if Johnny would be upset if he knew Ray had his feet on the desk. Probably not. Johnny didn't seem like the kind of guy to worry about little stuff.

"Sure, Joseph," Ray said. "I've got your phone number. What I'll do is call you from time to time and check on you, make sure you're all right." He lowered his feet to the floor, smiling in an almost amused way. Did he think this was funny? "I'll come by your place, make sure you're alive and all. In the meantime, you'll be at work most days, right?"

"Yes," Joseph said. "Taking care of clients. I have a lot of work with Genzer Labs right now, so I've been spending more time there the last couple days."

"All right. Please don't worry, Mr. Holmes," Ray said sincerely. "You're going to be just fine."

As he left the dojo, Joseph figured that was probably true. He headed back to the lab and found Mel in her office. She was sitting at her desk, frowning at some paperwork. When he entered, knocking softly on the door, she looked up. God, she was beautiful. He fidgeted where he stood, working up the nerve to see if she wanted to go to lunch with him.

He realized he hadn't said a word when she stared at him and spoke in a business-like tone. "Can I help you, Mr. Holmes?"

"Please, please call me Joseph. I...I was wondering if you'd want to go to lunch with me."

"No." The answer was abrupt. "I mean, no, I…I am afraid I can't." She gestured to the papers on her desk. "Too much work to do. Maybe another time."

"Right. Of course." Joseph smiled warmly, but as he left her office and walked down the hall, his cheer faltered.

*I can't catch a break*, he thought to himself.

\* \* \*

After his training the next morning, Johnny showered and returned to his bedroom to change while Yanagi took a nap. His phone buzzed on the bedside table. Picking it up, he slid his finger across the screen of his iPhone and read the text message. It was from Mel.

*Johnny, if you don't get back here soon, I am going to wring his neck.*

He chuckled. He didn't have to ask who she was talking about, because he knew she meant Joseph. He'd received an update from Ray, his business associate, stating that the nerdy little man was hanging around the dojo looking for protection. Of course, Joseph didn't realize the Feds were looking after him. He didn't have to know. They had to keep a low profile, so they kept tabs on Joseph without notifying him. He'd be fine.

He wasn't so sure about Mel. He was always protective of her, and he wished he could be there to help her with this. Instead, he had to finish the mission first. Then he'd have to figure out what to do about Joseph Holmes. He texted her back.

*Sorry, my friend. You're on your own until I get back. Good luck!*

He set the phone back on the end table, dressed, and headed into the kitchen where he found Meiko cooking a late breakfast. Their training had started early, and it was almost eleven in the morning.

"Do you want something to eat?" she asked.

"Sure. I never turn down good cooking." He was hungry from training, which always worked up a healthy appetite. He sat down while she cooked, breathing in the delicious scent of eggs sizzling in a pan.

"You know, an hour after you left last night, Mr. Tabata summoned me upstairs," Meiko said. "He told me that you work for him now, and you will be making a great deal of money. He said, 'Your future husband will fill you in with all the details.' " She eyed him curiously, her eyebrow quirking upward. "And he said that I will be making a lot of money as well, and between the both of us we shouldn't want for anything. He told me to move very slowly and cautiously and listen to you." Silence fell between them as she finished cooking. Then she brought the plates over, and sat down across from him. The steaming food made his mouth water, and he dug in.

Meiko took a small bite of her breakfast before asking, "What was that all about when I told you I would be home late? Do you dislike me dancing, or was it just part of the act?"

"Yeah, kinda."

"Kinda what?"

"I don't like it," Johnny admitted. "It wasn't part of the act. I like you a lot, and respect you, and I don't like that you're up there in front of all those sleazy animals."

"I think that's so sweet," she said, a blush creeping into her cheeks. He fought the urge to lean over and kiss her, just to see how she'd react.

Once again, they were quiet for a while, finishing their breakfast. But something passed between them, an unspoken bond, an intensity Johnny couldn't name. When the food was cleaned up, and the dishes put away, Meiko started to leave the kitchen.

Before she could walk away, Johnny caught her gently by the hand and said, "I am just worried about you." Looking deeply into her eyes, he could see that his affection was reciprocated.

She slid her arms around him and pressed her lips against his. They kissed passionately, and Johnny almost lost himself in the moment. Everything else seemed to disappear. They both startled, drawn back to the present, when they heard footsteps coming down the hall.

When they pulled away from each other, Johnny crossed his arms over his chest and cleared his throat.

Yanagi entered the room, announcing, "I am on my way to the village to shop at the market, but before I shop I have a luncheon appointment with a friend."

"Oh, yeah?" Meiko asked, smirking. "Who is she?"

"No one you know," her father answered sarcastically, glaring at her.

Meiko giggled and said nothing.

Yanagi huffed. "Don't you people have better things to do, besides worrying about my business?"

"Bye, Daddy!" Meiko said, patting him on the shoulder as he left the house.

# Chapter 34: Heated Encounter

Once they were alone, the silence of the house seemed to sink around them. Meiko fidgeted where she stood. "I think I am going to take a shower and freshen up," she decided. "I suggest you relax."

Johnny, having already showered and eaten, felt much better. He decided to lie down in his room and nap for a while. Just as he began to doze, his head against the soft pillow, he heard a knock on the door.

"It's me, Johnny," Meiko called out. "May I come in?"

Before he could consider the fact that he was bare chested and wearing only a pair of gym shorts, he called out tiredly, "Sure, come on in."

When the door opened, Meiko stepped inside dressed in a bright blue traditional Japanese kimono. She was stunning in the long robe with wide flowing sleeves, tied at the waist with a sash.

"My father just called and informed me that after his luncheon date, he will be going to a movie with his friend," Meiko said, smiling. "I thought I heard a familiar voice, so I asked him, 'Who are you with?' He said, 'I have to go now, and I will be home late, so don't wait up for me.' He has never done that before."

Johnny sat up on the edge of the bed. The old man must have a date. "Well, there's a first time for everything," he said, chuckling. "He is only human. After all, he is a man and he has needs."

"So do I, Johnny," Meiko said breathlessly, and before he could say a word, she untied her kimono and let it drop to the floor.

He gazed at her nude body, his heart rate increasing as he took in her supple breasts and slim form, her long hair hanging free around her shoulders. He stood and moved toward her, close enough that he could feel the heat of her flesh, and lowered his shorts so they fell at his feet.

"Meiko, you are so beautiful and I am hypnotized when I look into your deep brown eyes," he murmured. He took her into his arms and pressed her body against his, feeling her soft flesh on the hard muscles of his chest. He kissed her deeply, then nibbled at her neck, running his tongue along her skin until she moaned softly in his ear.

She pushed him into the mattress and straddled him, her eyes hooded, her chest rising and falling with each short breath she took. "I want you inside me," she whispered. Their heated lovemaking lasted for hours.

With his body pressed over hers, she gasped, "I wish this could last forever."

"Why can't it?" he asked. Soon, they fell asleep in each other's arms, tucked beneath the cotton sheets.

* * *

It was around six p.m. when Johnny's cell phone rang, and he realized they hadn't slept for very long at all. He knew it was Oshi Tabata calling. Answering the phone, he said, "Hello."

"Have I caught you at a bad time?" Oshi asked, perhaps sensing something in the tone of his voice.

"No, actually, you caught me at a good time."

Meiko giggled and hit Johnny playfully in the arm.

"Is that Meiko I hear?" Oshi asked knowingly.

"Yes, it is," Johnny replied. If anyone had doubts about the legitimacy of their relationship, this certainly proved their attraction. Johnny grinned, tugging her against him and relishing in her warmth.

"Now I know why it's a good time. You must be finished." Oshi laughed. "I'm just calling you to let you know that what we discussed in my office will take about two to three weeks to get together. It should be completed just before you go back to the U.S. Meanwhile, I need you to stop by my office at the club tonight. I want to show you something. Bring Meiko with you."

"Okay, how about eight o'clock?"

"That's perfect. I'll see both of you at eight."

Johnny ended the call. "Did you hear all that?"

"Yes, I did," Meiko said, running her fingers through the sparse hairs on his chest. All of a sudden, she sat up, looking around at the mess. "Oh my God. I have to clean up your room and wash the sheets before my father gets home. I also need to shower and be ready by seven-fifteen."

"I need to shower, too," Johnny said. "I'll help you make the bed when the sheets are ready. After all...I helped soil them." He chuckled.

"What do you think Oshi wants?" Meiko asked.

"I have no idea, but we will find out soon enough."

# Chapter 35: Secrets Of The Hornet

Johnny was glad Meiko didn't have to work as a stripper that evening. Instead, she just had to pretend to be his fiancée. At seven-fifteen, the two of them were dressed and ready to go.

"You look beautiful!" Johnny exclaimed, offering an appreciative wolf whistle.

She turned about, swinging her hips, showing off the simple black cocktail dress that displayed sparkling sequins around the hem and plunging neckline. "You don't look so bad yourself," she said, admiring his snazzy suit.

They took Meiko's sports car, and she slid behind the wheel, looking classy in the slim two-seater.

As she piloted the car out onto the roads, merging with traffic, Meiko said, "Why don't we go out and do something after we meet with Oshi?"

"Like what?" Johnny asked, squeezing her thigh through the sheer material of her dress. He was more in the mood to take her back to her house and spend some additional time in the bedroom, but he didn't say so. He didn't have to tell her; she already knew. Smirking at him, she gently squeezed his hand.

"How about an American steak house? There's a good one in downtown Tokyo." She winked, putting her slender hand back on the wheel. "My treat."

Johnny was unable to hold back his laughter.

"What's so funny?" she asked.

"I must have been really good in bed for you to offer to pay for dinner."

"You were incredible," she murmured, the husky tone of her voice suggesting she was reliving every moment in her mind.

"Well, I must be really good then…and you had the same effect on me." Johnny refrained from telling her to pull the car over before they reached the club, so they could have a little fun before meeting Oshi. However, he knew they wouldn't have time. It would have to wait. Exhaling heavily, he tried to dismiss his dirty thoughts as they pulled up to the valet at the club.

Guards escorted them to Oshi Tabata's office, where they started to frisk them both to ensure they had no weapons. Before the guards could get very far, Oshi emerged and shouted, "What are you doing? These are my friends and partners now, and we treat them with respect. Right, Johnny?"

"Yes, that's right, Oshi," Johnny replied, bowing politely.

The guards withdrew, each man tensing as if terrified they would be subject to punishment.

"Go," Oshi ordered, glaring at them.

The guards withdrew quickly, relieved to be dismissed.

Meiko bowed her head and said, "Thank you for your respect."

Oshi ushered them both into his office. "Have a seat. Can I get you two a drink?"

"No, we will pass, but thank you." Johnny leaned back in the soft leather chair, straightening his suit jacket.

"Let me get right to the point," Oshi said, lowering his large frame into his chair.

Johnny remained calm and composed, as did Meiko, but he couldn't help but wonder if she felt as anxious as he did. They watched the imposing man reach for a slim briefcase, placing it on the desk before him. He opened the case, turning it so his visitors could see it clearly. Inside, Johnny saw what appeared to be a small glass cube, perhaps six inches by four inches, carefully set in foam within the case, to keep it safe. Another sat beside it in the case. Within each glass cube was a small, round object, carefully contained.

Rather than inquire, Johnny waited for Oshi to explain. The man cleared his throat and said, "These are called Hornets." He indicated the objects, which appeared to glimmer in the artificial light of the office.

"No disrespect meant, Oshi, but why are you showing us these Hornets?"

Oshi chuckled. "Nothing to worry about. They do not sting like the insects you are familiar with. These, my friends, are mechanical Hornets."

"What do they do?" Johnny asked, feigning ignorance. Meiko leaned slightly in her chair, tilting her head to examine the objects.

"I will show you." Oshi opened one of the glass cases, and the Hornet jumped up, flying around in the air before going right to the computer. "The Hornet will attach itself to the hard drive and steal all the computer data, then transmit it to our home base. After the transfer of the data, the information is stored in our home base computer room."

"Once the Hornet sends all the data back to the home base computers, what happens to it?" Meiko wondered.

"Good question," Oshi said. "After the transfer is completed, a signal is sent to the homing device, the Hornet itself, and then it self-destructs."

"So, who invented this thing?"

"My brother and I invented it," Oshi replied proudly.

"That's ingenious," she remarked.

"Call it what you may, but that is how we perfectly execute industrial espionage. That is why I wanted your presence at this meeting with Johnny. I respect your computer savvy. Your reputation precedes you."

Johnny realized the Hornet that had flown out of the suitcase had seemingly disappeared. He'd seen it slide into the DVD drive of the computer, somehow, and then vanish. "What happened to your Hornet that went into the computer?"

Meiko placed her hand on Johnny's, and gave him a wink. "I will explain it to you over dinner."

"I am glad you are working on the computer end of this, Meiko," Oshi said, smirking.

"So am I," Johnny said, feeling more than a little silly.

"Well, that's what I wanted to show you," Oshi said, rising to his feet. "Now you have a better understanding of what we are doing." He walked them out. "Both of you, go out and have a good time together." He clapped Johnny on the back in a friendly gesture, and retreated into his office as the two of them left the club.

# Chapter 36: Safehouse

Johnny stopped when Meiko grabbed his hand in the parking lot, before they reached the car. "You really wanna get freaky out here?" Johnny asked, half-joking.

"That's not why I'm stopping you," Meiko hissed, scoffing. "I just wanted to remind you—though I'm sure you already know—do not discuss anything about the meeting in the car. You never know who might be an enemy of Oshi Tabata. The car may be bugged." She tugged on his hand, pulling him toward the vehicle. "Let's discuss it over dinner."

When they arrived at the Steak House Restaurant in downtown Tokyo, the hostess escorted them to a secluded table, and handed them each a menu.

"Your server will be with you momentarily," she said, smiling widely before stepping away.

Meiko glanced about, ensuring they were alone. The restaurant was large, but their table was set apart from the others, in a cozy corner of the room. "Johnny, we have a lot to talk about and we need to inform our superiors about what is happening."

"You're right," Johnny said, tapping his fingers nervously on the tabletop. "I was first shown the Hornet at a meeting in Miami by Oshi's brother Kazumi Tabata. Iraq had purchased the Hornet and it was put on a plane for delivery. I prevented the Hornet from being delivered there, but the Tabata brothers are looking for more buyers. It could cause astronomical problems for both our governments. But first I want to have something to drink so I can relax."

"I need something to drink, too." Meiko sighed heavily, her gaze scanning the establishment for their waitress, who had yet to arrive. "You know, Oshi is either stupid by divulging all this information to us prematurely in our business relationship, or the information we sold him about the two of us was very convincing."

"Maybe he is just very shrewd and savvy," Johnny replied, uncertain of where he stood on the issue.

"Yeah. Shoulda, coulda, woulda."

"Look, why don't we leave it like this," Johnny began. "We both know what we saw and what we talked about. You'll inform your superiors on your end and I will inform mine on my end. So, can we not talk about this anymore right now and enjoy our evening together?"

"Yes," Meiko said, visibly relaxing. She seemed to like that idea.

The waiter arrived, a short, lean man with dark hair. He nodded in greeting. "Good evening. My name is Gaku and I will be your waiter tonight. Would you and the lady like to start off with a bottle of wine?"

"Yes, I would like to order a bottle of your best champagne."

"What would the lady like to order as an entrée?"

"I would like an eight ounce prime rib with a lobster tail," Meiko said, straightening in her seat.

"Soup or Salad?"

"A Caesar salad, please."

"What would the gentleman like as his entrée?" the waiter asked, scribbling on his notepad.

"I will have a filet mignon with a rack of ribs and a Caesar salad."

"Thank you. I will return with your bottle of champagne in a moment."

As the waiter retreated, Johnny leaned forward and said quietly, "Eat and drink whatever you want because *my* boss is paying for it. I know you offered, but I prefer to put it on the credit card they gave me for expenses."

Meiko nodded, understanding what he meant. The Feds were footing the bill. "Oh, yeah? Then how are you going to explain the most expensive bottle of champagne on your expense report?"

"Whatever the bill comes to, you're worth it," he replied, winking.

Meiko leaned over the table and kissed Johnny on the cheek, whispering, "Thank you," against his ear. Her warm breath on his cheek almost made him shiver.

The waiter returned a moment later with a bottle of Dom Pérignon Champagne.

Later on during their meal, Meiko's cell phone rang and she checked to see who was calling. She cocked her head knowingly, raising one eyebrow as she glanced at the screen. "I have to answer this," she said. "It's my father."

The conversation was short, with Meiko saying "Uh-huh," and "Yes," until finally she said goodbye.

She slid her phone back into her purse. "My dad told me he's not coming home tonight. He is staying overnight with his friend. He also will not be home in the morning to train you, but he will be back at one o'clock for your workout."

"Great, so let's stay at a hotel tonight." The very idea of spending a night alone with her excited him. "Just in case your father decides to come home early."

"I know a hotel we can stay at and it won't cost you a dime," Meiko boasted.

"How's that?"

"Wait and you will see!"

After dinner, they left and headed for the hotel. When they arrived, Johnny wasn't sure what to think. The place didn't appear to be a hotel. It looked more like a giant mansion. The white two-story home was surrounded by immaculate Japanese gardens and had a circular driveway with a three-car garage.

After passing through the huge gate, they parked the car, and Meiko grabbed a set of keys from her purse and started to open the front door. Wanting to know what exactly she had in mind, and what was going on, Johnny grabbed her arm and said, "Wait a minute, what is this place?"

"Stop worrying," she chided him. "I know what I am doing. It is a surprise!"

Meiko opened the door and stepped inside, her heels clicking on the polished marble. She flicked the lights on and they entered the foyer.

"Oh my God!" Johnny gasped, looking up at the wide staircase. A sparkling chandelier hung above their heads. The mansion was decorated in cosmopolitan chic modern white furnishings with colorful Japanese print pillows and beautiful artwork hanging on every wall. The floors were marble, and Johnny peeked around the corner to see a living room with a fireplace and high ceilings with crown molding. There was a library, a chef's kitchen with an adjacent formal dining room, and a huge family room with fireplace.

"This is unbelievable. How many bedrooms does it have?"

"Eight. Let me show you the master suite." They walked up the huge spiral staircase and she said, "I also want to show you the spectacular Jacuzzi."

"You never answered me. What is this place?" Johnny demanded.

"It's my safehouse and I am the only person who has a key."

Opening the door to the master suite, Meiko put the lights on. Next to the king sized bed was an oversized Jacuzzi bathtub. She ran the water and mixed in some lavender bubble bath. Johnny couldn't help but be impressed. *This* was her safehouse?

Without saying a word, Meiko went to Johnny and began unbuttoning his shirt, tugging his clothes off. He pulled her against him, kissing her deeply, running his hands along her soft, supple body as he slipped her dress over her head. She kicked off her heels, pushing them out of the way.

Looping her arms around his neck, she kissed him and whispered, "How would you like to watch a porn movie while in the Jacuzzi?"

Johnny grinned. "Sure, but I don't see a TV in the room."

Meiko pushed a button on the wall and a panel opened from the ceiling. A huge TV screen was lowered, and she slid a DVD into the player.

"You do this often?" Johnny teased.

"Maybe. Maybe not." She giggled, sliding her naked body into the warm water. Johnny lowered himself into the tub as the movie began.

Drawing her close to him, he slid his hands up her soft thighs and pulled her onto his lap. "Oh my God, I know who you are!" He chuckled.

"Who am I?" she inquired, bewildered.

"The female version of me," Johnny joked.

After hours of sex, they fell asleep together in the bed, and Johnny couldn't remember when he'd had a better time. *Never*. With all the women he'd dated over the years, he'd never met anyone quite like Meiko.

# Chapter 37: Caught Off Guard

In the morning, they awoke to the sound of the doorbell chiming throughout the house. At first, Johnny mistook it for a part of the dream he was having. Yawning, he sat up in bed, and Meiko awoke beside him.

"I thought this was a safehouse and no one else knew about it?" he asked.

"That's true. I do have the only key, but a certain few in my agency know of its existence."

"You better find out who's at the door."

"I am getting dressed as fast as I can," she said, jumping out of bed and grabbing her panties and bra. She threw him a glare. "You stay here."

Despite her order, Johnny pulled his pants on and stepped outside of the bedroom when Meiko went downstairs. From here, in the cavernous house, he could hear the conversation taking place at the front door. He recognized Master Yanagi's voice.

"Why are you here?" he heard Meiko saying. She sounded nervous.

"You never came home last night, and you didn't call me, so I was very worried."

Johnny hung back, away from the bannister and out of view.

"What are you doing here?" Meiko countered.

"Don't you remember? One night you told me if you don't come home without calling, to check here first."

"I'm sorry, Dad, but I'm here with Johnny." Pausing, she added, "Wait a minute, how do you know I wasn't home last night?"

"Early this morning, I came home and there was no evidence of either of you being there. I started to panic, and remembered what you told me, so I came here. Maybe you don't remember, but you gave me a duplicate key just in case..."

"So, why didn't you just come in, if you had the key?"

"I decided to knock first," Master Yanagi said. "Johnny wasn't home either and I thought there may be a remote possibility that he was with you." He cleared his throat. "I did not want to...*interrupt* anything that was going on between the two of you. Apparently, I did!"

Johnny, hidden from view, covered his mouth with his hand to keep from laughing.

"So, who were you with last night that you avoided telling me?" Meiko asked. "Wait a minute, who is that in your car?"

Johnny slipped into his shirt, buttoning it as he walked down the steps and into the foyer, deciding it was time to come out and say hello. He nodded in greeting to Master Yanagi, but both father and daughter were distracted by the woman in Yanagi's car. Johnny followed Meiko outside. She turned and said, "Masako." Glancing at Johnny, she explained. "My mother's sister."

She turned to her father and said, "Daddy, what's going on here? I hope you're not dating Mom's sister."

"No, of course not!" Master Yanagi said, his face flushing.

"I hope not. My mother hasn't been dead for very long," Meiko snapped. "I don't think she would appreciate you dating her sister."

"Listen to me now! I told you, I am not dating your mother's sister."

"Then, what are you doing sleeping at her house?"

Yanagi appeared contemplative for a moment, as if he didn't want to explain. It was clear to Johnny that the truth had been concealed, probably at the behest of Masako herself. Yanagi hung his head. "Masako is dying of cancer and has no one to take care of her while she is undergoing chemotherapy and radiation treatments," he said, his voice low, but not so quiet that Johnny couldn't hear.

Meiko's eyes filled with unshed tears. "Oh, Daddy, I am so sorry. I accused you wrongly."

Even as he wrapped his arms around her to hug her close, her father spoke sternly. "You should never jump to accuse anyone without knowing the whole story."

"You're right, Daddy. I should know better."

When Meiko stepped away from her father, Johnny placed a reassuring hand on her shoulder and squeezed gently. This couldn't be easy for her. Master Yanagi nodded to him as if grateful for his presence.

"Come. I want you to see Masako, she wants to talk to you," Yanagi said to his daughter. When Johnny hung back, Master Yanagi ushered him forward as well. "Please," he said. "You are practically family, Johnny."

Johnny bowed his head in respect, stepping forward with Meiko and remaining silent. Masako climbed out of the car slowly, her thin face and sallow cheekbones illuminated by the sunlight. The blue cardigan she wore hung loosely around her slender frame. Without a word, she reached out for Meiko and pulled her close. Meiko could no longer hold back her sorrow. She began to weep on her aunt's shoulder.

"I am not going to let you die from this cancer," Meiko said brokenly.

Johnny's heart ached for her.

"Don't worry," Masako said. "I am too strong to die."

"I love you, Masako."

"I love you, too."

"I promise to see you soon and help take care of you," Meiko murmured, stepping back and wiping the tears from her face with the back of her hand. Masako squeezed her arm, and Johnny noticed how easily she trembled, her graying hair hanging around her face. He wished he could do something for her.

Masako climbed back into the car, needing to sit down, and Master Yanagi walked back to the foyer of the spacious house with Johnny and Meiko on either side of him.

"So, what's your excuse about staying with Johnny all night?" Master Yanagi glared at him, but his eyes betrayed his playful tone. "Is he sick, too?"

She broke into a grin. "No, on the contrary, he's very healthy."

When Master Yanagi left, grumbling under his breath, Meiko could not contain her giggles.

"I don't know why you are laughing," Johnny admonished as he watched the car drive away. "Now he's going to kill me during training!"

# Chapter 38: From The Outside Looking In

As they headed back upstairs, Johnny shook his head at Master Yanagi's morbid interest in their relationship. "I'm not going to your father's house tonight," he said. "I'll be safer at a hotel."

"Oh, that's ridiculous," Meiko said, hurrying toward the bathroom as she slid out of her clothes, dropping each delicate article on the shiny marble floor. "Stop being a pussy."

"Let's just shower and go out for breakfast," Johnny said, stepping into the bathroom behind her. Despite the lust surging within him whenever he saw Meiko's naked flesh, he was starving. His stomach grumbled.

"I know a good place for breakfast that the strippers brought me to after work," Meiko said as she turned on the shower. Hot water sprayed down as she climbed in.

Johnny couldn't help but wish every shower he took was this good.

During breakfast, he sat at the wide window in the diner, gazing out at the street. The restaurant was located in downtown Tokyo, a couple of blocks from Oshi's strip club. It was a popular place for locals, and had plenty of tables with red-cushioned chairs and smooth wood tabletops. As he glanced out the window, Johnny happened to notice two suspicious looking men taking pictures with long distance camera lenses. One of the men, clad in a black t-shirt and jeans, had long black hair and a full mustache and beard. His companion was dressed the same way, but his head was shaved. Johnny pointed them out to Meiko.

"Do you recognize those guys out there?"

"No, but I don't think they are taking pictures of us. It looks like they are taking pictures of the other end of the restaurant."

"I think I will just take a walk to the men's room and see who is sitting on that side," Johnny said. To his surprise, he noticed Oshi Tabata and two of his henchmen from the club.

When Oshi saw Johnny, he raised his hand in the air and called out. "Ah! My friend. Come join us. Where is your lovely fiancée?"

Johnny stepped up to the table, moving slowly and casually so as not to attract attention. He slid his hands into the pockets of his pants, keeping his gaze away from the windows in the restaurant. Other diners were nearby, ignoring their exchange. "Don't look out the window right now," Johnny advised, "but there are two men across the street taking pictures of you and your men. Meiko and I were sitting at the other side of the restaurant when we noticed them."

Oshi's smile disappeared, his expression turning grim. He nodded. "Okay, Johnny, let's stand up and I will shake your hand. Then you need to go back to your table, but don't look out the window."

Oshi rose to his feet and said to his henchmen, "When Johnny walks away, go into the kitchen and out the back door, around the block, and sneak up on the two cameramen." His voice was almost a whisper. "Find out who they are."

"What do we do after that?" one of the men asked.

Oshi shook Johnny's hand firmly to keep up appearances. Meanwhile, he replied to his henchman. "Take them by gunpoint into your van and tie them up. Then, bring the two men to my abandoned warehouse. I will meet you there shortly."

Johnny had learned the warehouse was located in a seclude area of Tokyo. After shaking Oshi's hand, he turned and walked back to the table to finish his breakfast. A short time passed as the cameramen were apprehended, and Oshi crossed the room to where Johnny and Meiko sat.

"Meiko, nice to see you." He squeezed her hand warmly in his large palm, then turned to Johnny and said, "Are you almost finished with your breakfast?"

"Yes, we are." Johnny took the last bite and slid the plate away.

Oshi glanced around to ensure they were alone. An old man was dining nearby, and the waitress stood behind the counter. He turned back to them and said, "I would like the two of you to follow me to an abandoned warehouse where my two men will be holding the cameramen."

After Oshi stepped outside, giving them a moment to gather their things and pay their bill, Meiko and Johnny exchanged a serious glance.

Time to go to work.

# Chapter 39: Sword Of The Samurai

When they arrived at the warehouse, Oshi instructed them both to put a hooded mask over their heads. When the three walked into the warehouse, they found the two cameramen, who were being tortured with waterboarding. A cloth covered the face of each man before water was poured overtop, causing a sensation of drowning.

The warehouse was dusty, with cobwebs hanging from high light fixtures. It hadn't been used in years and had puddles of water on the concrete floors from leaks in the ceiling.

"What information did you get out of them so far?" Oshi barked at his soldiers.

"Well, they are not cops but seem to be of Middle Eastern descent and were planning to kidnap you for ransom." One of the men shrugged, as if unsure of the reasoning.

"Who are you?" Oshi shouted.

The two men refused to answer.

"Who are you and who do you represent?" he snapped. It would do them no good to refuse his demands.

"We represent our God, Allah!" one of the men replied.

"What do you want?"

"We want one hundred million dollars and we will spare your life."

"Let me see if I got this straight. If I give you a hundred million dollars, you're going to spare my life, is that right?"

"Yes."

"So what the fuck is stopping me from killing you right now?"

"If you kill us, there will only be more of us. We have other cells infiltrated within your own organization."

"Bullshit! Who's your leader?"

"We are on a mission to collect one hundred million dollars for Allah!" The man refused to reveal details.

Johnny crossed his arms over his chest where he stood beside Meiko, and they watched as Oshi walked into the warehouse office and returned carrying a Samurai sword—a Katana with a distinctive appearance, a curved slender single-edged tapered blade. The terrorists shouted, "Jihad!" before Oshi swung the sword and swiftly cut their heads off. Blood splattered everywhere as their heads fell to the concrete floor.

"Get a burlap sack and write in their blood on the sack," Oshi ordered his soldiers, who immediately jumped into action. "Make sure it says *Yakuza* on the sack, and put the heads inside." He scratched his chin, frowning at the blood on his sword. "I will hold an emergency meeting at my warehouse at midnight. Make sure everyone gets the message to be there."

Then he turned to Johnny and Meiko. Johnny felt unsure why they'd been involved in the situation, but he said nothing. "I want both of you there tonight at midnight without fail," Oshi said.

"Of course," Johnny said, bowing his head.

# Chapter 40: Betrayed

Their next stop was Meiko's office, where they immediately tipped off the Tokyo Metropolitan Police Department about what they had witnessed, and about Oshi Tabata's meeting at midnight. It was decided they would have backup police at the warehouse. The police wanted to be able to follow members of Oshi's gang and put them under surveillance to track down which members of the crew could possibly be connected to a terrorist organization such as ISIS or the Taliban.

The situation was troubling for Johnny. First the Yakuza, and now this.

Earlier that evening, a warrant was issued for the Tokyo police to set up surveillance in the warehouse to install video cameras and audio.

Johnny and Meiko remained protected by their alternate identities. When they arrived at the warehouse for the meeting at midnight, numerous vehicles were parked outside. The Tokyo Metropolitan Police Department and the National Police Agency of Japan had the warehouse heavily guarded with hidden surveillance. Johnny did his best to suppress his anxiety as he slowly opened the warehouse door, Meiko following behind him.

He was astounded to see how many of Oshi Tabata's men and women showed up for the emergency meeting. He counted one hundred and forty men and eleven women, all standing around a large table in the dimly lit warehouse.

Oshi walked in, where his Yakuza members waited for his arrival. They bowed to him in respect, and Johnny and Meiko followed suit. Oshi sat at the head of a huge table along with ten other men and one woman who were his key members. The rest stood around the table facing him. No one was allowed to stand *behind* Oshi Tabata.

There were two silver buffet platters with lids located in the middle of the table. Oshi stood up and introduced his new associates Johnny and Meiko, and said, "Some of you may already know them." He remained standing and began to explain the situation. "Now, I need to tell you the main reason why I called this meeting. I recently found out some very disturbing news about traitors in our own organization that are linked to some terrorist group. Earlier today, I caught two men taking pictures of me from across the street from the restaurant where I eat my breakfast.

"Luckily, Johnny and Meiko were in the restaurant at the same time and observed the two men in a car with a high-power camera lens taking our pictures. I sent my two men around the building to capture them and throw them in the back of the van. We interrogated and tortured them and found out they were from a terrorist group and wanted money, and they would spare my life in return. I asked the terrorists what would stop me from killing them. They told me, 'If you kill the two of us, there will only be others. We have other cells infiltrated within your own organization.' "

A key member of the organization stood up at the table and yelled, "I am outraged to hear this. No Yakuza would do such a thing. It would mean treason. Where are these men now? I will question them myself!"

"Sit down, Fuyuki," Oshi shouted. "I will show you now. Johnny and Meiko, come to the table."

They both approached reluctantly, and Oshi instructed them to lift the covers off the buffet platters at the very same time when he gave the word. He then told everyone to come closer to the table.

"Remove the lids!" Oshi screamed, his face red with anger.

When the lids were lifted, the heads of the terrorists were revealed, bloody and pale, their eyes vacant and staring forward. Some of the men and women gasped in surprise.

Fuyuki stood up again, his back ramrod straight. "This is outrageous. You have gone too far. I do not want anything more to do with your organization!"

Oshi immediately signaled to one of his henchmen, who stepped behind Fuyuki and strangled him with a garrote. Fuyuki choked and struggled for only a moment before dropping down, his head resting on the table. Oshi reached under the table, retrieving his Samurai sword, and cut Fuyuki's head off with one swift movement. Everyone remained silent as they watched him reveal a burlap sack, grabbing Fuyuki's head by the hair and placing it inside the sack. He then grabbed the two heads on the platters and placed them back into the burlap bag along with Fuyuki's head. He tied up the bag with a long piece of rope, throwing the other end of the rope over the rafters of the warehouse, to hang over the table with the word *Yakuza* written on it in the terrorist's blood.

Suddenly, a man scrambled from the group, trying to escape from the warehouse, only to be quickly apprehended by a couple of Oshi's henchmen. The man's name was Sogen, and he was brought to the head of the table in front of Oshi.

He ordered his henchman to put Sogen's hands on the table.

"Give me the names of the other cells," Oshi demanded.

"I don't know," Sogen gasped, his voice trembling.

"Then why did you run?"

"I don't know. I was scared."

"I think you are lying to me." Oshi ordered his henchmen to hold the man's hands firmly on the table. He then pulled out a small knife and cut the tip of the man's pinky finger off at the joint. Sogen screamed as the knife removed part of the digit, spilling blood on the table. His face paled and he blubbered.

Finally, he cried out, "I know the names of the two men whose heads you cut off."

Oshi nodded. "Okay. Earlier this morning, in between torturing these two men, I gave them both a bottle of water and after I killed them I gave the bottles of water to a police officer who is a friend of ours and he was able to lift the fingerprints. He found the names of those two terrorists. I am going to ask you now what their names are. If you are lying to me, I will cut off your head as well and add it to my collection."

Sogen shouted their names, and Oshi grew silent for a moment before ordering his henchmen to release their grip on his hands. By testing Sogen to see if he would tell the truth and give him the real names, Oshi knew for certain the names of the traitors.

"He is telling the truth, but he is still a traitor," Oshi said. "Why did you do this to us?"

Sogen sank into a chair, his body limp and his skin covered in a sheen of sweat. "The terrorists have kidnapped my wife and children as well as my father. If I do not do as they say, they will kill my family."

"Was Fuyuki also involved?"

"Yes, they are also holding his wife and children hostage."

"I see," Oshi said, appearing contemplative. It was as though everyone in the room had stopped breathing for a moment; everyone remained still, waiting, watching for Oshi's next step. "Is there anyone else from the Yakuza whose families were held hostage?"

"No."

"This is what you are going to do," Oshi decided, and everyone listened raptly. "You are going to tell the terrorists that I am gong to be working on my racecar at my auto body shop on Thursday, late afternoon, which is three days from now."

"But…" The man gasped, clutching his damaged hand in the fabric of his now bloodied shirt. "What do I say when I am asked about my missing finger?"

"Wear a pair of gloves."

"It's only early September—"

"You figure it out!"

"And what if they ask where Fuyuki is?"

"Tell them that I sent him to New York for a week to take care of some dealings for me. I will take care of having his name appear on a flight list to New York. We will also take care of getting your family back, but you must tell me how many are in this cell and what places they frequent. Meanwhile, two of my men will take you to the hospital to sew your finger back on." With his knife, he nudged the digit toward the pale man, which one of the other henchmen had already tucked into a plastic bag filled with ice. "When this is over and you get your family back, I will ask you to move to the United States," Oshi continued. "You and your family will work for me at one of my factories, but you will no longer be involved in the Yakuza business. Your tattoos will be stripped from your back painfully and you will no longer be a Yakuza. Now go with my men."

As the men led him out of the warehouse, Oshi continued, this time speaking to everyone in the room. "Let this be a lesson to all of you. If anyone approaches you and your families are kidnapped, come to me immediately to avoid these consequences. The meeting is over and everyone can leave. Johnny and Meiko, you both stay." Once everyone had left, and the three of them were alone, Oshi spoke gravely. "I am very sorry you had to witness this."

"I think we all have bigger problems to worry about," Johnny said. "Not only must we be concerned about the police, but first and foremost, ISIS."

"Yes, you are right," Meiko agreed. "It has become a big problem for all of our countries. Are you sure the terrorists are from Syria?"

"Yes, my contacts at Interpol have confirmed what the two terrorists told me," Oshi said, inviting them both to sit. Meiko declined the invitation, perhaps shaken up from what she'd just seen.

Johnny lowered himself into a chair and leaned one elbow on the table. "There's one thing I would like to ask you. What are you going to do with the three heads?"

"I haven't made up my mind yet," Oshi admitted. "But I am going to put them on ice for now until I decide. Why don't you and Meiko go home and get some sleep, and I'll speak to you tomorrow."

They hadn't expected the day to be so long, but Johnny was relieved to be out of there. When Meiko sighed heavily in the car and leaned back in her seat, he knew she felt the same.

On the way out, she remained silent. They left the warehouse and decided to stop at a bar to have a drink, and discuss what had just transpired.

Meiko suggested a bar in downtown Tokyo that she'd been to with some of her co-workers from the Tokyo Metropolitan Police Department. It wasn't noisy like some of the other bars in town.

They walked into the quaint pub with its lacquered wood bar top. The back wall of the bar displayed mirrored panels with many brands of liquor bottles and glasses piled up on racks in front of it. The lights were dimmed and plush leather booths made it inviting for patrons to sit and unwind from a hectic day.

The couple chose a booth and sat down. "This whole situation is becoming overwhelming for me," Meiko admitted, distressed from what she had witnessed.

"I agree, I feel the same way," Johnny said. "It just goes to show you, when someone uses your family as hostages, you are liable to do anything to save them.

"Yes, that's true. I don't know what I would do if someone took my father hostage and threatened to kill him."

"I really think this is only the tip of the iceberg."

"Look, can we talk about this later?" Meiko sighed heavily. "I need to try to unwind my nerves."

They sat for a while, just trying to relax. It had been a long day.

# Chapter 41: Military Hop To Japan

When they arrived home, Meiko kissed Johnny goodnight. "I need to make a couple of phone calls before I can go to sleep."

Johnny shrugged. "I have phone calls to make, also."

Due to the urgent situation on hand, Johnny decided to call the Organized Crime Bureau Headquarters in Washington, D.C. He spoke to Thomas O'Keefe, the Head of the OCB who'd been put in charge of his case. Thomas debriefed him on the latest facts in the case and Johnny brought Agent O'Keefe up to date on what was going on with the Yakuza in Japan.

"This is going to get out of hand, unless I immediately send some back-up agents to assist you," O'Keefe remarked.

"I can't believe we are going to get the Yakuza and ISIS all in one package," Johnny said, running his hand over his tired eyes.

"When this is all said and done, I am going to recommend you for a promotion."

"That's great! Thank you. But...may I be bold?"

"Sure, Johnny. What's on your mind?"

"Here's my suggestion. Since you guys have cut a deal with Sonny DeSantis, wouldn't this be a great opportunity to send him and a few of his soldiers to intercept ISIS later this week at Oshi Tabata's auto body shop? After all, with the deal you cut for those guys, it's about time they start earning their keep."

"What do you have in mind?"

"Before I explain this to you, I got to know if DeSantis suspects. Does he know that I am an FBI agent?"

"We have convinced Sonny that you are a martial arts instructor, private investigator and a womanizer sleaze ball." O'Keefe seemed to chuckle, then thought better of it. The laugh became something of a cough before he cleared his throat. "As far as Sonny is concerned, we consider you one of the wiseguys working off his indictments for extortion, loan sharking, bookmaking, and interstate transportation of stolen goods from Chicago. You did a five-year stretch in Allentown, Pennsylvania. So, as far as Sonny is concerned, you are covered for all your arrests and prison time."

"That makes me feel a lot better!" Johnny said, breathing a sigh of relief.

"So, the next time you see DeSantis, he won't be surprised. I will get everyone together tomorrow morning and send DeSantis, his soldiers and additional OCB Agents for backup on a military hop to Japan."

"That sounds great."

"Take good care of Meiko and be careful out there."

"I will."

"Oh, by the way, I have one more thing to tell you. There will be a CIA operative who will introduce himself to you in Boston."

"How will I know who he is?" Johnny asked.

"His code name is Eagle One."

# Chapter 42: Okinawa

The next evening, the FBI agents, Sonny DeSantis and his crew landed at the airfield on Okinawa Island. They were greeted by several Marines and two Naval Officers. One of the Naval Officers directed the group into two large vans, which took them to the barracks on base where they would stay for the night. Transportation would be arranged the following day for the trip to their Tokyo hotel.

When the group arrived at the barracks, Sonny walked into his room and was immediately perturbed by the sleeping quarters. He glared at the nearest sergeant.

"Is this the best fucking accommodations the Marines can come up with?" he snapped. Sonny didn't want to be here, anyway, but he had no choice. He couldn't give up his own chance of freedom, and he certainly couldn't let terrorists win.

The gunny sergeant frowned. "I'm sorry you don't like your room, but this is the best officers' quarters we have here."

"Do you have any strip joints on this island?" Sonny retorted, hoping for at least some small reprieve.

"Yes, we do. Would you and your men like to go to a strip joint?"

"Is the Pope Catholic?

The tall, lanky Marine grinned. "Okay, let's go."

"You know something, kid? I'm beginning to like you," Sonny said, beckoning to his men.

"Thank you, Sir, I'm beginning to like you, too. I was worried there for a minute, when you were insulting the Marine Corp barracks. I thought I would have to remove my uniform and teach you a lesson," he replied, grinning.

"Hey, Sergeant, watch yourself," one of Sonny's men warned. "One word from my boss and I would have capped you right here!" He quickly added, "Just kidding," and snickered quietly.

"Let's get out of here and have some fucking fun with some of that Asian pussy," Sonny announced, spurring everyone to laugh as they exited the barracks.

"I will need to take a few of my Marine buddies. After all, there are ten of you and only myself. I will get one of my sergeants and two of my corporals who love strip clubs come along."

The gunny sergeant called his fellow Marines on his cell phone and within minutes they arrived, ready to party.

As they entered the strip club, Sonny shouted over the music, "Drinks are on me for the whole night." The men sat at a large table gawking at strippers. One of girls dancing up front was very limber, putting her head between her legs and looking at Sonny before signaling to him to slip his money between the lips of her pussy. Sonny placed a C note between her legs and she rubbed her tits in his face. She finished her dance and went into her dressing room, then returned to sit with Sonny. He asked her to round up the other dancers for his men and the Marines, telling her that he was buying everyone in his group a lap dance.

"What's your name, babe?" Sonny asked.

"My name is Kiko, and I am here for your pleasure." A wide smile spread across her face before she led him to a secluded room and performed several exotic lap dances for him. The seductive and lustful gestures made him want her so bad he could barely stand it.

"I'll give you five hundred American dollars if you have sex with me," he murmured in her ear when she moved close enough.

"I am sorry, but I am not a prostitute," Kiko told him. "I only have sex with a man if I love him."

"I am leaving tomorrow for Tokyo. May I have your number, so I can call you when I finish my business?" Sonny asked.

"What is it that you do for a living?"

He shrugged one shoulder and straightened his suit jacket. "A little this and a little that."

"Is a little this and a little that profitable?"

"Of course. Why else would I be here thousands of miles from home?"

"Where in the United States do you live?"

"Boston," he replied proudly.

"What nationality are you?"

"One hundred percent Sicilian."

"Oh, Mafia!"

Sonny fell silent, unsure if she was frightened or impressed.

"I like Mafia," Kiko added, causing him to relax.

"Give me your phone number and I will call you from Tokyo. I will let you know what hotel I am staying at and I will send for you."

"Sounds like a plan, Mr. Sonny!"

The next morning, Sonny DeSantis and his crew, along with the additional FBI agents, boarded a plane to Tokyo. Upon arrival, they were escorted to four stretch limos and driven to the Ritz-Carlton in Tokyo. The five star hotel was well-known in the area for its panoramic views atop Tokyo's highest tower in the Roppongi District. Sonny was impressed by the renowned club level lounge, with its spectacular views of Tokyo's skylines of Mount Fuji and the Imperial Palace Garden.

Everyone was checked into the hotel and assigned separate rooms. Sonny was given a suite to conduct business with his crew and the FBI team.

The first thing DeSantis did when he walked into his room was call Kiko.

"Hello?" she answered.

"Hi, Kiko. It's Sonny."

"I know, Mr. Mafia."

Instead of turning him on, the playful tone in her voice annoyed the shit out of him. She may not have been a prostitute, but she was clearly willing to be bought—as long as her purchaser was involved in organized crime. "Let's get something straight right now," he snapped. "Don't call me that anymore, especially over the phone."

"Sorry, Mr. Sonny, I understand."

"I am going to be busy for the next two days, so how about I send for you over the weekend?"

"Yes, that will be great!" she replied enthusiastically.

"I will also arrange for a limo to pick you up at the airport. I can text you all the information as soon as it's been arranged."

"Mr. Sonny, I am looking forward to seeing you this weekend."

"Yes, so am I," he said. Then he bid her goodbye, and hung up the phone.

# Chapter 43: Master Plan

Later that afternoon, Sonny had a three o'clock meeting with his men and the FBI agents in his suite. They went over their plans on how to apprehend the terrorist cell at Oshi Tabata's auto body shop, which was located in one of Oshi's warehouses.

During the meeting, the FBI agent in charge, Jeffrey Levitt, stated that his team would arrive at the auto body shop at ten o'clock in the morning, one hour before Sonny's crew arrived to get his men in place. Levitt had been able to obtain the blueprints of Oshi's warehouse, which the men studied to carry out their sneak attack.

"Sonny, you and your guys don't have anything to be concerned about," Agent Levitt assured him. "I will have twelve men in place for back-up."

"Thank you, but this is going to be fast and quick," Sonny said. "You won't even hear a pin drop because I have taken some of my best zips from Sicily. My men can cut a man's throat with a straight edge razor before a Jap can use a Samurai sword. They are professional killers. You will get a chance to see how the black hand of the Sicilians really moves."

Agent Levitt appeared somewhat uncomfortable. He coughed and wiped his hand across his mouth. "Look, Sonny, you will also need to carry some fire power."

"We already brought some with us," Sonny boasted.

"What do you mean, you brought fire power with you?" he shouted. "How the fuck did you ever get guns on a military plane and what kind of fire power do you have?"

Sonny opened up three huge suitcases with concealed AK-47s, along with various handguns and grenades.

The agent's face turned red. "For the last time, how did you get the guns on the plane?"

"Did you forget, Agent Levitt, who we are and what we represent?" Sonny said calmly.

"Oh, yeah, it slipped my mind for a minute," the agent retorted sarcastically. "When this is over, I will have to confiscate all the weapons you brought here."

"That's fine. I'll need additional room in my suitcases for clothes and souvenirs I plan to buy, anyway." The fact he wasn't bothered by the threat seemed to annoy the agent further.

"From now on, Sonny, there will be no more illegal activity unless sanctioned by the FBI. *Capisce?*"

Sonny tilted his head and said nothing. *Fuck that*, he thought to himself. *I will do whatever I want, and then some!*

The men continued to discuss their strategies for tomorrow's confrontation.

When the meeting ended, Sonny told his crew to go straight to their rooms and stay there using the hotel room service for their meals.

Before Agent Levitt exited the suite, he gave Sonny a glare that meant business. "I want the name of the person or persons who arranged the smuggling of weapons on a Military aircraft."

"Forget about it!" Sonny snapped.

"If you don't tell me before this trip is over, I will arrest and prosecute you."

"You won't arrest me or anyone else in my crew, dickhead. Your boss in Washington told me I have total immunity while this shit is going down. So, if you are done, get the fuck out!"

Just as Agent Levitt was about to close the door, he turned and spoke with a smirk on his face. "You should follow your own advice and stay in your room."

Sonny grabbed a paperweight from the hotel end table and threw it at the door as the agent left. "You fuckin' pig!"

\* \* \*

The following morning, Sonny and his men had an early buffet breakfast in the Ritz-Carlton hotel. After breakfast, the men went back to their rooms, got armored up, and met in Sonny's suite along with the FBI.

"Are you ready, Sonny?" Agent Levitt asked.

"Don't worry about us. Just worry about your men," Sonny remarked, his voice edged with irritation.

"Look, Sonny, let's talk out in the hall for a minute." He crooked his finger and indicated the door.

Begrudgingly, Sonny followed him into the hallway. After a cleaning lady passed by, pushing a cart filled with clean towels and other supplies, Levitt focused on Sonny.

"I'm aware that we both worry about our own men," Levitt said. "But we need to work together and watch out for each other at least for today."

"I realize that," Sonny grumbled, shoving his hands in the pockets of his pants.

"I know you don't like me." The agent frowned, the wrinkles on his brow crinkling. "It's not that I don't like you personally, I just don't like what you stand for."

"In that case, we can agree to disagree," Sonny said, doing his best to amp up his personal charm.

Levitt's thin lips quirked upward at the corner. "Fine. Thank you, Sonny." He extended his arm, and the two men shook hands, returning to the hotel room.

# Chapter 44: Body Shop Terror

The FBI left for Oshi Tabata's auto body shop to get the men in position. Then, they waited for the arrival of Sonny and his men. It was ten minutes to ten o'clock in the morning when Sonny and his men pulled up close to the garage. He immediately put on his headphones with a microphone attached. The communicator would allow him to keep in touch with Agent Levitt. "Are your men in place?" he asked.

"Yes," the agent confirmed.

"Has ISIS arrived?"

"Yes, they are here."

"How many?" Sonny asked from the safety of the car he'd been driving.

"We counted fifteen, but there could be more."

"My men and I are going to move in now," Sonny said. "We'll take the staircase at the back of the building."

The warehouse was located in a desolate area on the outskirts of Tokyo. The grassy field provided overgrown brush and trees to conceal the agents as they moved in on the wooden two story structure. Stairs in the rear led to a door on the second floor. Sonny and his zips climbed the stairs, moving stealthily, and used burglar tools to break into the back door on the second floor. Other men guarded the area, concealed by the darkness inside the warehouse. There were two staircases inside the back end of the building, parallel to each other with a catwalk going across.

The zips were eager to eliminate the ISIS cell. Sonny signaled his men that there were three terrorists to the left and two to the right. The shadows kept Sonny and his zips from being seen as they advanced on the enemy. Two of Sonny's men moved to the right toward the back of two ISIS terrorists. One of Sonny's men came up behind them and reached around to slice the throat of one of the men. The victim choked and gurgled before falling to the floor. Another of Sonny's men pulled out a silencer and shot the other terrorist between the eyes. The body crumpled to the floor. Since the other three terrorists were farther away, his other men decided to shoot them with silencers as well.

The five terrorists were left to bleed to death on the floor. Meanwhile at the other staircase, there were two terrorists standing guard. One was stabbed in the neck and the other was killed with piano wire and strangled to death.

"There are seven down and eight to go," Sonny whispered to Levitt.

"Be careful," the agent warned.

Glancing around, Sonny didn't see any sign of the other terrorists while he and his men stayed hidden in the shadows. Agent Levitt and his men remained outside. Suddenly, after a few minutes went by, eight men emerged from the office located on the ground floor in the middle of the warehouse. To the front of the warehouse were closed garage doors. He noticed one of the eight men was the leader giving orders to the other terrorists.

The terrorists' identities had been confirmed, and Oshi had planned to lure ISIS to his auto body shop in order to have them attacked by his own men, but the Mafia beat him to it. Now, this was Sonny's job.

Agent Levitt called Sonny and asked, "What's going on?"

Moving back where he couldn't be heard, Sonny explained the situation while observing the ringleader. He watched the leader of the terrorists looking at something dripping from the upper walkway above him. The leader swiped his finger across the wet substance dripping on the floor and brought it up to his face to examine it, realizing it was blood. The terrorist yelled in Arabic to his men who were positioned on the staircase.

Sonny glanced at the man beside him, who was listening intently. He nodded to a zip from Sicily, who spoke Arabic and could translate. He leaned close to Sonny and whispered, "He is trying to check on his men, see if they're okay. He knows something is wrong."

Sonny signaled in understanding. When there was no answer, the leader ran back to his other men, yelling in Arabic, telling them to split up and take cover.

Sonny got on the radio to alert his men. "Do not kill the ring leader," he hissed. "We need him captured alive to hand him over to the FBI for questioning."

Then he called Agent Levitt and said, "It's going down, and I know who the leader is."

Four of the ISIS terrorists including the leader ran back into the office and locked the door. The other three were ordered to check out the staircase and were apprehended by Sonny's men. Two were shot in the head and they plummeted to the ground floor below. Sonny grabbed an ax with a short handle, which had been hooked to his belt, and threw it at the third terrorist, hitting him in the frontal lobe. He tumbled to his death, over the staircase to the lower floor.

Peter, one of Sonny's henchmen, whistled in appreciation. "You got him. What a fucking shot that was!"

"Now you know why they call me Sonny 'the Ax Man' DeSantis," he quipped. His next action was to drop a grenade close to the office, not to kill the terrorists, but to draw them out. Sonny and his men stormed down the staircase, surrounding the office. The terrorists were forced out by the explosion, but emerged shooting. Three of the terrorists were picked off by Sonny's men. The leader was grabbed and thrown to the ground, screaming profanities in Arabic.

"Peter, take some of my men and go upstairs to carry the dead bodies down," Sonny ordered. "Line the bodies up on the concrete floor next to one another. Bring the large pad of white paper that we packed and write out the words 'ISIS sleeps with the fish.' "

Then he turned to another man and said, "Pauly, take one of our men and go out to the van and bring the two boxes of fish in here. Wrap each fish separately in the white paper and write 'ISIS sleeps with the fish,' also. And put one fish on each of the bodies." Sonny called Agent Levitt and said, "We're done, mission accomplished!"

A short time later, Levitt and his FBI agents rushed into Oshi Tabata's auto body shop and found fourteen dead terrorists lying on their backs, each with a fish wrapped in white paper, displaying Sonny's message to terrorists everywhere.

The fifteenth terrorist was the leader, kept alive and propped up on a chair, restrained by ropes. He was quickly taken away by the agents, brought into an FBI van and chained to the seat. Sonny knew he was being taken to an undisclosed location for interrogation.

Agent Levitt looked down at the fish, then at Sonny. "What's with the fish?" he asked.

"Sometime, I'll give you a history lesson on the black hand of the Sicilian Mafia," Sonny replied. "But right now I want to get back to the hotel."

Sonny observed several FBI agents taking numerous pictures of the dead terrorists and the various crime scenes throughout the building.

"Good job," Agent Levitt said. "We don't know anything about what happened here. Do we, Sonny?"

"Right!"

"You and your men need to get the hell out of here now."

"Ah shit, I would have loved to have seen Oshi Tabata's face when he walks into his auto body shop."

The FBI also departed before Oshi could arrive. While Sonny and his men were leaving in their van, Sonny asked Peter if he put the envelope he'd given him in Oshi Tabata's racecar where he would see it.

"Yes," Peter said, and Sonny couldn't contain his glee.

# Chapter 45: Mafia Intervention

One hour later, Oshi and his men arrived at the auto body shop. When he turned the light on, his eyes widened, and he shouted, "What the fuck is going on here?"

He walked up to the bodies and read the words on the white paper. "ISIS sleeps with the fish."

Sotaro, one of his men, shouted out, "Boss, what does this mean?"

"What it means is that somebody was sending us a friendly message."

"I am confused, boss."

Oshi rolled his eyes. "Someone jumped the gun and did us a favor by eradicating these terrorists, that's what happened."

"Hey, boss, I found this envelope on the dashboard of your racecar and it's addressed to you," Masaki called out.

Oshi turned and took the envelope from him, frowning. "Oshi Tabata, this is a gift for you from the black hand," he read aloud, breaking into a cold sweat, then closed the letter and stuffed it back into the envelope.

"Is everything all right, boss?" Masaki asked. The other men stepped around the bodies and began doing their best to clean things up. The doors were shut, everything concealed from those who might happen by.

"What the fuck is the Sicilian Mafia doing here?" Oshi said, unable to believe what was happening. At that moment, his phone ran. The caller I.D. told him it was his brother, Kazumi, in Boston in the United States.

"You would not believe the shit that just happened in my garage!" Oshi explained the situation, and then asked, "Do you know anything about this?"

"Yes, Oshi. The Sicilian Mafia are now our partners."

"It would have been appropriate for you to discuss this with me first," Oshi barked. "What else are they going to do for us?"

"For starters, the Mafia is going to provide assistance in gaining entry to all the computer companies. This way we can obtain access to many more computer labs and infiltrate their files with our Hornet," Kazumi declared, sounding proud of himself.

"That's great. It sounds like they will be very useful in our operation," Oshi admitted. Then, looking back at the mess before him, he grumbled, "I must now contend with the disposal of these bodies with the fish."

"Since ISIS sleeps with the fish, then why don't you dispose of the bodies in the ocean?" Kazumi suggested. "What about our goods? Are they ready for transport to the United States?"

"Yes, and everything has been tested and the items will not be detectable by Customs or K-9," Oshi said. "The shipment will be ready in just a few days."

"Contact me when it is shipped," Kazumi replied.

After he finished his call, Oshi told Sotaro and Masaki, "Take some of our men with you and get rid of these bodies. Put them in black garbage bags and transport them way out into the ocean. Use cement blocks to weigh the bodies down like our Sicilian counterparts and throw them in the water, so they can sleep with the fish."

Oshi Tabata and his men laughed. The new partnership was a surprise, but not an unhappy one.

* * *

When everything had been cleared away and taken care of, Oshi drove back to his strip club and called Johnny to explain what happened at his auto shop. "I have decided to send you and Meiko to the U.S. earlier than planned due to what has transpired." He leaned back in the seat of his car, watching patrons enter the club.

"What about our deal with the tires?" Johnny asked.

"Our deal is still on and your idea has been perfected and the goods will be ready for shipment in seventy-two hours." That was another good thing Oshi could be happy about. All in all, not a bad day. "You need to put your plans in place before the shipment arrives in the U.S.," he added. "I want the both of you on a plane by tomorrow."

"Okay, I will get on it right away," Johnny said.

With the call completed, Oshi climbed out of his car and headed into the club.

# Chapter 46: Debriefing

When Johnny told Meiko about the plans, she seemed concerned.

"What's wrong?" he asked, sitting with her in the living room area of Master Yanagi's house.

"Where will I stay when I get to Boston?" Meiko asked, appearing nervous.

"You are going to stay at my house." Johnny smirked, adding, "And besides, I have a huge king size bed."

"Oh, you do, huh? And will your boys be okay with that?"

"My boys will be cool with you staying with me. Besides, J. J. and Mikey will be crazy about you." She smiled. "They stay with their aunt when I am away on assignments and during the school week. I get to see them on the weekends depending on my schedule."

"It will be good to meet them." She picked her phone up and dialed, calling her boss at the MPD, Organized Crime Control Bureau, to explain the reason for her sudden departure to the U.S. Johnny listened as she attained his approval, then he called Thomas O'Keefe at the Washington Organized Crime Bureau to fill him in, as well.

"What do you think of taking Daddy out to dinner tonight to tell him?" Meiko asked. "I can't leave him here by himself."

"He will come with us," Johnny said.

"What if he doesn't want to?"

"I think he will be interested."

At dinner that evening, in a nice restaurant in town where they sat in a secluded, comfortable area, Meiko explained the situation to her father.

Master Yanagi appeared to be considering things. Finally, he said, "I would like to visit the U.S., but I can't be ready by tomorrow. However, I could be ready in just a few days. You two go ahead of me, and I will follow you once I am ready. I need to get a nurse for my wife's sister while I am gone, and I have to tie up a few loose ends." Master Yanagi glanced up at Johnny, then asked, "Can I run your dojo in Boston while the both of you take care of business?"

"That's actually a really great idea," Johnny said. "I hadn't thought of that. My students will be excited that my master will be teaching them. Master Yanagi, I want you to stay at my house. I have plenty of room."

Immediately, Meiko kicked Johnny's leg under the table.

Yanagi shook his head. "No, that will not be necessary. I will sleep in your dojo."

Johnny raised an eyebrow. "All right, if that's what you want. I do have a sofa bed downstairs and a small kitchenette with a stovetop and refrigerator."

"Okay, then it's settled. I will teach your students and make them better than you, Johnny Son." He chuckled, and Meiko just shook her head.

\* \* \*

Upon their arrival in Boston after clearing Customs, they were greeted by Thomas O'Keefe and another FBI agent from Washington, D.C.

"We are here to escort both of you to the Boston FBI Headquarters for a debriefing," O'Keefe said, his expression stern. He indicated the burly man standing beside him, whose thinning brown hair had been neatly combed. "This is Frances White, my counterpart in solving crime."

Johnny grinned. Placing his hand on the small of Meiko's back, he introduced her. "This is Meiko who was my contact and assistant in Japan and my counterpart in crime. She is Master Yanagi's daughter."

"It is a pleasure to meet you, Agent O'Keefe," Meiko said. "I have heard a lot about you. All good things, of course."

"The pleasure is all mine," O'Keefe said, shaking her hand. "I've heard good reports in regards to your work in Japan."

"Wait until you hear all the evidence we have for you," Johnny said, his voice low as he stepped close to the two men.

They left the airport and drove together to the Boston FBI Headquarters for the debriefing. When they arrived, Agent Thomas O'Keefe led Johnny and Meiko into the debriefing room. Hours went by in which many questions were asked about the Yakuza operation and the unexpected ISIS involvement.

After all the questioning had ended, and they stood from where they'd been sitting in the large debriefing room, Agent White signaled to Johnny to get his attention. "Can you teach me some of that Judo and Jujutsu stuff?"

Johnny frowned. "Didn't they teach you martial arts at the FBI Academy?"

"Yes, but I would like to learn more techniques."

"Any particular Judo or Jujutsu move that you want to learn?"

"Yes." Without warning, he initiated a demonstration of an attack move as he held a knife to Johnny's back. "I want to know how to defend myself from such an attack." White attempted grabbing Johnny around the neck with his right arm, the knife in his left hand, while he lunged toward Johnny's lower back.

In a spit second, Agent White found himself on the floor with Johnny standing over him holding the knife.

"What the fuck just happened?" White shouted. A few of the other agents watched from outside the debriefing room through a window. A few mutters could be heard in the hallway. Johnny guessed this would be a topic discussed at the water cooler that afternoon.

"Listen, White, you don't point a real knife at someone's back especially without defending yourself," he retorted, pissed off. "You *never* demonstrate with a real knife."

"Who taught you that technique?" Agent White asked as he caught his breath and clambered to his feet.

"An old friend of mind, Phil Porter, who was a former Olympic Judo coach." Johnny cracked his knuckles, and White cringed. "Phil was the man who actually put all the rules and regulations together for Olympic Judo. He started the Armed Forces Judo Association and later formed the USJA, United States Judo Association."

"Do me a favor," White snapped. "Don't show me anymore of Phil Porter's techniques, USJA, or whatever the fuck else you know." He straightened his suit jacket and his tie, while grimacing at Johnny.

"Well, White, don't stick a knife in my back anymore." He glared at him pointedly. "Let that be a lesson to you in the future."

Meiko steadied Agent White, who seemed dizzy from the fall, and brushed some dust off the back of his coat.

O'Keefe chuckled as he watched the three of them. "Are you certain you won't change your mind about learning Judo and Jujutsu from Agent Macchia?"

"I'm not sure," White said. "I have to give this Judo and Jujutsu some more thought."

Meiko gave him a warm, disarming smile. "Would you rather I teach you?"

"Um, that might not be a bad idea!"

"Let me show you something that's more gentle," she suggested. "Go ahead and grab my wrist." When he did as she instructed, she brought him to his knees with technique and speed, setting him up once again.

In moments, White was begging for her to release the wrist lock, *Kote Gaeshi*, or wrist reversal, an Aikido technique involving the twisting of the wrist. As everyone watched, chuckles could be heard in the hallway. White continued to yell out for Meiko to release the lock, and when she finally did, she wore an effortless smile as if the move had taken none of her energy whatsoever.

"And that technique was taught to me by my father, Master Yanagi."

"You two are fucking dangerous," White shouted as he stumbled for the exit. "I think I'll stick to using my gun." Everyone laughed. "If you guys are done beating up on me, I'd like to go home," he added.

Agent O'Keefe nodded. "Yes, I think you've had enough excitement for one day." He turned to Johnny and Meiko, adding, "I'm sure you are both tired and want to go home, also. I'll see all of you tomorrow."

# Chapter 47: Eagle One

It was already dark by the time they arrived at Johnny's home and noticed another car parked in his driveway. A strange man suddenly stepped out of the car and Johnny quickly drew his gun and yelled out, "Who are you and what are you doing here?"

Meiko remained behind Johnny, ready to pull her own gun if necessary. The intruder couldn't be seen until he stepped into the dim light of the moon that shone through the gray clouds.

"Johnny, I'm Eagle One!" the man exclaimed, holding his hands up. "Don't shoot!"

"Get his I.D. and weapon," Johnny said to Meiko.

She stepped around him and took the man's identification and grabbed his gun, which was in his shoulder harness concealed under his suit jacket. She first looked at the I.D. and then handed it over to him.

"Mark Hunt," Johnny read aloud. "CIA, Special Operations." He glanced up at the man. "Okay, Meiko, return the gun to Mr. Hunt." Johnny walked over to the CIA agent and handed him back his I.D. "Sorry about that, Agent Hunt, but one cannot be too careful these days." Johnny extended his arm and they shook hands.

Agent Hunt appeared extremely relieved. "Thank you, Mr. Macchia."

"I'd like you to meet Meiko," Johnny said. "She's working with me on this case, and she's with the Japanese police." The Tokyo Metropolitan Police Department, MPD, Organized Crime Control Bureau, was fortunate to have such a talented agent among their ranks.

"Let's go inside," Meiko said, glancing around. "We're under cover of darkness, but you never know who could be watching."

Johnny invited them into his home. The one-level brick building with its small yard welcomed Johnny, and he felt immediately relaxed when he entered. Flicking on the lights in the foyer, he stepped across the polished wood floors and led his guests into the cozy living room. He was glad the boys were still at Kate's house, as he had yet to tell her that he'd arrived. Once business was finished for the night, perhaps he'd send her a quick text message.

The curtains were already drawn, shielding them from the outside world. One could never be too careful.

"Can I pour you a drink, Agent Hunt?" Johnny asked, approaching the pristine liquor cabinet in the corner of the room.

"Sure," Hunt said, lowering himself onto the couch, while Meiko took a seat in a plush armchair.

"What's your poison?"

"Scotch, straight up."

"Meiko, what about you?"

"I'll have the same as Mr. Hunt," she responded with a smile.

Johnny poured himself a scotch on the rocks. "Okay, let's cut to the chase, what's going on?"

"Well, first of all, let me commend you and Meiko along with your FBI counterparts for a job well done back in Tokyo. However, Sonny DeSantis and his band of thugs made a huge mistake."

"What mistake?" Johnny asked, his brow crinkling.

"Apparently, one of Sonny's zips lost his wallet in the upper walkway of the auto body shop and it got in the wrong hands."

"Who has the wallet?" Meiko asked. Johnny handed them both their drinks, and Meiko sipped hers.

"When the terrorists didn't return from their mission, they sent out another cell to investigate."

"How do you know all this?" Johnny asked, taking a seat.

"We have had a CIA operative undercover with one of the ISIS cells for the past year now. Of course, I had to inform your boss, O'Keefe, of this major screw up. He has taken action by briefing Sonny on all the facts of this crucial situation and was doing so right before I came here."

"Now what do we do?"

"O'Keefe will send Sonny and his crew additional security as back-up surveillance. I don't believe that you or Meiko have anything to be concerned about."

"Maybe Johnny and I don't have anything to worry about, but my father is back in Japan," Meiko said. "He was planning to follow us over here, but we had to leave right away and he needed a few extra days."

"We do not believe any of these cells have any knowledge of Johnny, you, or your father," Agent Hunt explained. "Please, try not to worry."

Before Meiko could utter another word, Agent Hunt's phone rang and he said, "Excuse me, I gotta get this." When he was finished with his phone call, he returned to the living room. "My undercover agent gave me more bad news. He informed me that the terrorists had set up video surveillance prior to the massacre. They set it up on the inside and outside of the auto body shop. The terrorists' investigation team picked up the surveillance tapes and brought them back to their headquarters to review. However, my undercover agent is going to try to intercept these tapes and destroy them before the terrorists get a chance to review them. Otherwise, this whole fucking mission will be compromised and everyone involved will be in danger, including Meiko's father."

Meiko bit into her lip, her body tensing and her expression becoming impassive. Johnny recognized her attempts to calm herself despite her distress. Another woman might've wept in fear, but Meiko's training kept her from falling apart.

"Pardon me, I need to make a phone call to our American Embassy in Japan and to my other CIA operatives to snatch up your father and put him on a military hop to bring him to the U.S. We want to keep him out of any possible danger until such time we all get a handle on this situation," Agent Hunt said.

"Thank you. I appreciate all you can do to help my father," Meiko replied. Johnny squeezed her hand in reassurance.

When Agent Hunt got off the phone, he informed Meiko that someone had been sent to pick up her father. "They are taking him to the American Embassy first for a new passport because our records showed his passport expired. He will also need a Visa. We will then transport him to Okinawa for his military flight to the U.S."

"Thank you, Agent Hunt," Meiko said. "I truly appreciate it."

He seemed to notice her distress despite her attempts to hide it. "Don't worry. Everything will be okay." He glanced at the screen of his cell phone. "Well, I have to go now. As you can only imagine, I have a million things to prepare," he said, then left and shut the front door firmly behind him.

Johnny sent a quick text message to Kate, letting her know they were in the area but he wouldn't be over to visit this evening. Leaving his phone on the coffee table, he tugged Meiko against him.

"Your dad will be okay," he assured her. "He's one of the toughest old geezers I know."

"Old…geezer?" Meiko smirked, looking up at him with a mixture of confusion and amusement. Instead of explaining, Johnny kissed her, pressing her body against his.

# Chapter 48: Hunt's Cell

Some time later, as they dozed on the couch, the doorbell rang and Meiko said, "You relax and I'll see who that is." Johnny knew immediately that his sister-in-law had responded to his text message with a visit.

As Meiko opened the door, she was met by a jovial looking woman with wide blue eyes. "You must be Kate," Meiko said.

J. J. and Mikey pushed past their aunt, and all three yelled, "Surprise!"

Kate entered the house carrying a large cake box and the boys held casserole dishes with dinner she had prepared to celebrate Johnny's homecoming. As they burst inside, Johnny emerged from the living room and gave Kate a one-armed hug, kissing her on the forehead.

"What are you guys doing here?" he asked.

"When I got your text message, I thought we should come over and surprise you," Kate said, leading them into the kitchen where she set the cake down on the table. The boys placed the casserole dishes beside the dessert. "So good to see you again, Johnny. I hope your trip to Canada was successful."

Johnny grinned. "Everything went well." He put his arm around Meiko. "This is Meiko."

"Hi, I'm Kate, and these are Johnny's sons, J. J. and Mikey," Kate said, giving Johnny a conspiratorial wink.

"Nice to meet you," Meiko said, giving Kate and the boys a hug.

Johnny embraced both boys, holding them tightly. He was so glad to see them again, and told them as much.

"Dad, we're so glad you're home," J. J. shouted excitedly. "You've been gone a long time and we really missed you!"

"Yes, Dad, I missed you so much," Mikey shrieked.

"I missed you guys, too. Come on, let's sit down."

"I'm glad your home," Kate said. "I couldn't resist bringing dinner." She revealed a paper bag, and pulled out a bottle. "And some nice wine for the adults!"

"Thank you so much. I'm starving. I wasn't sure what we would do for dinner," Johnny admitted.

"How long have you been hiding this beauty from us?" Kate inquired, her brow crinkling.

Johnny had to think fast. At twelve and thirteen, Mikey and J. J. were loyal to their father and often picked up on details about the nature of his work. He figured he could let the truth slip because they would figure it out, anyway. "She is Master Yanagi's daughter." He took a deep breath before adding, "Listen, guys, you cannot tell anyone, but I was really sent to Japan, not Canada like I led you to believe. I haven't seen Meiko or her father in about twenty years." He smiled. "It was a good reunion."

"Well, Johnny, she is absolutely beautiful. You outdid yourself this time."

"Yeah, I guess I did."

"You better hold on to this one. She's a keeper," Kate said.

Meiko offered to help Kate in the kitchen, so Johnny could spend some time alone with his children.

"Does she know martial arts, too?" J. J. asked.

"Yes, she's a blackbelt."

"You better watch out, Dad, she may kick your ass!"

"No, *you* better watch out, she'll kick *your* ass." They laughed.

Mikey put his arm around his dad's shoulder and patted his back. "Hey, Dad, if you marry her, will we have Japanese brothers and sisters?"

"Let's not get carried away. Meiko is my friend and she is staying with us for a while. Tomorrow, her father will arrive."

"You mean Master Yanagi, your teacher?" Mikey asked.

"Yes, Master Yanagi will be staying at the dojo and teaching my students when I am busy with a new case."

"Dad, that is so cool!"

"Yes, that is cool, Dad," J. J. added. "Can Master Yanagi teach us, too?"

"Sure, he will enjoy teaching you techniques, so you can try them out on your father."

The boys continued to ask him a million questions about Japan. They all had dinner together celebrating Johnny's return home. It was a school night and it was getting late, so Kate decided to take the boys back to her place, but they didn't want to leave. They finally said their goodbyes reluctantly.

After they left, Meiko and Johnny started unpacking. When they finished, they began getting ready for bed, knowing they had a long day tomorrow. Just as they put their heads down on the welcoming feather pillows, Johnny's phone rang.

He groaned, reaching for it, and answered without lifting his head. The conversation was mostly one-sided, and Johnny offered a few grunts and said "okay" a couple times. After a few minutes, the phone call ended.

"It was Agent Hunt," he said, dropping his phone on the bedside table. He rolled to his side to face Meiko, whose eyes were fluttering shut.

"What did he say?"

"An undercover operative was able to intercept video and audio, and that lost wallet, from one of the terrorist cells."

"Oh, good."

"He destroyed the tapes and the wallet, but not before getting into a fight with the terrorist. He killed him by breaking his neck and had to dispose of the body. After hearing what happened, Agent Hunt advised him to shave his head and beard and go underground for his protection."

"The operative saved our mission," Meiko said. "Okay, what about my father?"

"He has his renewed passport and necessary Visa for his trip to the United States," Johnny said, squeezing Meiko's hand. "He is already on the military plane that just took off from Okinawa and he's headed to the U.S. as we speak."

"Oh, thank God." Meiko pressed her head into the pillow, a tear rolling down her cheek. "I hold it together well, don't I?"

"You sure do," Johnny said, kissing her cheek. "I admire your strength, but everyone has a breaking point."

"Was there anything else Hunt told you?" Meiko asked.

"Yes, one more thing. They intercepted a conversation about the shipment of tires from Tokyo that we arranged. It was changed from transporting by sea to air via cargo jet. Oshi Tabata will probably be calling. We don't know why he changed the mode of shipping, though."

"Hmm," Meiko murmured. "I guess we will find out soon enough."

Moments later, they were both asleep.

# Chapter 49: Change of Plans

Early the next morning, Johnny's phone rang again, waking him. This time, it was Oshi Tabata, just as he'd anticipated. "Our shipment to the U.S. is now being transported via air cargo," Oshi said.

"Why have you changed the mode of transportation?"

"It would have taken too long to get my materials to the U.S. by cargo ship. This way the shipment will get there within two days and we can go into operation sooner."

"But this will cause problems at my end. My contacts are all in place for arrival at the docks." Beside Johnny, Meiko stirred and sat up in bed, watching. "When is the cargo plane scheduled to leave?" he asked.

"It is leaving now as we speak, and is scheduled to arrive in Boston tomorrow at four o'clock in the afternoon, Eastern Standard."

"Thanks for giving me the heads up with such a short notice." He couldn't hide his annoyance.

"I have faith that you will get it taken care of. After all, you only have to juggle a few people around from one place to another. Besides, I am on my way to the airport to take a private jet to meet with my brother Kazumi in Boston." He paused, adding, "I have a lot of money riding on this deal and I need to make sure that everything goes as planned."

"What is your itinerary, so I can have someone meet you at the airport?"

"Kazumi will meet me at the airport. He has taken care of all the arrangements. You will meet him soon. I spoke very highly of you and he is anxious to meet you."

"Well, in that case, I need to get off the phone and start preparing for the shipment's arrival." After hanging up, he turned to Meiko and said, " I need to call Agent O'Keefe about my problem with meeting his brother, Kazumi."

"What are you going to do about it?"

Johnny shrugged and dialed the phone. "Hello, Agent O'Keefe, this is Macchia. Do you mind if I put you on speaker phone, so Meiko can hear what's going on?"

"No, not at all."

"Oshi Tabata is headed for the United States right now on a private jet. His brother Kazumi will be picking him up in Boston tomorrow morning. Kazumi will be taking Oshi to their hotel and will then head back to the airport to meet the cargo plane by four o'clock."

"Yes, I know. Our intelligence picked up the communication of this just a few hours ago. We are way ahead of you!"

"That's good, but there is a slight problem you may not have thought of."

"What's that?"

"You remember when Joseph Holmes was attacked in the limo and his driver was shot? Well, when I came to their rescue, I was engaged in a martial arts confrontation with the assailants. They were Kazumi's henchmen and I'm sure they can recognize me as well as the driver. Kazumi will also know what I look like, because he was at my home trying to have me killed. Now he's been told he'll be meeting Johnny Rizzo. When he sees me, he'll know otherwise."

"That can be a real problem. Do you have any suggestions?"

"What do you think about calling Sonny?"

"That might be a good idea. Can you hold on the phone a moment while I call him?"

"Sure, no problem."

O'Keefe called Sonny and informed him about the problem. He had the pictures of Kazumi's henchmen from the hospital surveillance tapes, which had already been identified by Macchia. The pictures were sent to Sonny in order to arrange the elimination of the three assailants to protect their mission.

"Johnny, are you still there?"

"Yes, I'm still here with Meiko."

"I advised Sonny of our problem with Kazumi's three henchmen and he assured me that by nightfall your problem will be solved," O'Keefe said. "In regards to Kazumi, we will have him arrested when we conduct our raids on his office and Marine Shipping at the docks, simultaneous with the raid at the airport cargo hangar. We plan to detain Kazumi with one of his dirty cop friends who will do it to save his own ass. This will prevent Kazumi from going to the airport with his brother Oshi to meet the cargo plane with his shipment, protecting Johnny's cover."

After he ended his call, Meiko said, "Johnny, I am concerned with our well being. We are getting very close to wrapping things up and it could get very dangerous in the days to come. I...I love you, Johnny...and I would not want anything to happen to you."

Warmth swept through him, and he realized he hadn't felt this good with a woman since his wife had been alive. "I love you, too," Johnny said. "We have grown so close in such a short time. I feel like you and I have become one person. Since my wife's death, I have never met anyone who came close to fulfilling me the way that she did...until I met you."

They kissed, and Johnny held her close, reveling in the feel of her against him.

"Meiko, I have something I need to do. You look like you didn't sleep that well last night, so why don't you rest while I'm gone?"

"That's a good idea," she said, yawning.

He embraced her, kissing her goodbye. "I promise to be back in plenty of time, so we can pick up your father at the airport."

Johnny knew that what he had to do next would help him move on. He hadn't mentioned it to Meiko, but when he'd woken up that morning, one thought had crossed his mind: it was the third anniversary of his wife's death.

In the living room, he picked up the urn from where it sat above the fireplace. His wife's ashes—her last remains—were in this urn.

Things were changing, and he had to let her go.

# Chapter 50: One Hundred Miles

The sun rose higher in the blue sky as Johnny drove to Quincy Boatyard where he had always kept his sailboat docked. As he walked toward the boat, he focused on the name of the craft, scrawled across the side in beautiful blue calligraphy: *Kimberly*. Seeing the name of the boat immediately brought back many memories of his wonderful life with Kim, the fun they had sailing, and the tragic way she died.

Johnny untied the boat from the dock and set sail for the open seas. He took the boat out a few miles and dropped anchor, then placed his wife's urn lovingly on the bow. The water lapped gently against the side of the boat. Gulls flew overhead.

"Kim," Johnny began, "it's been a long time since I had the chance to be alone with you and talk. I have met a wonderful woman. Her name is Meiko. She is from Japan, the daughter of my master instructor, Yanagi. I think you would approve of her and the children really like her." He listened to the waves for a moment before continuing. "When you died, I lost my soul mate...the woman I loved dearly. I never thought I would meet anyone else who could ever come close to you. Even though your sister Kate has been wonderful for the boys, they still need another mother. No one can take your place as their mother, and the boys will never forget you. Neither will I."

Johnny hung his head, a tear rolling down his cheek. "Please give me some kind of a sign! I need to know whether you approve of Meiko, so I can move on with my life. Also, I wrote a poem for you, and I would like to recite it to you. I hope you can hear me, Kim."

He tugged a paper out of his pocket and read aloud. "My Everlasting Love." He paused, his voice cracking.

*"They say you can see one hundred miles.*

*For one hundred miles you can see.*

*For I can see not one mile, for I am blind you see.*

*I've wanted to see for oh so long, so long I've wanted to see.*

*But now I have seen the hatred of hell, no longer do I wish to see.*

*I saw my love fall apart at sea, at sea my love fell apart.*

*Now, she has seen the hatred of hell, no longer do we wish to see."*

After Johnny recited the poem to Kim, huge gusts of wind came from nowhere and blew heavily across the bow of the boat. He shoved the paper back into his pocket. The sunny skies turned dark, filling with massive clouds while strong winds swirled around. Suddenly, the winds died down and the sun shined brightly again.

Johnny gazed intently at the urn. "Was that the sign?"

Then, instantly, the urn started to shake repeatedly for about fifteen seconds and then finally stopped. Johnny decided that must have been the sign he was looking for and said, "Am I right in accepting this sign as your approval?"

Unexpectedly, the urn began to tremble again, confirming to Johnny this was indeed the sign. He picked up the urn and held it close to his heart. "I will never forget you, my first love and the mother of my children." Deciding not to scatter the ashes after all, he pulled up anchor and sailed to port, reflecting on his encounter.

# Chapter 51: Mo, Larry, And Curly Get Hooked

When Johnny arrived at his house, he placed the urn back over the fireplace. He walked into the bedroom and noticed the bathroom door was open and Meiko was in the shower. Johnny undressed and joined her, startling her at first. He pulled her close, so happy to have her in his life. They kissed, touched, and made love beneath the warm water.

Afterward, as Meiko dried off, she grabbed her watch from the bathroom counter and said, "Oh my God, Johnny, we have to be at the airport in one hour! We need to rush out of here."

Johnny remembered he promised J. J. and Mikey they could go to the airport with them. He told Meiko they needed to swing by Aunt Kate's house and pick up the boys, then he called ahead to make sure they would be ready, waiting outside.

When they arrived at her house, the kids swiftly hopped into the SUV and sped away. Johnny parked his vehicle in the garage and hurried into the airport. They headed toward the waiting area nearest Master Yanagi's gate, and waited. A few minutes later, Meiko noticed her father coming down the walkway from Customs.

"There he is," she said, pointing.

Johnny could hear the excitement and relief in her voice.

Master Yanagi walked over to them, and Meiko wrapped her arms around him. "Oh, Daddy, I am so glad to see you."

He kissed her on the cheek. "My daughter, it is good to see you again, too." He glanced at Johnny, then at the two boys beside him. "This must be J. J. and Mikey. It is a pleasure to meet both of you."

"I am very happy to meet you, Master Yanagi," J. J. said.

"Yes, me too," Mikey agreed.

He hugged both boys, as well as Johnny, and they continued to the luggage area. The airport was busy, and people were bustling past them with rolling luggage, talking loudly into cell phones. They had to wait for a few minutes before Master Yanagi's luggage came around on the conveyer belt. The boys helped Yanagi take his bags off the turnstile.

After placing all his luggage on the cart, Mikey yelled out, "You have a lot of clothes, Master Yanagi. Are you planning to move here permanently?"

"I will be here as long as your father needs me, Mikey Son," Yanagi replied.

"You're going to stay at the dojo, right?"

"Yes, that's where I am going to stay."

"Do you want some company? I could stay with you."

"Dad, that's a great idea, can we stay at the dojo with Master Yanagi, please?" J. J. asked as they took the luggage past the crowds of people and out into the sunlight.

"That is totally up to Master Yanagi."

"Yes," the old man said, grinning. "It would be nice to have some company."

"Well, tonight might not be such a good idea, because he had such a long flight and he should rest."

"Johnny Son, I insist that they stay with me. Besides, I understand you and Meiko will be very busy tomorrow."

"Well, okay, but when we get in the SUV, I will have to call Aunt Kate and explain you will be staying at the dojo for the next three days. Kate told me there is a teachers' conference tomorrow, so there is no school and you kids have the weekend to spend with Master Yanagi."

They arrived at the dojo and unloaded all the luggage and he showed Master Yanagi around his dojo. He was very impressed and was looking forward to teaching Johnny's students. He showed him the room downstairs where he could sleep, as well as the kitchenette and a sitting room with books and a television. Then he led him back upstairs.

"Master Yanagi, when you start teaching at my dojo, remember all new members need to be registered with the USJA, United States Judo Association, before they are allowed to step on my mats," Johnny warned. "They carry one million dollars liability per student, and that covers my ass. If one new person steps on my mat without being a member of the USJA, I'm fucked."

Master Yanagi nodded. "Understood, Johnny Son."

Johnny squeezed the man's shoulder. "Let's all go out and have some dinner," he said. "There's a real nice place right on the corner, just across the street."

Victorio's Italian Restaurant wasn't too busy that night. The delicious scents made Johnny's stomach grumble as he opened the door.

"You will love the food here," Johnny said. "This place belongs to my friend Sonny."

Once they were seated, the server brought them water and stepped away so they could review the menu. When she returned, they ordered. As Johnny handed his menu to the server, he glanced up and saw Sonny crossing the room toward their table.

Johnny started to stand up to greet him, but Sonny shook his head. "Please, don't get up. Relax," Sonny said.

"I'd like to introduce you to my friend and teacher, Master Yanagi," Johnny said. "He is my Jujutsu instructor."

"Master Yanagi, so good to meet you. I've heard a lot about you."

"He is my father," Meiko said, and Johnny introduced her as well.

"Oh, you have a beautiful daughter," Sonny said, glancing from Yanagi to Meiko, and then allowing his gaze to rest on Johnny. It was clear he was assessing their relationship. He could tell they were seeing each other. He looked back at Master Yanagi and said, "Your wife must be beautiful, also."

"She was, but she is gone now. She is no longer with us."

"I am sorry. I know what it is like to have someone close to you gone," Sonny replied. He looked right at Johnny and said, "You know what I mean?"

"Yeah," Johnny said, and Meiko squeezed his hand beneath the table.

"I am going to let you guys finish dinner," Sonny said. "I have something to do in the kitchen. I want you to know dinner is on me tonight and I am sending over another bottle of wine."

"Thank you, that's very kind of you," Yanagi said, bowing his head.

"Johnny, meet me in the kitchen in a couple of minutes. I have something to show you." Without another word, he turned and headed to the back of the restaurant.

"What a nice friend," Yanagi commented, before sipping from his glass of water.

Johnny rose from his seat a moment later and whispered in Meiko's ear. "This ought to be good." He rolled his eyes, wondering what Sonny was up to. "I'll try to be back by the time the food gets here."

"Okay." She patted him on the hand.

When he entered the kitchen, Sonny waved him over to a far corner. "Follow me into the freezer," he said. "I don't want anyone to hear what we are talking about."

Inside the freezer, he pulled back a curtain to reveal three Yakuza henchmen hanging on meat hooks by the backs of their necks. "Are these the three Yakuza men you had a battle with?" he asked.

"Yes." Johnny raised an eyebrow. "Sonny, what the fuck are you going to do with these bodies now?"

"Johnny, Johnny…don't get all upset. After all, I kept them on ice just for you." Sonny burst into laughter right in his face, and Johnny could smell garlic on the older man's breath.

"No, really, what the fuck are you going to do with the bodies?"

"Well, I think maybe we will chop them up and use them for our lunch special tomorrow. What do you think?" A menacing grin crossed his face. "We can call the special of the day Italian Style Oriental Ribs, all you can eat!" He placed a hand on Johnny's shoulder. "Listen, I am going to tell you what I am really going to do with these bodies. I have three tubs all side by side with their names on it—Mo, Larry, and Curly. I'll dump them in the tubs filled with sulfuric acid and in a matter of minutes the bodies will disappear."

"Okay, okay." Johnny gestured to the door. "I need to get out of here and back to my family."

Sonny's amused cackle followed him out of the freezer and back into the kitchen.

# Chapter 52: Security Council

Johnny returned to the table, the image of the three dead Yakuza burned into his brain. People sat around the dining room, clinking their glasses together, eating, laughing, and enjoying each other's company, while the corpses were hanging ice cold in the back of the building.

"Is everything all right?" Meiko asked as he slid into the seat beside her.

"Everything is good. Sorry it took me so long. I was just hanging around with Sonny…and three other guys."

The food had arrived while Johnny was in the back, but by this point he had lost his appetite. All he could think about were the dead Yakuza. It felt strange eating dinner so close to three frozen corpses. When the server arrived, and everyone else had finished eating, Johnny asked for a to-go box.

Afterward, he drove everyone back to his dojo to drop off the boys and Yanagi. Before the kids could jump out of the SUV, he snapped, "Hey, now. Hold it."

"Yeah, Dad?" J. J. asked.

"I want you both to be on your best behavior and listen to Master Yanagi." He turned to Meiko's father. "There's a supermarket one block away where you can find just about everything you will need. The boys can show you where it is, and anywhere else you need to go."

"I am sure we will be just fine, Johnny Son."

As Johnny drove away with Meiko in the passenger seat beside him, Master Yanagi and the boys waved from the sidewalk.

"Johnny, are you going to tell me what Sonny wanted to talk about?" Meiko asked as the vehicle slowed at a red light.

"Remember the three Yakuza henchmen I told you about who were after Joseph Holmes?"

"Yes."

"Sonny had them strung up in the freezer on meat hooks."

"Ah." Meiko glanced down at the take-out bag she was holding on her lap. "So that is why you did not finish your dinner."

When he explained what Sonny planned to do with the corpses, Meiko grimaced.

"That reminds me of something," she said. "You told me a story about a man named Whitey from South Boston who was very ruthless. Well, he sounds like a popcorn next to this guy Sonny who I think probably invented the word ruthless."

"I agree with you."

The rest of the drive was quiet. When they arrived back at the house, Johnny said, "Let's try to forget this for tonight and get some sleep."

The phone rang at nine o'clock the next morning. It was Agent Hunt.

"Good morning, Agent Macchia. I have a couple of things I need to run by you. We have four agents tailing your sons and Yanagi. Early this morning, they went grocery shopping and Master Yanagi prepared breakfast for your sons. Later on this afternoon, they are going to Aunt Kate's house for lunch."

"How do you know all this?"

"We have the phones bugged at the dojo in case they get any suspicious calls and we have video surveillance set up."

Johnny frowned as he sat up in bed. "I don't know if I should be pissed off or thankful you took the initiative to protect my family,"

Agent Hunt seemed to ignore his comment. "Oshi arrived a few moments ago and was greeted by his brother Kazumi. His brother seemed very upset and spoke to Oshi in Japanese about three of his best men who have disappeared and can't be found anywhere. I'm sure you know what three men he is referring to."

"That's for sure, but how'd you know what they said?"

"We had an FBI agent posing as a baggage handler who spoke Japanese fluently."

"You guys think of everything," Johnny said.

"You and Meiko must meet us at the airport by eleven o'clock this morning at gate six. Besides myself and two other CIA agents, FBI, Homeland Security, and other Federal agencies will all be there to be briefed on today's three raids."

"Sounds good, we'll be there." He hung up the phone, and started getting ready.

# Chapter 53: The Big Bust

Johnny and Meiko arrived at the airport that morning to discover every Federal agency including the Massachusetts State Police and the Boston Police in attendance. When they both walked into the conference room, it was filled with chitchat from everyone speaking at once before the actual meeting commenced. Agent Hunt was there to conduct the conference, briefing all Federal agencies on their part in the operation. Three raids would be conducted simultaneously at the airport, Marine Shipping located at the docks, and Kazumi's office.

Johnny and Meiko took their seats and listened.

Just before the meeting ended, Hunt excused himself and momentarily walked out of the room. He returned with Master Yanagi and introduced him to the group.

Meiko whispered in Johnny's ear. "I knew it, I knew it! My father was too quiet and I just knew he was going to be involved in this raid."

"I had the same feeling," Johnny said.

After his introduction, Hunt explained to the assembly of government agencies that the Master would be a great asset to them.

Suddenly, he was interrupted by Captain O'Reilly, head of the Organized Crime Bureau of the Massachusetts State Police. "No disrespect, Master Yanagi, but what are you going to do if someone attempts to pull a gun on you from a distance?"

"Well, Captain O'Reilly, why don't you show me what you're talking about?" Yanagi asked.

The captain reached for the gun inside his holster, which was snapped closed, and before the blink of an eye, a shuriken—a ninja star with projecting blades—flew from Yanagi's hand, embedding itself right in the holster and preventing him from drawing his gun. Laughter broke out in the conference room, but Captain O'Reilly only frowned in irritation.

"A point well made, Yanagi!" Agent Hunt exclaimed.

"Captain O'Reilly, maybe sometime you come to dojo and I teach you," Yanagi suggested.

"Can I bring my gun?"

"No, leave gun home." Everyone laughed again.

"Okay, back to our meeting," Agent Hunt said. "I will be in charge of coordinating all three raids. Thomas O'Keefe will be at Marine Shipping located on the docks, Steven Flannigan at Kazumi's office building, and I will be here at the airport. Everyone has been briefed and knows the plan of operation, so get positioned in your assigned locations and wait for my command."

As everyone got moving, Johnny stepped to the front of the room. He spoke in a hushed tone to Agent Hunt. "Where's Master Yanagi going to be in all this?"

"You and Meiko will be paired together, and Yanagi will be close behind you out of sight. Now, get in position and wait for my order."

Approximately an hour later, Agent Hunt notified everyone that the cargo plane carrying the tires had landed. The plane was taxiing on the runway and stopped on the tarmac by the cargo hangar. The aircraft was met by ICE, Immigrations and Customs Enforcement. The flight crew departed the aircraft and were immediately detained, then taken by black van to a secluded hangar where they would be interrogated.

A limousine pulled up to the cargo plane and the chauffeur opened the door. Oshi stepped out, followed by Kazumi's henchmen in a black Lincoln town car, which stopped directly behind the limo. Oshi's brother had sent the men along for protection. The four body guards exited the vehicle and walked over to join Oshi, who was irritated that Kazumi had been detained by a dirty cop about the three henchmen who'd gone missing. Nearby, the cargo was being removed from the aircraft, to be transported to a hangar for inspection.

Oshi and the four henchmen followed the cargo back to the hangar along with the members of ICE, DEA, and state police. As they assembled inside the hangar, the state police released their K-9 dogs to sniff out possible drugs.

At that moment, Johnny and Meiko entered and Johnny shouted, "What's with all the badges around here?"

"Who the hell are you and how did you get in here?" the Customs inspector snapped.

"I'm Johnny Rizzo and I work for the Tabata brothers."

"And who are you, lady?"

"My name is Meiko, and I also work for the Tabata brothers."

The inspector glanced at Oshi. "Do you know these people?"

"Yes, they are employed by me." Oshi nodded in greeting.

Agent Hunt approached, posing as a U.S. Customs inspector. A state police officer walked over to the Customs inspector and announced, "My K-9s have inspected all the freight and it seems to be free of drugs."

"Let's clear this load so it can be delivered to Tabata's warehouse," the inspector stated.

Suddenly, he was interrupted by Agent Hunt. "First, I want to personally inspect one of these tires." He proceeded to pull out a large hunting knife from his jacket and started to remove the paper cover off the tire.

He took the knife, sliced it wide open, and yelled out, "What do we have here?" He straightened and said, "I think I'll tell you what we have here. A bag of heroin and little containers filled with metal objects that resemble small insects." Hunt continued to open one of the plastic containers, pulling out a Hornet. He examined it, finding an electronic homing device. Agent Hunt stepped over to Oshi, holding a bag of heroin and the Hornet in front of them. "What do you have to say?"

"I don't know how that got there!" Oshi said, spreading his arms wide.

Hunt pulled out his wallet and flashed his I.D. and badge. "I am Agent Hunt of the CIA and I am putting you under arrest for drug smuggling and possible industrial espionage, including your flight crew and four body guards."

Oshi started to reach for his gun, but he was instantly hit by a knife thrown from a distance by a man dressed as a ninja. Then, Kazumi's henchmen pulled their guns out and started to fire at the ICE agents and state police.

Hunt dropped to the ground after being wounded by a bullet from a sniper's rifle hidden in the rafters. He grabbed his radio and shouted, "I've been hit! Officer down."

The unknown ninja threw himself into the fray, engaging in a martial arts battle with Tabata's four henchmen, then pulled out his Samurai sword and beheaded one of the henchmen before swinging it around and castrating another henchman. Swiftly, he took four white smoke balls and threw them in front of him, creating a thick white cloud and effectively camouflaging himself. Then he stood behind the other two assailants and killed them both by means of a blowgun loaded with poison darts, hitting them each in the base of the skull.

Oshi ran out of the hangar, followed by Johnny and Meiko, but they were unable to escape the DEA and FBI agents. The three were taken into custody and put under arrest. Meanwhile, the ensuing battle continued with six more Yakuza fighters who were hidden in the hangar's rafters. Eventually, four of the Yakuza were killed by Customs agents and the Massachusetts state police. The other two Yakuza were wounded by flying bullets and apprehended by the FBI.

Oshi, Johnny, and Meiko were transported to FBI Headquarters. They were booked, fingerprinted, and put in holding cells. At the same time, Kazumi's two wounded henchmen were brought to the Mass General Hospital to undergo surgery. The Yakuza henchmen were closely guarded by the Boston Police.

Later on, Johnny and Meiko were escorted from their separate holding cells and brought to an interrogation room and asked to wait.

\* \* \*

Meanwhile, Oshi was brought to another interrogation room where FBI Agent O'Keefe, CIA Agent Hunt, and Boston Director of the FBI, Steven Flannigan, were waiting for them. Flannigan had been the Director for the last ten years, having worked his way up from Captain of the Massachusetts State Police. Oshi was not impressed. He leaned back in his chair, annoyed.

"Why was there heroin and electronic devices in your shipment of tires?" Hunt demanded.

"I told you before. I don't know how they got there."

"I find that hard to believe."

"Believe what you fucking want, but I am not saying another fucking word until I see my lawyer," Oshi snapped.

The three men left the room with two agents guarding the outside door.

\* \* \*

Johnny and Meiko glanced up as O'Keefe, Hunt, and Flannigan briskly enter their interrogation room. They all sat down on the opposite side of the table.

O'Keefe folded his hands on the table before him. "Okay, you two, I want to make something clear right now. The only reason you were apprehended was so your cover wouldn't be blown. You do realize you're not actually under arrest, right?"

Johnny and Meiko exchanged a baffled glance. "I wasn't quite sure when I was being fingerprinted and booked," Johnny shouted.

After that comment, the agents continued staring with rigid expressions, but then burst out in laughter.

"Our plans are to keep you undercover long enough to get a conviction," Flannigan stated, shaking his head as he forced himself to stop laughing.

At that moment, there was a knock at the door and it was one of the other agents. "I'm sorry to interrupt," he said, peeking around the slightly open door, "but I just received this information from an FBI informant. This afternoon, thirty-six Yakuza arrived at the Logan International Airport from Tokyo which was approximately two hours after the raids."

"Johnny, did you know anything about this?" Flannigan said.

"No," he replied, amazed.

"How about you, Agent Meiko?

"No, sir."

"Would someone please fucking tell me, how the fuck did thirty-six Yakuza fly in here under our radar?" O'Keefe demanded. "You mean to tell me the C fucking I-A didn't know anything about this? Otherwise, it must be information that you fucking didn't want to share with the FBI."

Hunt smirked at O'Keefe after his last remark.

"Okay, the look on your face answered my question. Does the CIA at least know where the thirty-six Yakuza are hiding?"

"Is it my turn to talk now?" Hunt asked sarcastically. "Yes, we do know where the thirty-six Yakuza are held up. We have them under surveillance."

The phone rang and O'Keefe answered it. It was loud enough that Johnny could hear the voice on the other end. "I am Samuel Clark, the U.S. Attorney in charge of your case against Oshi Tabata. Everyone who has been arrested during the airport raid must be released immediately." He went on to say, "It seems that whoever made out these warrants failed to put the correct address for the location of the raid at the airport, so that warrant is null and void. However, the seizure of the heroin and the electronic devices will remain in our custody as evidence until such time a hearing by a federal judge can be scheduled."

"What about Kazumi Tabata?" O'Keefe asked, sounding irritated.

"He is in custody, now in general population at the prison until his hearing," Clark said. "The other two warrants for Kazumi's office building and Marine Shipping were accurate."

After he hung up, O'Keefe briefed everyone on his conversation with the U.S. Attorney. They were all upset and arguing. O'Keefe yelled out, "Now what the fuck do we do?"

Hunt interjected. "First of all, we need to send Johnny and Meiko back to the holding cells before their presence here becomes suspicious." An FBI agent was called immediately to escort them.

Oshi asked about their interrogation and commented that they'd been in for a long time.

"Nothing was revealed by us," Johnny told him. "It fucking frustrated the Feds and they kept asking the same questions over and over again."

\* \* \*

The three agents were still in the interrogation room, discussing another strategy. Agent Hunt spoke up, rapping his knuckles gently on the surface of the table. "As we all know, Sonny DeSantis and his crew did a great job in Tokyo taking down ISIS. Therefore, I have taken it upon myself to notify DeSantis to meet us here. After all, our original agreement with Sonny was to take down the Yakuza in exchange for dropping their indictments. We need Sonny to eliminate the Yakuza from Boston once and for all. Our national security is being breached by the Yakuza organization with industrial espionage through their electronic flying hornet."

\* \* \*

Oshi, Johnny, and Meiko were soon released from custody. The three of them left the Federal Building together and climbed into a limo headed to a hotel owned by Kazumi.

Oshi proceeded to plan their next move with Johnny and Meiko.

While they were in the limo, his phone rang. He recognized the voice of the dirty cop his brother sometimes dealt with, William Dugan.

"Mr. Tabata, I'm sorry to inform you that your brother is gone," Dugan said.

"What?" Oshi barked. Across from him, Johnny and Meiko exchanged a curious glance.

"I wanted to call you personally and let you know," he said, sounding hesitant. "Kazumi Tabata was found dead in his cell this morning."

"How?" Oshi said, his stomach churning.

"He stabbed himself in the abdomen with a long shiv he got from one of the other inmates."

"That's impossible," Oshi shouted. "My brother would never kill himself." *Hara-kiri*...The stabbing fit right into the ancient Japanese custom practiced by warriors who'd been disgraced. The thing was, Oshi knew his brother would've never done such a thing. It was impossible.

The man on the other end exhaled loudly. "I'm afraid it's true," he said. "You'll be hearing from the medical examiner soon to arrange his last wishes. I'm sorry to have to tell you."

Oshi said nothing, and after a long moment of silence, the line went dead.

*Impossible*, Oshi thought. His brother had lost many friends to death, and he'd lost money, business assets—but it wasn't like him. Someone's made it look like suicide. Oshi was certain. His brother had been set up.

"Johnny, Meiko…you're not gonna believe this," he said, and told them both what had happened.

# Chapter 54: Social Club Gathering

Sonny DeSantis was at his social club when he received the call, and he felt a little put out about the short notice—especially since he'd been enjoying a night of playing cards with his men and winning. He also didn't want to leave the hot women who were serving food and drinks, and massaging the backs and necks of the men. Sonny had been looking forward to an evening with one of them, and he had his eye on a blonde with crystal blue eyes who kept smiling at him. Instead of a night with a beautiful woman, he had to go to FBI Headquarters.

It didn't bother him one bit that he'd be killing the Yakuza criminals, or anyone else for that matter. Sonny just wanted to make good on his agreement with the Feds and get rid of the indictments against him and his crew. His anxiety heightened, knowing that after he heard what O'Keefe had to say, he would need to get everything put in place to eliminate the Yakuza once and for all.

When he arrived at the FBI Headquarters, he was briefed on the Yakuza situation by O'Keefe.

"It's all up to you, Sonny, and your crew to take down the Yakuza," Hunt said. "If something goes wrong, remember one thing. You are on your own, and we will not admit to any dealings with the Mafia."

"Don't worry. I will keep the code of silence," Sonny promised. He understood the need to keep some things under wraps. In his line of work, this was essential.

"After your attack on the Yakuza has been successfully orchestrated, we will execute our end of the deal and clear all pending indictments against you and your crew. Is that understood?"

"Yes. Understood."

"The attack must be completed by five in the morning, before a judge can schedule a hearing on the Tabata case," O'Keefe explained.

"Not a problem. Consider it done." Sonny was confident he could follow through with what the Feds wanted. As far as he was concerned, he'd completed more difficult jobs than this.

*Bring it on*, he thought to himself, as he rose from his chair and was escorted out of the building.

After leaving the Feds, he returned to his social club in Boston's North End where he met up with his underboss, his capos and Slavic Androposky, his security expert. They gathered in the back room.

The club consisted of a full size bar and additional seating throughout, with tables and chairs covered in linen cloths. Everything was tastefully decorated. Framed pictures on the walls showed Sonny's family, his mother and father, sisters and brothers. Coming to the club was like going home, and he felt comfortable there. He wasn't married and he had no children of his own, so this club was his home away from home. The images of deceased associates and friends reminded him of who had come before him.

In the back, a private room with ample seating and clean tables provided plenty of room for the men to partake in their usual card games. Passing the huge kitchen, he waved hello to Emillio, his Italian cook and a trusted member of his crew.

After taking a seat in the private room, he and his men got comfortable. Sonny cleared his throat to get everyone's attention. "We are all here to discuss our strategy on how to contain thirty-six plus Yakuza all in one sweep, including Oshi Tabata," he began. "I have already secured twelve reservations for twenty-four of my men at the hotel Kazumi owns, and we've made sure no civilians will be around for this. If anyone's there, they'll be evacuated in such a way that Oshi and the Yakuza won't be aware. There will be two men in each room on each of the twelve floors. I will have an additional twelve men in the back of the hotel on the fire escapes, one man for each floor, six more men on the roof of the building, and eight men in the front of the building parked across the street in two black Escalades. All the men will have headphones with a microphone attached, and will carry pieces with silencers along with piano wire and knives. The quieter the better.

"Two men will sneak into the video surveillance room to kill Kazumi's security men who monitor the video cameras in the hotel. A couple of you will stay there to monitor the cameras to avoid any problems and freeze the pictures. I have contacted our hitman and explosives expert, Guido. With six of his men, he'll set up C-4 explosions in different key areas of the hotel, connected to one central detonator."

Captain Franco Del Ponte raised a hand. "Sonny, do we really need all these fucking men to take down thirty-six plus Yakuza?"

"Who the fuck are you to question me when you haven't heard the entire plan?" Sonny growled. "Now, shut the fuck up and listen! Once everyone is in place, Guido and his men will wire this place for sound. If any Yakuza go outside for any reason in the front or back of the hotel, you are going to pop them. If some of Kazumi's men go into the hall, pop them and drag the bodies back to your room.

"We have been advised that Johnny Macchia and Meiko have already finished their meeting with Oshi and are heading home." Sonny instructed his captains to brief their men and get them armed and in position at the hotel for one o'clock in the morning. As he pondered the situation, Johnny kept popping into his head, and he wondered again if the man was a double agent. He had his suspicions, but nothing had been confirmed. It disappointed him to think this way about his childhood friend, but sometimes a man could deceive you. He tried not to think about it. He had a job to do.

Soon, at Kazumi's hotel, Sonny's men were ready and in place, waiting for their command. Sonny gave his orders for everyone to move in.

When his men reached the roof, they discovered four of the Japanese Mafia positioned there, so his men had to sneak up on them. They shot three Yakuza in the back of the head with their silencers, but ended up in a battle with the fourth guy. The fight was stopped by another of Sonny's men by shooting the Yakuza right between the eyes. The force of the bullet knocked the Japanese mobster over the roof and onto the pavement below.

Thirty minutes later, Sonny received a call from one of his men on the seventh floor.

"Yeah?" he said, answering gruffly.

"There was a man walking to the ice machine and when he was bending over I strangled him and dragged his body to our room. Another Yakuza bites the dust."

"Good," he replied, ending the conversation.

Two of the Yakuza on the tenth floor walked down the hall toward the elevators and Sonny's men shot them both in the head using their silencers. The two men dragged the bodies back to their room.

When Sonny heard about it, he called Guido, who answered on the first ring. "We just killed some of the Yakuza," he told him. "It's only a matter of time before they are missed. How much longer?"

"I need five more minutes. I'm on the last explosive," Guido replied.

"All right, call me back when you're finished." Sonny disconnected the call and waited.

Five minutes seemed like forever while he counted down the seconds. Finally, the call came in, and he answered hurriedly.

"Boss, it's Guido. Everything is in place and we are ready to go when you give the order."

"I'll call you back when my men are out of the building," Sonny said.

As soon as he disconnected the call, he contacted one of his men and gave the next order. "It's time to evacuate the hotel by using the fire escapes. Let me know when everyone is out and accounted for."

Ten minutes went by and Sonny received the call that all of his men were out of the building. Guido was ready and set up fifty yards away from the hotel, waiting for his order.

# Chapter 55: Down In Thirty Seconds

Down the street about seventy-five yards from Kazumi's hotel, Sonny was positioned with his zips in three black SUVs ready to give his command. It was time and Sonny gave the order to Guido. "Press that button and level those fuckers once and for all."

The Feds mandated a secure bombing, so adjacent businesses would not be affected by the blast. However, hotel courtesy vans, vehicles parked directly in front of the hotel and in the parking lot out back, were severely damaged and covered by the heavy debris. It was necessary for the Feds to disable all outside video surveillance cameras from the surrounding area to cover up evidence of the bombing.

When he hit the button, it made Sonny think of the London Bridge falling down. The rumbles shook the earth, and Sonny called Guido back, his voice edged with excitement. "It was perfect! The hotel came down just like a deflated accordion," he said, guffawing loudly.

The rubble from the building came straight down with clouds of concrete debris spreading across the surrounding areas. There were no civilian casualties and the Yakuza were flattened like pancakes—including Oshi Tabata.

Sonny shouted to his crew. "Get the fuck out of here, get out now, I can hear the sirens from the police and fire department!"

He hurriedly opened an ISIS flag and laid it on the area where the front of the hotel used to be.

Then he attached an envelope to the flag, which read:

*This is in retaliation for killing our cells in Japan. We will not stop until we kill every Yakuza and keep them from drawing their swords.*

The fake evidence Sonny left behind would surely shift the blame to ISIS. He left feeling confident with himself that he'd completed a job well done.

* * *

The following day, headlines in the Boston Herald announced the news exactly how Sonny had intended it.

### ISIS Destroys The Yakuza Gang In Retaliation

Sonny chuckled to himself as he read the paper over coffee that morning. He was at his social club with the rest of his crew and partners in crime. They patted each other on the back and congratulated themselves for a job well done. Some of his crewmembers relaxed at the bar counter while others sat at the tables eating breakfast and drinking coffee, discussing their successful mission.

When his cell phone buzzed on the tabletop, he picked it up. It was Agent O'Keefe.

"Yeah," he said.

"Sonny, that was real cute what you did with the flag and note. Hopefully it doesn't start a whole new problem for us with ISIS."

"Forget about it!"

"Yeah, forget about it, until something happens. You know it is just a matter of time before ISIS realizes that it wasn't one of their cells," O'Keefe warned.

"Don't worry about it. When the time comes, we will take care of those sand fleas also."

The derogatory comment was met by a brief silence. Then, O'Keefe cleared his throat.

"You know something, Sonny, I don't like you. Maybe your trouble is over for now, but if you make one single mistake or slip up, I will nail you to the fucking cross."

Sonny said nothing. He just waited.

Finally, O'Keefe spoke again. "Your indictments have been lifted this morning and our agreement has been met. However, we will never admit to any wrongdoing."

"Thanks, nice doing business with you," Sonny said sarcastically, before abruptly ending the call.

# Chapter 56: Taken

After a busy few weeks, Johnny wanted to spend some time with Meiko—alone. He planned a romantic dinner, and brought her to a restaurant near the Boston waterfront. Sharing this city with her was an absolute joy.

They pulled up in the parking lot and climbed out of the Corvette, turning when they heard a vehicle pulling up behind them. It was a van with high beams which shined brightly, blinding them both.

For a moment, Johnny lamented the fact that his evening with Meiko had been interrupted. More than anything, he feared for her, pulling her behind him to shield her. He knew instinctively that something was wrong.

They'd been followed.

A cell of six ISIS members swiftly jumped Johnny and Meiko, placing white rags filled with chloroform over their mouths and noses, knocking them out. In a dark dream world, Johnny reached out for Meiko, wanting nothing more than to protect her. He had lost Kim. He couldn't lose Meiko, too.

The terrorists wore black masks and carried AK-47s strapped to their shoulders, along with their pistols. Johnny and Meiko were thrown into the back of the van, tied up, and black pillowcases were pulled over their heads, leaving a small hole for air. The van sped away to an undisclosed area in Boston where the hostages were interrogated, then tortured with electrical shocks inflicting excruciating pain, and water boarding.

All that Johnny could think of was Meiko.

All he'd wanted was a romantic evening with her. Now, he could only see her out of the corner of his eye—bloodied, bruised, her eyes half open. It terrified him. But more than anything else, it pissed him off.

The terrorists seemed puzzled by the fact that after repeated torturing, Johnny and Meiko refused to divulge any information.

"You mother fuckers," Johnny growled, blood seeping between his teeth. "Why don't you dig a hole and bury yourselves in it?"

One of the men punched him square in the jaw, and he felt a bone crack. He spat a tooth out on the floor, and for a few moments, they were left alone.

\* \* \*

After a few hours passed, Master Yanagi became concerned when Johnny and Meiko didn't show up at the dojo. Neither of them were answering their cell phones. He had called Johnny at least six or seven times by now. Once again, he tried Meiko's number, but it went straight to voice mail.

Yanagi decided to call the restaurant and was told they had never showed up for their reservations. A tremble of deep concern coiled in his chest and his shoulders tensed as he paced back and forth in the dojo.

He then called CIA Agent Hunt, giving him the name of the restaurant, so he could go there and investigate. It was nearly an hour before Yanagi heard from Hunt again.

"Master Yanagi, I'm at the restaurant now."

"Did you find them?" Yanagi had never felt so panicked before. Sure, his daughter had a difficult job that could be frightening at times, but he'd never lost touch with her like this.

"They aren't here," he said. "Master Yanagi, I'm afraid they've been taken."

"Taken?"

"Kidnapped."

Yanagi lowered himself to the floor, sitting in the Lotus position. "Go on."

"I met with the owner to view the surveillance video. Some men in a van attacked Johnny and Meiko in the parking lot, knocking them out before they could fight. I was able to get the license plate number of the van." He had then called Agent O'Keefe and advised him of the situation. O'Keefe immediately ran the plate number and was able to get a make on the license plate for the registration and address. It was registered to a known terrorist on the FBI watch list.

Master Yanagi gasped. "Now what?"

"We put out an APB to all government agencies including the Mass State Police and the Boston Police. We found where they're being held."

Yanagi exhaled heavily as he was told the warehouse where they were being held was now surrounded by many law enforcement agencies.

"Hang in there," Hunt said. "We're going to get your daughter out of there."

Yanagi disconnected the call, and waited.

# Chapter 57: Meiko's Revenge

They soon discovered the whole outside of the building had been wired with explosives. Soon, an agent reported to O'Keefe and Hunt that there was no way to raid or break into the warehouse until such time as the Boston and ATF bomb squad defused all of the explosives. One mistake would blow the warehouse sky-high, killing the hostages and terrorists along with the agents.

"ISIS cells don't give a shit about their own lives," Hunt grumbled. "They think they're going to Heaven and will each have twenty-seven virgins." He shook his head. "You can't even find twenty-seven virgins here on earth!"

O'Keefe cracked a wry smile, then his expression turned serious again. "Our bomb squad just arrived with the bomb robots." He promptly got on the police radio, informing his people that he wanted all personnel to get back at least one hundred yards, while the bomb squad with their protective gear prepared to defuse the explosives.

\* \* \*

Inside the warehouse, the torturing of Johnny and Meiko had stopped for a while, since it was late at night and even the terrorists were getting tired.

Johnny tried to keep himself awake so he could watch Meiko, who sat beside him tied in a chair. No one was aware of what was happening outside the building. Everything was quiet until Meiko abruptly went into a seizure, startling Johnny and the terrorists. Johnny tugged against his restraints, panicking as he yelled out, "Meiko, Meiko, what's wrong?"

Her body trembled and he watched, powerless to help her, her eyes rolling back in her head.

Johnny screamed. Despite all the torture he'd endured over the past hours—his skin bloody and bruised—he was discovering there was no worse pain than the fear of losing her. "I think she is having a seizure! She'll die if we don't help her."

The terrorists untied her, knowing she wouldn't be any good to them dead.

Johnny tugged at his restraints, feeling the rope tear off a layer of his skin. "Untie me! Untie me, I know how to help her."

Two men exchanged wary glances, but it was clear they didn't know how to deal with a seizure. Reluctantly, one of the terrorists released Johnny, but they were still surrounded by men who aimed guns in their direction in case their hostages decided to bolt. Johnny rushed to Meiko's side as her slim form crumpled from the chair to the floor. On the cold concrete, her trembling subsided, but he realized her breathing wasn't good. He started to give her CPR, mouth to mouth resuscitation, while an AK-47 was held to the back of his head by a terrorist who wore cargo pants and a gray t-shirt.

After the fifth time applying mouth-to-mouth resuscitation, Meiko very carefully whispered to him while he had his lips on her mouth. "Now," she said. "It's our only chance."

He realized he had to act without delay.

His heart hammered in his chest, even as he discovered that the seizure had been Meiko's ploy to give them a chance to escape. As his lips left hers, he turned suddenly and moved his left arm in a circular motion, confiscating the AK-47 from the extremist. He shot and killed the gunman before the man knew what was happening. He turned on his heel, firing the AK-47 and killing three more ISIS fighters.

The other two terrorists ran for cover behind pallets of crates piled high. Meiko ran and grabbed the rifles from the dead gunmen, then dashed with Johnny to the other side of the room and hid behind the stacks of crates. A large-scale battle erupted between the two agents and the terrorists, all of them firing until the gunmen found themselves out of ammunition. They came out from behind the crates, and after Johnny yelled out to the gunmen to throw out there weapons, they threw their AK-47s including their pistols into the middle of the warehouse. Then, the terrorists came out from behind the crates and proceeded to walk forward with their hands over their heads. Johnny and Meiko emerged and ordered the two gunmen to drop their knees to the floor.

"Now, lay yourselves down flat on your stomachs, put your hands behind your heads, and don't you dare move, you fuckers," Johnny commanded.

As they walked closer and closer to the terrorists, he turned to her and spoke in low voice. "Be very careful. They may be up to something." When he reached the first gunman, he stood over him, pointing his gun at him and demanded, "Release your left hand and slowly put it behind your back and now take your right hand and put it behind your back."

This enabled Johnny to successfully handcuff the gunman. Just as he clamped down on the cuffs, the other terrorist swiftly rolled over, sweeping Meiko's leg from under her and she fell, losing control of the rifle and dropping it to the concrete floor. Johnny thought fast and kicked the weapon across to the opposite side of the warehouse.

Meiko shouted, "Don't shoot him, he's mine!"

A large-scale martial arts battle ensued between Meiko and the terrorist, complete with flying kicks, sweeps, and grappling techniques. The ISIS fighter pulled out a pair of knives used in Filipino knife fighting.

Johnny noticed Meiko's Japanese expandable nightstick lying on the concrete floor along with the other contents of her handbag. The expandable nightstick closed small enough to fit in Meiko's bag, and she always carried it with her for protection. The terrorists had been stupid enough to overlook the nightstick when searching through her bag for weapons. Johnny quickly scrambled to pick it up and called out to Meiko as he threw it to her. The assailant repeatedly tried to stab her with his knives, but Meiko was able to block all of his attempts to cut her.

She hit his forearms and wrists so hard with the nightstick that he lost his grip on the knives, dropping them. Then she threw her nightstick aside and fought off her assailant in unarmed combat. During the intense fight, she applied *Kansetsu-wasa*, a Judo elbow joint manipulation, in order to break his elbow. Then, Meiko executed a Judo rear naked choke, *Hadaka-jime*, which cuts off blood supply to the brain.

Johnny yelled out to her, "Enough!" and handed her the other set of handcuffs. Meiko restrained the assailant and tied him around the ankles, then took the other end of the rope and tied a hangman's noose around his neck.

"You are under arrest and coming with us," Johnny said. He began reading them their rights and was suddenly interrupted by one of the terrorists.

"Unless you two want to die, don't try to leave the warehouse, which is wired with C-4 explosives. There's enough to take out a city block."

Johnny and Meiko glanced at each other, wondering if they were telling the truth.

"We have no choice," Meiko said. "We'll have to believe them for now."

"So, what do we do, just sit here and wait?"

"Where are our phones?" Meiko demanded of the assailant.

"Look in the jackets of the dead men. One of them had your cell phones," he replied.

Johnny searched in the jackets of the dead terrorists and eventually found them. He gave Meiko her phone and she immediately called her father who was already outside the warehouse and explained the situation.

"The Feds and the police have the warehouse surrounded," Master Yanagi said. "But do not try to leave. It is wired with C-4 explosives."

"I guess our two prisoners were telling us the truth," Johnny said, having overheard Yanagi on the cell phone.

"How many terrorists were there?" Yanagi asked. Johnny leaned close to the phone so he could listen, while keeping an eye on the two handcuffed terrorists.

"There were six. We killed four and captured two of them," Meiko replied.

"The ATF and the Boston Police bomb squads are doing everything they can and as fast as humanly possible," Yanagi said. "But actually they are not all humans, some are robots which find the bombs and put them in a large bomb kettle and detonate them. So, it will probably take until daylight to complete this procedure, but knowing that both of you secured the warehouse, it should go faster now. I will explain everything to Agent Hunt and O'Keefe."

"Dad, Johnny and I were brutally tortured and growing very weak. We are in need of medical attention, so please tell them to hurry."

Johnny remained strong, but he was exhausting quickly. He hoped the rescue team would arrive soon.

# Chapter 58: Promotion

An hour went by. They were sitting on crates while holding weapons on the terrorists, who were restrained before them. Johnny's phone rang, and it was O'Keefe.

"All of the explosives have been secured and we are coming in, so stand down," the agent said.

Moments later, an FBI SWAT truck equipped with steel plows broke through the warehouse doors and apprehended the prisoners. The dead terrorists were brought to the morgue for identification. O'Keefe, wearing a dark suit and tie, walked over to where Johnny and Meiko sat.

"Wow, the both of you look like shit, but a job well done," he said. "Meiko, when you are feeling better, I want you in my office so I can talk to you about staying in the U.S. and working for the FBI directly under the new Boston Director of the FBI, since Steven Flannigan is retiring."

"Who will be the new director?" she asked as several EMTs approached them.

"None other than Johnny Macchia," O'Keefe replied with a smirk on his face. He stepped aside to allow the EMTs to look at them both.

Johnny's jaw went slack. "I'm pretty messed up, so maybe I heard that wrong."

"No, you didn't," O'Keefe said, chuckling.

"Does that mean a raise?"

"Yes, a substantial raise, enough for you to start a new family." He winked at Meiko.

The couple exchanged a warm glance.

"Now, let the paramedics treat you and I will see you in a couple of days." O'Keefe and his men, along with CIA Agent Hunt, swiftly hustled out of the warehouse to go back to the FBI Headquarters to conduct their interrogation of the prisoners.

While the EMTs looked them over, Yanagi rushed into the building, embracing his daughter and Johnny. Tears were in his eyes, and he was relieved they were alive. Yanagi told Johnny that he would pick up his children and Kate and bring them to the hospital.

Johnny and Meiko were treated by the paramedics and sent in an ambulance to the Mass General emergency room where they both were examined and later admitted.

# Chapter 59: Room 306

Johnny tried to relax against the floppy pillow on his hospital bed, but with all the sounds—phones ringing, monitors making noises, and nurses chatting—he found it difficult to rest.

There was a knock at his door.

"Come on in."

"Hi, Agent Macchia. Let me introduce myself. I am John Wooten, Director of the CIA, Special Operations." He flashed his badge. "Agent Hunt has told me good things about you. I wanted to stop by personally to see how you are doing and to thank you for a job well done. Also, congratulations on your promotion."

"Thank you, I appreciate it. Actually, I haven't had a chance to accept the promotion."

"Well, I have some information I would like to share with you, but let's wait until you are feeling better. Then, we can get together and share intelligence."

"It would be my pleasure to meet with you in the near future," Johnny said.

"Good. I wish you a speedy recovery." He said goodbye, and left.

Master Yanagi, Kate, and the children soon arrived at the hospital to visit with Johnny and Meiko. J. J. and Mikey walked into their father's room and Mikey gasped.

"Daddy, are you all right?" he shouted, his eyes red-rimmed. He looked as if he'd been crying when he heard his father was in the hospital.

J. J. shrugged. "Of course he's all right, he's a Macchia." When he focused on his father, however, his expression appeared uncertain. "You *are* okay, right, Dad?"

"Yes, J. J., I'm fine." He realized his voice sounded scratchy. He rubbed his throat, eyeing the IV that was attached to his arm. "You don't need to worry."

"Then, how come you look like shit?"

"It's a long story. Maybe I'll tell you when your brother's not around." J. J. was the oldest, and he could handle more of the truth, but Johnny was reluctant to inform Mikey of how he'd gotten hurt. The truth was, he couldn't really tell J. J. either. Though, the boy was nosy enough that he might find out on his own, anyway.

"I'm old enough to hear what's going on with my father," Mikey snapped, glaring at his brother.

"Listen, guys, this is FBI top secret stuff and I can't divulge any information to either of you." That ended that. The boys grumbled, and J. J.'s shoulders sunk.

All of a sudden, there was a knock at the door and Johnny said, "Come in."

"Hello, Mr. Macchia, how are you feeling?" An older man clad in a white coat and tan slacks entered the room.

"Who are you?" Johnny asked, still feeling a little disoriented. He wondered what kind of medication they'd given him for the pain.

"I am Doctor Phillip Saxon, chief of staff at MGH," the man replied, "and I will be overseeing your case."

"Good, when can I go home?"

Mikey interrupted the doctor and said, "Yeah, when can my dad go home?"

"Well, son, your dad can go home tomorrow, if all the blood work and CT scans come back normal."

"What if the tests don't come back normal?" Mikey asked, clearly worried.

"We will cross that bridge when we come to it," Dr. Saxon stated.

"I am sorry, Doctor, but my younger brother asks a lot of questions and talks too much," J. J. said, rolling his eyes.

"J. J., that's not true," Johnny said, chuckling. "You are on the phone talking with different girls all day long."

The doctor grinned. "Well, Mr. Macchia, I can see you are in good hands and I'll stop by again on my morning rounds."

There was another knock at his door, and Johnny called out, "Come on in."

The doctor ushered the newly arrived visitor into the room before leaving.

Kate hurried inside, carrying a bright bouquet in a glass vase. She placed it on the end table and gave him a kiss on the forehead. "Hi, Johnny, I thought I would get you some flowers from the hospital gift shop to cheer you up."

"That was so nice of you."

She hugged and kissed Johnny again, then took a moment to fix a few of the flowers in the bouquet.

"Excuse me, Kate." He held out a piece of paper. "I would like the boys to take this envelope down the hall to Meiko in room 306." He directed his gaze at his sons. "Kids, make sure she reads it while you are there and stay for a visit." Kate took the envelope, turning it over in her hand, before giving it to J. J.

"Do as your father asked," she said.

"I would like to talk to your aunt Kate for a little while."

"Okay, Dad." J. J. carried the envelope, and Mikey followed him out of the room. Their chatter could be heard as they hurried down the hallway, the door shutting behind them.

"Johnny, I heard from Yanagi that you got a big promotion," Kate said, sitting in the chair beside his bed. "Are you going to accept the job?"

"I think so, but I would like to discuss it some more with Mieko first."

"That's a good idea," Kate said. She examined her fingernails for a moment before adding, "Yanagi also told me that Meiko was offered a job here in the U.S. to work under you. How do you think she feels about it?"

Johnny could tell Kate was curious about their future together, and questing for information. He smiled. "I believe she will be fine with it."

"What about the children? Would you have them live with you?" She gave a small half-shrug. "They're at my place so much, and they have their own bedrooms. They practically live at my house."

"Well, I'm going to have more responsibilities as the director of the FBI and Meiko will also be very busy heading up OCB, Organized Crime Bureau, for the Feds directly under me. Kate, if it's all right with you, I'll still need your help taking care of the boys with our busy schedules," he said, smiling at her. "The boys can stay with me and Meiko when we are home either during the week, or on the weekends."

"Sounds good to me," she said, squeezing his hand. "Let's see what Meiko has to say about all this."

# Chapter 60: Letter Of Importance

Johnny had been resting when Mikey and Master Yanagi entered his room.

"Hey, Dad," Mikey exclaimed, shoving an envelope into his hands. "Meiko replied to your note." He grinned, bouncing back on his heels. "J. J.'s visiting with her now."

Johnny stared at the envelope for a moment. He was almost afraid to open it. In all his years of casual dating since Kimberly had died, he never thought he would settle down with another woman. But Meiko was different. She was so much like him—truly a female version of himself. He wanted her in his life.

Opening the envelope, he tugged out the letter and began to read while Yanagi lowered himself into a chair and Mikey chattered away to the old man.

*Dear Johnny,*

*I have given much thought to all of your questions. Yes, I will take the job with the FBI to work under you and assist you with OCB.*

*Now, the answer to your second question, I love you and I would be proud to be your wife. However, you have to ask my father for my hand in marriage. He is very old fashioned. He loves you like a son and I am sure he will approve of our marriage.*

*I have not said anything about getting married to him yet. I know
my father was very happy for both of us about our job offers. He told
me if I accepted, the two of us would be too busy and you wouldn't
be able to run the dojo properly. My father told me that it would be
his pleasure to continue running your dojo and he can increase your
student membership. Besides, he would miss me too much if he went
back to Japan and I would miss him terribly. So, I think this is a win-
win situation for all of us.*

*Ah, Mr. and Mrs. Johnny Macchia.*

*I just love the way it sounds.*

*Love, Meiko*

Meiko's letter warmed his heart, but Johnny knew there was
something else he had to do. When the boys went back to spend time
with Meiko, leaving Johnny alone, he picked up his cell phone and
called a friend. The letter rested on his lap as he reclined against
pillows in his hospital bed.

"Hey, Johnny." Mel answered after a couple rings. "You back
from Canada?"

He cleared his throat, a sheen of sweat developing on his
forehead. "Uh, yeah. Listen. Got something to tell you."

"What's up?"

"First of all, you goin' steady with Joseph yet?" He glanced at the
door as a doctor wandered past, a clipboard in his hand. On the other
line, Mel scoffed.

"I haven't heard from you in a few weeks, and that's the first thing you ask me? Nah. I finally got the little guy to leave me alone. When are we getting together again?"

Johnny chuckled. "That's why I called you. Playboy Johnny Macchia is off the radar. I'm getting married." A moment passed, and he thought he heard a gasp, then loud coughing. "Mel? You okay? Mel?"

"I…I choked on my coffee. I'm fine. You're…you're getting married?" She cleared her throat. "Guess this means no more…benefits."

Feeling uncomfortable with the direction of the conversation, Johnny glanced toward the door again, but no one was there. "Well, you and me been friends a long time. I wanted you to be the first to know." Pausing, he added, "I'm sure you'll find somebody adequate to fill your needs. Nowhere near as good as me, of course, but—"

She laughed loudly. "No worries. I'm happy for you, Johnny. Am I on the guest list?"

"'Course you are. As an old friend."

"I gotcha, Johnny. As an old friend," she confirmed. "So I guess you've been good, then?"

Johnny decided not to tell her he was in the hospital. Otherwise, she'd only ask more questions. "Everything's fine. Talk to you soon, okay?"

"Sure. Take it easy, buddy."

"You too, Mel."

When he hung up, he read Meiko's letter again, knowing they had a bright future ahead.

# Chapter 61: Cat Out Of The Bag

In Johnny's room, Master Yanagi, the boys, and Kate all spent time talking with Johnny. When visiting hours were over, they headed home, and Master Yanagi went back to the dojo.

When everyone left, Johnny picked up the phone and called Meiko's room. She knew it was him right away.

"Hello, Johnny."

He smiled. "Tonight, you and me are going to have a wonderful dinner together."

"How are you going to manage that?" she asked, giggling.

"Well, I just talked to Sonny, and he is sending us a full course meal with a bottle of wine from his restaurant to celebrate our engagement."

"Wow, that sounds great! My room or yours?"

"Since I'm in better shape than you are, let's have dinner in your room," Johnny said, unable to contain his excitement.

"Okay, that's great. I love you, Johnny."

"I love you, too," he replied.

An hour later, Sonny and three of his men showed up at Johnny's room. His zips carried an array of Italian food and a bottle of wine past his room and into Meiko's, where they would have dinner. Johnny inhaled the scents that wafted in from the hallway. Sonny greeted Johnny with a hug and a kiss on the cheek while a couple of his men stood guard outside the room to protect their boss.

Sonny clasped his hands before him after smoothing the wrinkles out of his button-down shirt. "How do you feel, Johnny? Are you doing all right?"

"I am doing okay, Sonny."

"You know something, I know all about you, Johnny. Or maybe I should call you Agent Macchia."

"What do you mean?" He held his breath for a moment.

"I know you are a fucking Fed. I suspected it a while ago," he declared with a stern expression on his face. "I had a long talk with Agent O'Keefe and Agent Hunt, and they filled me in about who you are and what you do." He offered a half shrug. "But, that's okay, because if it wasn't for you, I would not have gotten this deal for me and my crew. At first, I was disappointed in you, but not surprised. So, I think that makes us even now." Sonny extended his arm, and they shook hands. Johnny felt immediate relief. He had not lost his old friend, after all.

Sonny sat down in the chair beside his bed. "As you must know, O'Keefe made a deal with me to assist you and the FBI in our fight against ISIS."

"I am glad, Sonny. It's great we are going to be working on the same side together."

"Yeah, yeah, I know all that! But, you need to realize, Johnny, that it is business as usual for us. After all, a man has to make a living."

"Sonny, I don't want to know what you're doing, but keep it toned down to bookmaking, loan sharking, and prostitution," Johnny said. "Stay away from the white powder stuff. It makes you and your crew too vulnerable. One more thing, I don't want to hear anything about your organization committing murder on civilians, unless we sanction it. Do we understand each other?"

"Yes, Johnny, we understand each other fully." He grinned. "I brought a small bottle of champagne, so let's you and me along with Meiko have a quick toast to celebrate your engagement."

When it came to getting out of his bed, Johnny refused help from a nurse, insisting he didn't need it. The pain medicine and his conditioning from martial arts kept him strong despite all he'd gone through. They all went to Meiko's room and opened the champagne to celebrate.

# Chapter 62: Priorities

The next day, Johnny and Meiko were released from the hospital with a clear bill of health except for their many bruises. They met with O'Keefe and both of them accepted their new positions at the Boston FBI Headquarters.

Meanwhile, business continued like any other day for Sonny DeSantis and his crew, just as Sonny said it would.

Kate continued taking care of Johnny's boys and Master Yanagi kept telling Johnny how much he enjoyed teaching and running the dojo. Before heading to the states, he'd decided to rent his home in Japan to his dear friend, Master Hiroshi, who would run his dojo and continue training both their students while Yanagi was in the U.S. Yanagi wanted to leave his options open in case he decided to return to Japan in the future.

Meiko and Johnny both found time to practice martial arts with Master Yanagi, J. J., and Mikey.

Six months went by, and Master Yanagi finally gave his permission to Johnny to marry his daughter. On their wedding day, Meiko looked radiant in her white traditional modern strapless full-length fitted wedding gown with a low intricate back, delicate lace woven along her train. She appeared elegant as she walked down the church aisle holding her proud father's arm.

Johnny looked very handsome and distinguished in his tuxedo.

J. J. and Mikey were the ring bearers, Kate was Meiko's maid of honor, and Johnny asked Thomas O'Keefe to be the best man. The father of the bride gave his daughter away to his beloved student, Johnny. In the audience, Mel sat with Johnny's closest friends. He'd been nervous telling her about his plans, but her excitement for him was clear, and she'd even gushed over Meiko's wedding gown.

Sonny DeSantis and his crew also arrived at the St. Anthony Shine Church in Boston for the wedding. Johnny's FBI family, CIA agents Mark Hunt and John Wooten, police, friends, and students were all there for the big day.

Toward the end of the ceremony, the priest asked, "Is there anyone who knows why this man and woman should not be wed? May he or she speak now or forever hold their peace."

At that moment, everyone turned to look as a woman charged into the church and ran down the aisle. People gasped and murmured amongst themselves. The priest looked up, raising an eyebrow. Meiko turned, frowning. Johnny, his hand around Meiko's thin fingers, turned to see what the woman wanted. He didn't know her personally, but he had seen her before at FBI headquarters and knew she was a fellow agent.

"Yes?" he said, more than a little perturbed that his wedding had been interrupted. The crowd of onlookers waited, and a low chatter began in the audience.

"Agent Johnny Macchia," the woman said, stepping close and trying to catch her breath. "There has been a terrorist attack at Fenway Park in Boston, in the middle of the game. The whole stadium was under siege and terrorists were shooting at the fans as they tried to escape."

Johnny and Meiko exchanged a glance before running down the aisle holding hands, along with all the Feds, police, and other agencies who had attended. The wedding would have to be put off until a later date.

The tragic incident became a national security crisis. They had to protect the state and its citizens.

* * *

The church was nearly empty. Master Yanagi frowned as he adjusted his suit jacket. He turned to the priest, who still looked dumbfounded as he closed his bible.

"Did you say enough in the ceremony to marry them?" Yanagi asked.

"No, I wasn't able to finish the ceremony and complete the marriage vow."

Yanagi smacked his forehead with the back of his hand, and said, "*Mamma mia,*" with a Japanese accent.

Sonny stepped up beside him, shaking his head. His men were still milling about, watching out for their boss. "You got that right," Sonny said. "I guess me and my crew gotta go, too."

Soon, the church was totally empty, and the priest, Master Yanagi, Kate, and the boys were all left at the altar.

# About the Author

John Wooten writes novels inspired by his own past in the realm of organized crime. He is also a screenplay writer, actor, producer, and a Grandmaster in Jujutsu. He is a Professor in Judo, with a black belt in Aikido and Karate. As the World's Strongest Man, John is the holder of 143 World Strength Records. He has appeared on many television shows, commercials, national news broadcasts, newspapers and magazines all over the world.

54754665R00183

Made in the USA
Charleston, SC
12 April 2016